the THIEVING COLLECTORS of FINE CHILDREN'S BOOKS

Adam Perry

YELLOW
JACKET

 **YELLOW JACKET**
an imprint of Little Bee Books

New York, NY
Text copyright © 2021 by Adam Perry
All rights reserved, including the right of reproduction
in whole or in part in any form.
Yellow Jacket and associated colophon are trademarks of Little Bee Books.
Interior designed by Natalie Padberg Bartoo
For more information about special discounts on bulk purchases,
please contact Little Bee Books at sales@littlebeebooks.com.
Manufactured in China RRD 1020
First Edition
10 9 8 7 6 5 4 3 2 1
Library of Congress Cataloging-in-Publication
Data is available upon request.
ISBN 978-1-4998-1124-7
yellowjacketreads.com

To Mom, thanks for all the books
—AP

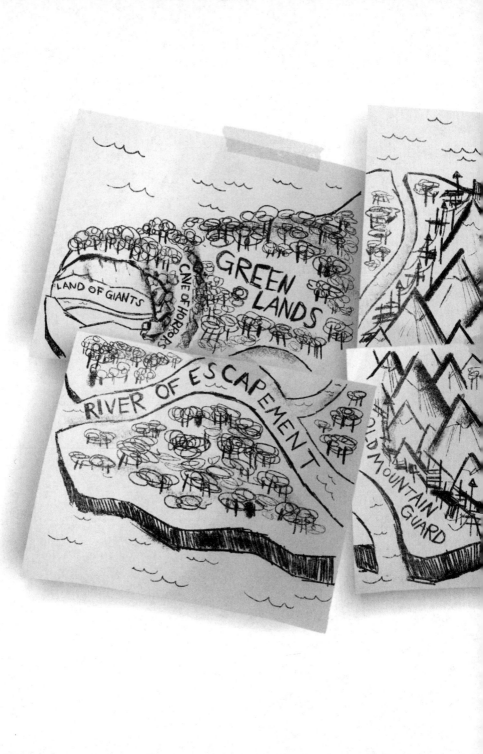

INTRODUCTORY QUOTES—
MOST PEOPLE SKIP THESE.
THAT IS ILL-ADVISED.

Quote #1

Very young children eat their books, literally devouring their contents. This is one reason for the scarcity of first editions of *Alice in Wonderland* and other favorites of the nursery.

    —A. S. W. Rosenbach (collector of fine children's books)

Quote #2

Mr. Rosenbach was right!

Children are the worst thing to happen to books, and if it were up to me, would never be allowed within spitting distance of them.

Why, if you give a child a book, you can expect it to be bent in half, torn apart at the seams, and drooled over until it is reduced to a wet pile of quivering pulp.

Children are animals.

Have you ever seen a child's hands? Filthier than a swamp crocodile.

Children have no regard for the finer things in life and have no desire to keep books in mint condition, on a shelf, in a temperature-controlled room where they belong. And they simply refuse to wear reading gloves or turn the pages with tweezers!

Not that it matters. It's unlikely that children could even understand what was written inside. Most doctors agree that the imagination stopped evolving decades ago, so there is little point in encouraging them to read. That is why I prefer *showing* them what to think.

Children's books, I fear, are a dying breed and should be reserved for us adults who can properly enjoy them.

Keep away, young ones.

Good riddance, I say.

Toodle-oo.

Now, can someone point me in the direction of the nearest restroom?

—Mr. Edmund R. Pribble (inventor/investor/collector of fine children's books) speaking at an anti–children's literacy convention in New York City, New York, October 24, 2059

AN OVERLY DRAMATIC PROLOGUE

A Bloody Start

Blood.

Oliver Nelson could taste it in his mouth. It dripped down his face and pooled in the little crevice above his chin, a shock of red against his skin. He felt dizzy and weak, and his legs wobbled as he walked. The world around him was a strange and dreamlike place, skewed slightly but oh-so-very real.

Oliver tightened his grip on the backpack, could feel the weight of the contents inside. He knew what he had to do. He paused to steady himself and looked down the long, twisting wings of the mansion until he saw the bright glow of the foyer's glass atrium. He ran toward it as fast as he could, through the book-lined hallway, rubbing his fingers across rows of perfect little spines. Things were coming into focus now.

He flew past enormous reading rooms and storage vaults where great stacks of books waited to be cleaned and sorted. Paintings of familiar characters and scenes lined the halls. Workers milled about, their mouths agape as they watched this strange and bloody child sprint through their kingdom of impeccably maintained literature.

"Oliver, wait!" a voice yelled from behind him, echoing in the halls. "We must talk this instant! Don't leave!"

Oliver did not obey. He pressed on, crossing a giant logo embroidered in the purple carpet, which was surrounded by outlines of books and pens and blobs of black ink. He slid onto the marble floor of the atrium, where towering bookshelves extended toward the domed glass ceiling. Diagonal slices of light reflected throughout the room, highlighting the gold-foil titles of invaluable first editions. A clock above the doorway told him the time.

An hour and a half. That was how long it had been since he first stepped inside the Pribbles' mansion. It seemed impossible that it had only been an hour and a half, but the proof was there, displayed by the twisted brass hands on the face of the clock. *Tick tock tick.*

Behind him, Mr. and Mrs. Pribble turned the corner of the hallway and pointed at him. Mrs. Pribble yelled, "Someone stop him!" and Mr. Pribble wheezed in agreement.

The Pribbles' butler was fifty feet in the air, standing on a sliding ladder attached to a metal railing that ran the circumference of the room so he could dust the high bookshelves. He surveyed the situation and kicked off from a pillar. The ladder spun around the room and the butler slid down it, toward the ground, toward Oliver, his fingers curved like the talons of a hungry hawk.

The Pribbles advanced, too, but Oliver was already at the door, leaving a bloody handprint as he turned the handle and ripped it open. His eyes adjusted to the brightness of the outside world, and he watched as a tiny blue car came up the driveway. His father was inside, sipping from a can of soda.

Oliver ran to the car, not waiting for it to stop under the portico before he clawed at the door, his bloody fingers slipping on the handle.

"Oliver?" his father asked. "Done so soon?"

Oliver opened the door and threw his backpack inside before diving onto the passenger seat, which was cluttered with hamburger wrappers.

"GO!" he yelled, but by now his father's interest had shifted from his son's premature exit to the blood dripping from his hands and face, and he asked the obvious question that a loving father would ask, given the circumstances.

"What *happened* to you?"

"*GO!*"

The Pribbles appeared in the doorway and advanced toward the car, and it must have been the look on Oliver's face that made his father decide that there was a time for questions and a time for fleeing, so he punched in their home address and the car sped away from the mansion, down the driveway, and onto the road, spurting gray smoke in its wake.

This was not the last time Oliver would see the Pribbles.

Rewind

G oodness! What an unnecessarily dramatic start to our story. I apologize for all the blood and excitement, though, if you're squeamish, I must warn you that there will be quite a bit more before we reach the final page.

The story you hold in your little human hands is full of murderous monsters and perilous caves, gangs of children, nasty rodents, gorgeous birds, towering mountains, evil villains, and several horrible deaths. And, of course, books. Lots and lots of books. But perhaps I should calm down and start at the beginning before I ruin any of the surprises.

Let's take a breath and go back in time. A month should suffice. But read fast, because the hours move quickly.

Tick tock tick.

PART 1

WHERE WE MEET OLIVER, THE PRIBBLES, AND A HOST OF OTHER CHARACTERS WHO MAY OR MAY NOT BE IMPORTANT

The Pribbles

Oliver first saw the Pribbles at the Garden Grove Library last winter. He was hidden away in a reading loft that overlooked the front lobby and had gathered up pillows and stacked them in a pile, curling up to read the final book in the Swordflinger Saga. Large puffs of snow stuck to the windows above him. The library was warm and quiet and nearly always empty. He was the only child that ever visited after school, and Ms. Fringlemeier, the librarian, told him it would hardly be worth keeping the lights on in the children's section if not for him.

He had just arrived at the point in the book where it looked like all hope was lost—the dragon was about to finally destroy the entire village of Cromwell—when the front door bell jingled. In stepped Mr. and Mrs. Pribble, appearing exactly as they did in their commercials, magazine covers, and billboards. It was a strange thing to see famous people in such an ordinary place, and Oliver found himself unable to look away from the peculiar pair.

Mrs. Pribble was tall, thin, and pale, with raven hair streaked with white. She wore a bright purple dress that clung to her legs and a silk shawl draped across her shoulders. She teetered as she walked, like the slightest bump might knock her over. Her smile was tight and sharp and not the least bit friendly. She held the door for her husband, who walked under her arm. He was so short that he didn't even need to duck— his head hardly passed her stomach—and was as round and bloated as an overinflated beach ball. His nose was a putrid mass of red flesh, and a thick brown mustache sprouted underneath it, curling up in a gravity-defying swoop. His beard was long enough to touch his tie, and he wore round glasses and a small bowler hat. He snatched the hat from his head and bowed to a surprised Ms. Fringlemeier.

"Good heavens!" Ms. Fringlemeier said. "Are you the—"

"Pribbles, yes," Mrs. Pribble said.

"You weren't expecting us?" Mr. Pribble asked. He pulled a chair from a nearby table and slid it to the desk, climbing on top so he could see above the counter. "We called your boss. She must not have relayed the message. Perhaps she thought it was a prank. That often happens to us."

The Pribbles were famous around the world and were also filthy rich. They were known for their vast collections of anything able to be purchased, as well as for their inventions, philanthropy, and business sense. It was also common knowledge that they loved books above everything else, and they were known to buy them by the truckload, sometimes relieving stores of their entire inventory with one thrust of a wallet.

Mrs. Pribble tilted her head back and sniffed the air. "Wonderful. How utterly wonderful! The *aroma* of a classic library! All mold and glue and ink. I thought this smell had gone extinct."

Ms. Fringlemeier tried to remain composed.

"No . . . I . . . well . . . sorry . . . How can I help you?"

"We made arrangements for next week, but we couldn't help ourselves. Patience is not a virtue we possess. We're looking for a very particular book."

Mr. Pribble removed a piece of paper from his breast pocket and thrust it at Ms. Fringlemeier.

"This one," he said.

Mrs. Pribble tapped her fingers on the counter and giggled. "To think, all this time and it was right under our noses. Oh, I can't wait, dear. I simply can't wait!"

Ms. Fringlemeier glanced at the note and typed it into the computer. "Mm-hmm. Let me see. . . . Yes, it says it's here."

"Where is it? *Where is it?*" Mr. Pribble asked, clapping his hands and jumping up and down on the chair.

Oliver stood to look through the slats in the loft's railing.

"It's in the loft. Shelf B. Come with me."

Oliver fell backward, knocking over a stack of books and making a horrible racket. He scrambled to clean up the books. He scanned shelf B. It was practically empty, save for a few books and balls of dust, and his heart began to pound. *No no no*, he thought. *Not today. Not shelf B.*

"Did you hear that?" Mrs. Pribble asked, her hand frozen in midair.

"Probably rats," Mr. Pribble said.

"No, that's just Oliver," Ms. Fringlemeier said. "He's reading in the loft."

"There's a *child* here? *Reading?*" Mr. Pribble asked, clearly taken aback by this revelation. "Whatever for?"

"Oh, Oliver loves to read! He's such a wonderful boy." Ms. Fringlemeier turned toward the loft and called out, "Oliver? Are you still here? We have visitors I'd like you to meet! Oliver?"

Oliver did not reply. He had already crawled down the loft's ladder and escaped out the library's rear exit, racing through the alley and across the street, along the winding roads that led to his home with the bent copy of *The Swordflinger: Volume III* shoved into his back pocket.

Oliver did not want to meet the Pribbles. Not today, not ever. Blood pumped through his veins faster than usual.

Shelf B. Why did it have to be shelf B?

His body tingled in fear, and the book in his pocket seemed to burn red-hot. You may have guessed, but Oliver Nelson had a terrible secret, and he feared that if anyone discovered it, he would be thrown in jail for the rest of his miserable life.

Oliver's Terrible Secret

Oliver was poor.

No, that was not his terrible secret, but I feel a need to provide some context to the little lad before I reveal all the scandalous details. Oliver's father was a hard worker, but good jobs were difficult to come by, and with the ever-rising cost of living, the Nelsons found it challenging to keep money in the bank and food on the table. Oliver knew better than to complain—he much preferred to stay quiet. What was the point of complaining when it was clear that things could get worse? And things *always* got worse. That had been Oliver's experience, at least.

Why was he so cynical? Well, for a ten-year-old boy, his little life had been a series of Roald Dahl tragedies and Lemony Snicket misfortunes. Take last summer: his father worked overtime every day for a year so the Nelson family could have a weeklong vacation at Wacky World (the Wackiest World north of Orlando), and his mother died of a sudden heart attack on a roller coaster regrettably named the Sudden Heart Attack. The news reports on the ordeal seemed to relish this detail, ignoring the fact that a young child lost his mother and that his entire world changed in an instant.

Time moved on.

Shortly after returning from the trip, his father lost his job, and the two of them were forced to move to a smaller house in a worse part of town. Oliver didn't have friends. Grief was a powerful thing, and he mostly kept to himself, scared of becoming close to anyone for fear they might leave him, too.

But then, in the midst of tragedy and misfortune, he found a refuge. *Books.* Books provided all the friends he could ever want, a place for his imagination to run wild, for his dreams to soar twice as high as a butterfly in the sky. Oliver loved books more than anything else, because it was in their pages that he could escape from his sad world.

Now, with that little piece of backstory given, I feel you can handle Oliver's secret: *He was a thief.*

Before you judge him too harshly, you must consider that Oliver was not a vicious and violent thief who plunders solely for the joy of it. He was the honorable type of thief, the kind who follows an unbreakable code of conduct, and the first and most important rule in his code was that *he only stole books.*

His life of crime began like many others, with a slight lapse of judgment and then a quick descent into irredeemable transgressions. The library had a policy that limited children to borrow only two books at a time, and that simply wasn't enough to keep up with Oliver's prodigious reading speed. What else could he do but steal?

I'll just take one extra book, he reasoned. *And no one ever comes to the library anymore. Ms. Fringlemeier will never notice. I'll bring it back someday.*

So one afternoon when Ms. Fringlemeier was making tea, Oliver slipped a book under his shirt and ran out of the library, waving goodbye and giggling with the strange glee that is common in first-time thieves. And once he took one book from the library, it was easier to take a second and third, and then he took another, and another, and another. With each passing month, it became harder to stop, and he soon found himself a petty criminal with a mountain of loot stashed under his bed. And since his name wasn't on record as having borrowed the books, there was no point returning them within the usual two-week window. Even if he wanted to, how would he manage to bring them all back without Ms. Fringlemeier noticing? It was safer to keep them, and his collection of stolen material quickly grew.

The second rule in his code was that *he only stole books that deserved to be stolen.* What, you may ask, makes a book deserve to be stolen?

Good question. Let's explore the characteristics of books that made Oliver's thieving little fingers tremble in delight.

Old. Of course, this was a characteristic of every book Oliver pilfered, as new books were a rare thing and certainly not present in the Garden Grove Library.

Musty. Old books have the most wonderful smell, don't they? When locked in a damp room for years, books acquire a truly pleasant stink. His copy of *The Swiss Family Robinson* had a potent aroma to it, in part because of the mold growing along its spine and the bits of old cheese that had become embedded in its pages.

Ripped. Most of the time, the books had broken bindings and were held together by tape and rubber bands. Take his copy of *The Mysteries of Grimshire Manor,* for instance. That beautiful book clearly had been gnawed by some feral child and was missing half its cover.

Yellowed and brittle. This should go without saying.

Incomplete. His favorite book, *The Timekeeper's Children,* was missing the final chapter. He could tell from the table of contents that the chapter title was "A Timely End," but the pages had been torn out, leaving only a few ragged inches of paper with enough words and sentences for Oliver to guess how the story ended. He had checked out the book eleven times and nearly had it memorized before he finally nicked it one crisp autumn afternoon.

The Timekeeper's Children was about two children named Cora and Jack whose mother had died unexpectedly. When the evil sorcerer, Sigil, killed the king and took over the kingdom of Dulum, the siblings set off to collect the pieces needed to build a magical clock that could turn back time to before anything bad had happened.

But Sigil had other plans. He wanted to build the clock in order to speed up time so he could rule over a land with no children. Why? Children were the only people in Dulum who were entirely unaffected by magic.

Perhaps it was because Oliver had something in common with the siblings, or maybe it was because he also wanted to turn back time, but there was something about this book that stuck in his imagination and never shook loose. The world of Dulum was alive in his mind. Oliver covered his bedroom wall with drawings of the characters and maps of the land. There were Cora and Jack racing through the trees and the hideous giants guarding their jewels in the valley. There were the Cave of Horrors and the rich foliage of the Green Lands. He drew the wooden cities of the Old Mountain Guard and the snow-covered mountain ridges to the west of the main city of Dulum, with the castle where King Gerard once ruled. He taped pages together to create the Dark Forest and the Twisted Tower, which lay in the middle of a swamp far in the north where Sigil hatched his evil plots.

And though Oliver never *technically* finished reading the story, he had still drawn a clock in the center of it all, its hands moving in reverse, and the children back in the arms of their mother.

Books, you see, were very important to him. But being a thief was a heavy burden for Oliver to carry. He lived in fear that his father would discover the stash of books in his room or that he would get caught in the act and be thrown into prison or, even worse, banned from the library forever.

So that is why Oliver ran from the Pribbles that fateful afternoon in the library and why he had no desire to meet them. Shelf B had been a particular target of his larceny, and he didn't want to see Ms. Fringlemeier's reaction when she discovered how sparse the selection had become.

He had to return the books and clear his conscience. He promised himself he would. *Someday.*

But that day would never come.

Books!

Weeks later, a school bus was headed toward Garden Grove Elementary, packed tight with children. They wore metal goggles that glowed like the glistening blue light of the ocean on a hot summer morning. Their fingers wriggled in the air like baby worms waiting to be eaten.

They were quiet, mostly, their heads tilted slightly back and their mouths held open at just the right angle to prevent drool from dripping down and splashing on their trousers. For the most part, they all looked the same. Oh yes, hair and skin color varied across the usual human spectrum and their clothes were slightly different cuts of a similar style, but by and large it would be difficult to tell any of the little creatures apart.

Except, of course, for Oliver.

His clothes were old—last year's style, *the horror*—and his face was missing the sparkling goggles that were so prevalent among his peers. Oliver sat on a seat with an old book open on his lap. He turned the pages slowly, spinning a clump of his dirt-brown hair with his pinky finger as his eyes darted across the sentences.

He loved the bus ride to school. The goggles made his

schoolmates so quiet and peaceful, and for the most part they never even saw him. Each morning he could read for thirty-seven minutes without being bothered, enjoying the meditative hum of the school bus's wheels on the road as it careened past empty parks and city streets.

It was pure bliss.

On this day, however, he was interrupted at the exact moment his book took an unexpected plot twist.

"What is *that*?" the boy next to him asked, pulling up the left lens of his goggles to peek out. His skin was a pleasing brown, and he rubbed one of his fingers on the page, whispering, "Ohhhh."

"It's a *book*," Oliver answered, somewhat sarcastically. "You *read* it."

"Why would you wanna do that?"

Oliver was annoyed by the question and scooted over a bit in the hopes that the boy would take the hint and leave him alone.

He didn't.

"But where are your goggles?" the boy asked, tapping the strap that wrapped around his head. The words *Pribble Entertainment Co.* were laser-etched onto the side. Oliver flinched at the sight. It had been several weeks since he had seen the Pribbles in the library, and he hadn't returned since. He yearned for a new book.

"I don't have a pair."

"*You don't?*" the boy asked, as if the notion were so preposterous that it was almost like Oliver had told him he had fingers sprouting from his nostrils. "Well, this here is the newest model. Just got it last week for my quarter birthday. Very expensive. I told my parents I'd hold my breath until my *actual* birthday if they didn't buy it right away. Pribble Entertainment Company added a ton of new worlds to *Boom, Explode, Dragon* that you can *only* play on this model. You want to try?"

Oliver shook his head.

We've already established that Oliver was poor, so let's not belabor the point, but to *try* the goggles might mean he would *want* the goggles, and as any poor child knows, wanting something you can't have is a terrible curse. An unreachable itch. An unbelchable belch. Besides, he could see the scenes from his books so vividly in his imagination that he couldn't possibly think what benefit the goggles might have.

"Ah, come on," the boy said, and he removed the goggles and slid them over Oliver's eyes. He adjusted the strap so they formed a tight seal across the bridge of Oliver's nose. Through the semiopaque blue lenses, Oliver could see the children on the bus. Out the windows, the city raced by.

"Try them."

Oliver's little heart pattered in his chest. Is this what all the fuss was about? It didn't seem so—

A Brief Demonstration of the Pribbles' Remarkable Alternative Reality Goggles

S uddenly, the world around him seemed to melt away. His ears hummed. The bus began to tremble in his vision. Windows stretched, smearing color and sunlight around him.

"What's happening?" he asked. He felt like he was falling, falling, and his belly rose up to his throat.

"It's beginning," the boy answered, but now he didn't sound like he was seated next to Oliver; he sounded like a great booming voice from the heavens, light-years away and yet still able to whisper into Oliver's ear.

Blackness crept in from the corners of the goggles and letters spun around in the sky, coming together to form words.

PRIBBLE ENTERTAINMENT CO. PRESENTS
SPACE, DARK AND DEADLY

"Whoa," Oliver said. He held out his hand. It was covered in a thick white glove. He wiggled his fingers as the words CONTINUE and NEW EXPERIENCE and OPTIONS appeared in front of him.

"Don't overwrite mine. Start a new one," the boy said, and Oliver reached out, wrapping his hands around the words

NEW EXPERIENCE. They tickled his palm and exploded in light so bright that he had to squint and look away.

The light faded, and he noticed he was standing on the dusty surface of some desolate moon. Looming large in the sky above him was a giant planet swirling in purple gases.

"What do you see?" the boy asked.

"Dirt," Oliver answered. "And space."

"Nothing else?"

"No."

"Then you better start running."

"How do I—"

The ground in front of Oliver exploded, sending a cloud of gray dust in the air. He spun around and saw two giant figures looming on a mountain ridge. They were tall and gnarled and covered with eyes and strange folds of wet flesh. Their mouths opened, revealing rows of dripping, red teeth.

Oliver reached up to remove the goggles, but his hands bumped against the thin glass dome of a space helmet.

"How do I take them off?"

The boy laughed. The sound echoed in the helmet.

"You can't just grab them. These aren't those stupid old *virtual reality* goggles. These are *alternative reality* goggles. I'll show you. Run like you would in the real world."

"I want out!" Oliver yelled. He looked down and saw his legs were covered in a white space suit. The alien creatures jumped into the air, landing and running toward him. They shot beams of red light at the ground around his feet. He stepped forward and saw his foot move on the ground. How was this possible? He'd been sitting on a bus a moment ago and now he was standing, and it was almost like—

Another beam struck near his foot, grazing the side of his boot. He felt pain and jumped into the air, floating a bit before settling back on the surface.

"They're shooting at me!"

"Don't worry, this is only the first moon. They still have have terrible aim. But you need to run!"

There was no time to argue. The alien monsters ran forward, unearthly noises coming from their wretched bodies.

To Oliver's left, a small spaceship had crashed nosefirst into the dust. Smoke poured from its engine, and beside it, stuck into the moon's surface, was the curved handle of a blaster. Oliver ran toward it, taking powerful leaps and rolling on the ground to avoid the aliens' blasts. It truly felt like he was moving, like he was actually *here* in this place, far away from the real world. His fingers wrapped around the handle and he jumped into space, arching his body in the air and sending a wave of blue beams back at the monsters. They exploded in light, their screams piercing through his helmet.

"How are you doing in there?" the boy's voice asked.

"I'm . . . I think I'm safe."

The boy laughed.

"No, you're not."

The mountain ridge that surrounded him began to squirm, almost like it was alive, and an army of alien creatures appeared, too many to count, their shapes visible against the starry light of the galaxy.

Oliver's knees went weak.

"I don't want to play anymore."

"Come on, don't be a wimp. At least get to the moon base. Then I'll show you how to exit."

Oliver turned and saw the base behind him. It was built into the ridges of the moon and was constructed from clusters of cubed, white buildings. Diagonal pillars poked from the top, adorned with flags of fictional planets.

"You'll have to run."

Oliver did run, faster than he ever had before, his body flailing through the moon's thin atmosphere. Screams came from all around him, and hundreds of red beams of light struck the ground at his feet.

Pssssttt.

He felt a sting on his arm. A beam had hit the sleeve of his space suit, and oxygen was beginning to leak from the hole.

He ran harder.

"Are you there yet?" the boy asked.

Oliver couldn't answer. He felt a great weight pressing down on his chest, and his mouth flapped open and closed, but no sounds came out. As he approached the moon base, he hit the ground and crawled to a triangular door, slamming his palm on a blinking red button. A robotic voice said, "Biochemistry analyzed. *Human.* Pressure off. Doors open in three . . . two . . . "

Red veins appeared in the corners of Oliver's vision.

"One."

The doors slid open, and Oliver pulled himself inside.

"Pressure on," the voice said, after the doors sealed shut.

Oliver ripped off his helmet and sucked in the rich, cold

air. It felt real and luxurious sliding down his throat and filling his lungs.

Banging sounds came from the door, and the indentation of an alien fist formed in the thin metal.

"Get me . . . out of . . . here," he wheezed.

"Don't you want to go down the hall and find the—"

"NOW!" Oliver yelled.

"All right. Fine. Take off your gloves and I'll show you the exit motion."

Oliver did. The door buckled and groaned and bent on its hinges. Alien fingers slid through, their fingernails clicking against the frame.

"Place your index finger right above your left ear and hold it."

"What?"

"Just do it."

Oliver obeyed, pressing his finger hard into his skull. He heard a beeping sound.

A beam of light hit the door and smoked poured into the hallway.

"Hurry!"

"Now trace that finger in a straight line to the middle of your forehead. Stop right between your eyes."

The door ripped from the hinges, flying out into the dark expanse of space. There was a *whoosh* and Oliver slid toward the doors, wedging his feet on the frame. The alien creatures grabbed him and pulled him near their mouths.

His hand shook, but he slid his finger to his forehead.

"Now what?" he screamed.

Alien teeth wrapped around his ankles, sending a dull pain throughout his body.

"Press down," the boy said.

Oliver did, and his finger seemed to sink into his forehead like it was made of melted butter. Everything around him froze in place. The pain in his leg disappeared, and the aliens turned to dust and blew away as the world slipped to black. His body seemed to turn inside out, and the words RESUME, RELOAD LAST CHECKPOINT, and EXIT appeared around him. He reached for EXIT, wrapping his fist around the word. Light shone from between his fingers. He began to fall, and his body lurched forward. His head bumped on the soft rubber of the seat in front of him. The world around him came into view through the blue lenses of the goggles. The city whizzed by, and his classmates continued to sit in neat, quiet rows, absorbed in their own worlds.

"What do you think? You want a pair, don't you?" the boy asked. He held up Oliver's book and waved it around. "Makes this seem pretty dumb, right?"

Oliver shrugged. He didn't want to be rude, but no, he absolutely did not want a pair. He reached for the book and laid it in his lap, rubbing his hand against the pages, his heart still beating from the nightmare he had just experienced.

"Whatever," the boy said, slipping the goggles on and tilting back his head. He disappeared into his game and the bus continued toward the school.

One thing was certain: Oliver never wanted anything to do with the stupid Pribbles or their stupid goggles ever again.

The Invitation

S o you can understand how, when Oliver received an invitation to visit the Pribbles' mansion later that week, he nearly tore up the letter and threw it away.

They're onto me! Oliver thought, clutching the exquisite envelope, which had arrived in the mail. A gold-foil logo was printed across the top, and the paper smelled like a mixture of cinnamon and blueberries.

Dear Oliver, the letter began, handwritten in ebony ink.

As you may know, we are the world-renowned Pribbles—inventors, philanthropists, and collectors of fine children's books. You have recently come to our attention in a most unusual way, and we would simply <u>love</u> if you would join us for a meal at our home. We believe there's something special about you, Oliver, even though you may not realize it. I'm afraid we can't give any more details, but it would be an absolute honor for us to have you as our guest and "pick your brain," as the saying goes. I've written our personal phone number on the back of this letter.

Please R.S.V.P. as soon as possible. We are (quite literally) trembling in anticipation.

Your friends,

Edmund and Sophelia Pribble
Founders, Pribble Entertainment Company

P.S. Please do not tell anyone about this letter.

P.P.S. And do try to stay safe. If you ride a bicycle, remember to wear a helmet.

At first glance the letter seemed quite positive, though Oliver rightly suspected there was some other, more sinister motive behind it. It couldn't be a coincidence that the Pribbles had happened upon his library, the very scene of his crimes, before inviting him to their mansion. Ms. Fringlemeier must have discovered the truth and ratted him out.

No, nothing good could come of this.

"Well, what is it?" Oliver's father asked, snatching the paper from his fingers. His eyes widened as he read the note. "Is this for real? An invitation from *the* Pribbles?"

Oliver nodded.

"What do they want with *you?*"

"I have no idea," Oliver lied. He suspected they would be waiting with police officers and Tasers and attack dogs and—

"Amazing! We have to go," his father said, sniffing the

envelope. "Can you imagine? The Nelsons meeting the Pribbles. What good luck!"

As I've already mentioned, good luck did not happen to Oliver Nelson. Panic began to course through his limbs. He ran upstairs and crawled under his bed, pulling out his stash of stolen books. He had to return them. He grabbed a box from his closet and piled them inside. Today was the day. He'd return the books to the library, and he'd never steal again. He considered writing a note to Ms. Fringlemeier, apologizing for his crimes, but decided against it. No, it would be best if he simply left the box at the door and ran away. She'd find the books and put them back on the shelf where they belonged and everything would go back to normal, just as it had been. He'd no longer be a thief, and his conscience would be clear.

Oliver picked up the box. It was heavier than he expected. He gripped it by the bottom and tiptoed down the stairs to the back door. He was about to exit his house when he heard his father on the phone.

"Yes . . . yes . . . that sounds wonderful! We will be there. Saturday at noon it is! Thank you *so* much, Mr. Pribble!"

Oh no! Oliver's heart raced. Why did bad things always have to happen to him? He slammed the door and ran down the alley just as his father yelled, "Oliver! Did you hear? We're going to visit the Pribbles this Saturday! Isn't that exciting? Oliver?"

But Oliver didn't answer. He ran as fast as his little human boy legs could carry him, lugging the heavy box toward the Garden Grove Library, where, I'm sad to say, things were about to get much worse.

CLOSED—FOREVER

By the time Oliver made it to the library, his arms were aching from the weight of his box of purloined books. He set it down on the stairs that led to the side door of the library and opened it, running his fingers along the pages of the books one final time.

That's it, he thought. *It's over.*

But then he noticed something odd. There were other boxes stacked all the way to the curb, full of alphabet posters and metal bins and old Dewey decimal charts.

Strange, he thought.

He went to the door and pulled at the handle. It was locked. *Even stranger.*

He ran to the front door and discovered that it was locked as well, and just he was about to knock, he noticed a sign on the door that said CLOSED—FOREVER and underneath, in Ms. Fringlemeier's loopy handwriting: *Sorry, Oliver.*

Through the windowpanes he could see the racks, once covered in books and magazines and archival newspapers, were now bare. Scraps of paper lay on the floor, and a lone fluorescent light bulb flickered in the ceiling. The loft was empty except for a single ripped beanbag chair. Without books the library was just a sad, gray room with streaks of water damage dripping down the walls.

Oliver wanted to cry, but he bit his lip to stifle it. He had become skilled at that.

"Where have you been?" a voice asked behind him. Oliver turned to see Ms. Fringlemeier standing beside her car. "I wanted to tell you in person, but I haven't seen you for a few weeks."

Oliver stuffed his hands in his pocket and kicked at a weed. "I've been busy."

"I'm so sorry, Oliver," she said. "I never thought it would come to this."

"What happened?"

"No one came," she said. "We couldn't keep it open anymore. Libraries are closing all over the country, I'm afraid, and we had an offer from a generous couple to buy all of our books. It wasn't my decision."

The Pribbles, Oliver thought.

Ms. Fringlemeier pulled a gift-wrapped box from her car and handed it to him.

"I got you a present. Open it."

It had been a long time since anyone had given him a present. Oliver ran his fingers along the paper and tore it away, revealing a beautiful leather-bound journal. His name was stamped on the cover, and the paper was lined and brown and gorgeous.

"It's time for you to write your own story, Oliver," she said. "I know there are amazing things happening in your mind."

Oliver shook his head. Nothing he could ever write would

be worthy of its pages. But the journal felt wonderful in his hands, perfect in every way.

"Thank you," he whispered.

"Goodbye, Oliver," Ms. Fringlemeier said. She sat in her car and started the engine, waving from the window as she puttered away.

That was the end of the Garden Grove Library. Ms. Fringlemeier's car disappeared down the hill, and tears began to flow down Oliver's face. He felt more alone than he ever had before. Was it possible that things could get worse? He doubted it. This had to be the absolute lowest he would ever feel in his entire life.

A loud squealing sound came from the side of the library. A garbage truck had parked, and workers were shouting and scraping boxes across the ground, heaving them into the metal back of the truck.

"No," Oliver whispered, and his heart felt like a woodpecker beating against his ribs. "No no no no."

He ran around the building, watching as a man in an orange safety vest picked up his box of stolen books and heaved it into the back of the truck, then wiped off his hands and jumped onto the side, signaling to the driver.

"Wait!" Oliver screamed, but the truck began to move, rumbling away from the library, its engine so loud that the workers inside never looked back to see the screaming child racing behind them.

"No, you can't! My books! Stop!" Oliver yelled, waving his arms.

The truck continued on, taking with it Oliver's broken

copy of *The Mysteries of Grimshire Manor*, his incomplete copy of *The Timekeeper's Children*, and his green and stinky copy of *The Swiss Family Robinson*.

Gone. All of them—gone!

The horror hit him in waves. He'd never read *The Westing Game* again. *Matilda* was lost forever among mounds of smelly garbage. His complete series of *The Borrowers*—vanished. He'd never finish volume three of the Swordflinger Saga, never get a chance to revisit the familiar friends in volumes one and two. They were gone now, only existing as distant memories in his mind.

He collapsed on the ground, and then another horrible realization washed over him: he was stuck as a thief forever. He was irredeemable. A scoundrel. A sinner. Alone and without his books.

Now it was *surely* impossible for things to get worse for Oliver, right?

Keep reading.

The Pribbles' Mansion

The Pribbles lived an hour away, far away from the dingy row homes with boarded-up windows and eviction notices to which Oliver was accustomed. Their mansion was located on the top of a majestic, green hill that could only be reached by way of a long, narrow road surrounded by hedges and marble fountains.

"This is really something," Oliver's father said, arching his neck out of the car window to take in the view. It was the first week of spring, and tall trees sparkled with multicolored fruit, their limbs twisting against the sky. Everything seemed brighter and more radiant here, like the colors had been amplified, turned up to their highest setting, capable of burning out your eyeballs if you looked too long.

"It sure is," Oliver said, swallowing several times to calm the throbbing pain in his stomach. He didn't see any police cars around. Yet.

The mansion was made of marble and was roughly the same size as the town's shopping mall. The main building was a large, monolithic rectangle with a domed glass atrium sticking from the top. Smaller wings jutted out from its sides, covered in conical turret roofs that stabbed at the sky and were topped with colorful flags.

Oliver's father parked the car under a large portico near the front entrance, its roof held up by stone pillars carved to look like mermaids and horses and ogres.

"How classy," his father whispered.

Oliver grabbed his backpack. Inside was a handwritten confession, should the need for it arise.

The front door opened and a tall man appeared. He was dressed in black and white (clearly a head butler), and his hair was perfectly combed to the side. He folded his arms in front of his chest and stuck his nose straight in the air.

"Welcome," the butler said in a deep drone. "It is my *deepest* pleasure to welcome you to the Pribbles' domicile."

"Domicile?" Oliver's father asked.

"It means house," Oliver whispered. He had learned that word on page thirty-two of *The Executioner's Young Apprentice*.

"Would you like a hot towel to clean the grease and grime off of your little child fingers?" the butler asked, extending to Oliver a pair of kitchen tongs that held a steaming white towel.

Oliver looked around, still convinced that this whole thing was a trap and he would soon be swooped up and arrested for his thieving ways. There was no one else around. He grabbed the towel and wiped his hands.

"Let me inspect," the butler said, grabbing Oliver's wrists and lifting up his palms to his face. He gave them a sniff and examined every wrinkle, finally nodding and releasing his viselike grip.

"Acceptable. Now, if you are ready, I will show you in."

The butler turned on his heels and walked toward the

large front doors. Oliver followed, his father close behind.

"*Excuse me*," the butler said, glancing back. "Forgive me if I'm mistaken, sir, but I don't believe your name was on the invitation."

Oliver's father stopped, clearly taken by surprise.

"The invitation was addressed to *one* Master Oliver Nelson. What is your name?"

"David."

"It isn't Oliver?"

"No. It's David."

"Then I believe my point has been made. I do not have the authority to let you enter. That would have to come from—"

"Who is *that* on my porch?" a loud voice bellowed inside the house. The butler slid to the side and bowed, extending his arms to reveal a figure waddling toward them.

"Mr. Pribble," the butler said.

Mr. Pribble appeared in the doorway wearing a sparkling blue tuxedo and a matching top hat that added an extra foot to his height. A blood-red handkerchief peeked from his jacket pocket and was the same color as his crocodile-skin shoes. His round nose hung over his mustache, which had been artfully greased into two swooping arches, and his round glasses reflected the sky like luminescent planets.

"Good to see you, my boy!" Mr. Pribble said. "We've been so excited for you to arrive!"

He was shorter than Oliver remembered, and his legs seemed to blend with his midsection. His little arms stuck out from his torso like small twigs on a snowman. He stood on his tiptoes and extended his arm as far as he could to pat Oliver's head.

"Come, come. What's the holdup?" he asked the butler, who raised an eyebrow at Oliver's father.

"It's just . . . I was talking to your *employee* here . . . and he told me . . . well . . . I don't want to get him in trouble, but . . . Mr. Pribble, was I not invited?"

"Good heavens!" Mr. Pribble yelled, letting out an uproarious laugh. Oliver's father joined in, uneasily. "I can see how that might be uncomfortable. *Of course* you weren't invited. Imagine! Having to explain proper invitation etiquette to a grown man."

The butler covered his mouth.

"I just assumed I could join him. I'd feel better if I could—"

"Sir, your name was not on the invitation, and that is as clear a sign as I can give as to *who* is invited and *who* is not."

"Well, what do you want with Oliver, anyway?" his father asked, as if the thought had only just occurred to him.

"Was I unclear in the invitation? I'd like to pick his brain. Your son is a fascinating boy who has many things rattling around in that head, I am sure. Please wait out here," Mr. Pribble said, pulling a wallet from his coat pocket and throwing a few dollars on the ground. "There are a plethora of fast-food establishments down the road. Buy yourself some hamburgers or something."

Oliver's father bent to pick up the money.

"Well, I guess I could—"

But Oliver wasn't listening. He stepped into the grand foyer and walked into the glass atrium, mesmerized by the sight. The room was at least fifty feet high. Large oak shelves were attached to every wall, stretching all the way to the ceiling. Light poured down on the marble floor, illuminating the ground like stars fallen from the sky. Everywhere Oliver looked he saw books, books, and more books. His head buzzed with delight.

"Wow," Oliver said.

Ladders of varying heights were attached to metal rods that ran in circles around the length of the room, and workers dressed in black-and-white uniforms spun around on them, delicately dusting the spines of the books.

"Wow indeed," Mr. Pribble said, laying his hand on Oliver's shoulder. "My favorite room—the *jewel* of the mansion. I use it as a holding tank for new arrivals. Once they are properly categorized and sorted, they will find a permanent home in the one of the main wings."

He pointed east.

"Picture books are over there, for instance."

North.

"Juvenile literature. A personal favorite."

West.

"Books intended for young adults."

South.

"Miscellaneous things. Adult fiction. Thrillers. Graphic novels. Oh, Mrs. Pribble does have the disgusting habit of reading graphic novels with a glass of Pinot Grigio, though I can't fault her the occasional guilty pleasure. Mine happen to be cheese curls and alphabet books."

"Excuse me," Oliver's father said, cupping his hands and yelling into the atrium from outside. "Are you all right in there, Oliver?"

Oliver was more than all right, though he was feeling a bit dizzy from spinning in circles, taking in every detail of the remarkable room. For once he had forgotten all of his misfortunes, forgotten the fact that police might be waiting to arrest him at any moment for his crimes, forgotten the fact that he had lost his collection of books. Now he was surrounded by more books than most people would see in a lifetime, and his eyes greedily scanned the titles, bouncing from shelf to shelf.

"I think he's quite fine," Mr. Pribble answered.

"How long will you be?"

Mr. Pribble pulled his other hand from his pocket and consulted a gold wristwatch. Gears and springs spun and whirled beneath the hands. "Hmph, well . . . general tour . . . followed by lunch . . . yes, yes . . . a few hours should be enough time, I suppose. How does that sound, Oliver?"

"I never want to leave," Oliver whispered. He walked to a ladder, grabbing a rung, his eyes widening at a pristine first edition of *Alice in Wonderland*.

"Excellent, then we will see you later this afternoon, sir. Toodle-oo," Mr. Pribble said, abruptly turning toward Oliver. "Step away from that ladder, young man! You might fall and crack your skull. And what a tragedy that would be."

Oliver's father waved.

"I'm going to get some food and then I'll be waiting out—"

The butler stepped inside and slammed the giant front door, locking it with a definitive *click*.

"Finally," Mr. Pribble said, through an oddly malicious smile. "Follow me for a tour. Our meal is almost ready, and time is ticking."

A Tour

They entered the picture book wing first, a grand hallway with neon-purple carpet adorning the ground. The carpet was covered in patterns of majestic flying books, fireworks, and pens squirting blobs of black ink. The ceiling was painted with world maps, modified to show landmarks from classic stories. On both sides of the hallway were shelves stacked as high as the ceiling, packed tight with books of all colors and widths.

"Everything is in perfect alphabetical order by author," Mr. Pribble explained, walking briskly and flapping his arms. "You can imagine the strain it places on the staff when new books are added. When I purchased the complete works of Katherine Applegate, everything had to shift downward by several inches. The resulting upheaval took weeks to handle, hence the need for a holding room. But it's worth it, Oliver, to be able to grab nearly any book ever written at any time."

They continued on, entering the juvenile fiction wing. Oliver's eyes widened at the titles, and pangs of guilt and sadness shot through him. He spotted familiar books he had stolen, remembered them being driven away in the back of the garbage truck.

"Ah, yes, I can see you're as much a connoisseur as I am.

Name a book. Anything you want. My gift to you."

"Really?" Oliver asked, still awestruck by the greatness of the mansion and the quantity of books. He thought hard. "I . . . well, I suppose . . . um . . . do you have the Swordflinger Saga?"

"Book one, two, or three?"

"Is there a volume with all of them?"

Mr. Pribble's eye twitched.

"You must mean the hardcover, leather-bound, twentieth-anniversary special edition. Autographed by the author."

"Yes, that one!" Oliver answered.

Mr. Pribble winced as if he'd been smacked, then his face morphed back into a smile. He grabbed Oliver's hand and ran down the hall as fast as his short legs could carry him.

"Oh, I do so love the Swordflinger Saga. Written by Kenneth Wachsman, originally published between 1992 and 1996 by DreamStar Books, New York City, New York. An excellent and wholly unexpected choice!"

They arrived at a shelf labeled *W* and Mr. Pribble grabbed a stepladder, slid it over, climbed up, and removed a large book.

"Extremely limited," Mr. Pribble said, holding it out and panting slightly. He opened the cover to reveal a handwritten note and signature. "A magnificent piece."

Oliver reached for the book and found it difficult to take, mainly due to Mr. Pribble's unclenching grip on the book's spine.

"My apologies," Mr. Pribble said, his eye rapidly twitching

behind his round glasses. "Arthritic fingers. Sometimes they make it hard to let go of things."

He thrust the book at Oliver and pulled a phone from his pocket, dialing a number and whispering, "Get me another anniversary edition of *The Swordflinger Saga*. Leather-bound. Of course I want it signed! I don't care what it costs. Yes, I know Mr. Wachsman is dead. Hunt down his children and take one from their personal collections if you must."

Mr. Pribble directed his attention back to Oliver and smiled. "Shall we?"

Oliver slipped the book into his backpack and they continued down the hall, exploring each wing of the mansion. Occasionally Mr. Pribble would stop to note a particularly rare or unusual book. They passed large, glass-walled reading rooms filled with chairs, reclining sofas, hammocks, and benches. Giant screens that curved up and over the ceilings were mounted on the walls.

"Certain books require different atmospheres," Mr. Pribble explained. He pushed a button by the door to one reading room, and seagull noises played from a sound system. A vibrant video of an empty beach appeared, depicting water gently lapping the shore.

"For a lighter book, I prefer the ocean and a hammock." He clicked the button and the video changed to the inside of a wooden cottage. A fireplace glowed golden orange, and out a window was a cold, blue winter scene. Other cottages were peppered around the landscape, their roofs covered by mounds of snow. Smoke curled from their chimneys. "And some books go better with a hot cup of cocoa while snow pounds away outside."

Oliver blinked, amazed at how real the scene looked. It looked so comfortable, and he longed to curl up on a sofa and crack open his new copy of *The Swordflinger Saga* and—

Mr. Pribble pushed him by the small of his back. They walked on, passing loads of books, heaps of books, mountains of books, more books than Oliver would have guessed existed in the world.

At the end of the final hall was a dead end blocked by another monstrous bookshelf.

"I find doors to be such a waste of space," Mr. Pribble said, walking up to the shelf and pushing on the blue spine of a copy of *One Thousand and One Nights*. "Open sesame."

The bookshelf moaned and shook, rumbling the floor under Oliver's tattered brown shoes. It raised into the ceiling, revealing a dining room with a large, wooden table covered in the finest food he had ever seen.

Mrs. Pribble sat in a high-backed chair and tapped her long fingers on the table.

"It's about time! Oh, you do take *forever* on your tours," she said.

Mr. Pribble lightly punched Oliver on the arm. "It's important I build rapport with the young lad before—"

"Come, Edmund, the food is getting cold," Mrs. Pribble said.

The Pribbles' butler glided around the room, laying out knives and forks and arranging napkins. He extended his hand toward a seat.

"After you," Mr. Pribble said.

A present had been placed next to Oliver's plate, wrapped in shiny paper that reflected every color of the rainbow, and Oliver walked toward it, into the room that would forever alter his miserable little life.

And, as you already know from the prologue, would leave him covered in blood.

A Delicious Dinner
and Another Generous Gift

It's exceptionally tedious to read about people eating, so I'll skip over the details except to say that the roast beef, potatoes, and green beans the Pribbles served that day were some of the best-tasting things that Oliver had ever squeezed through his gullet.

Forks clanged against plates, water glasses sparkled with condensation, and napkins were dabbed at the corners of mouths.

The butchered beef sat in a bowl, swirling in its juices. Steam rose from the potatoes. Everything was heavenly.

"Of course, we have our own private chef," Mr. Pribble explained, slurping down the remnants of his gravy and licking his sausage fingers. "We snatched him from a five-star restaurant in France. Keep him locked in the basement, mostly."

"Sometimes, if you want something, you have to *steal* it," Mrs. Pribble said, giggling. She cut her food into tiny wedges before lifting them to her thin red lips.

"That's true, I guess," Oliver said, and felt his face grow warm. *Why did she say that? What does she know?* "Thank you so much for having me. The food is delicious, and I really appreciate the book."

Mr. Pribble erupted in laughter, slapping the table with his palm.

"Did you hear that, Sophelia? So polite, isn't he, dear? I've never known a child to talk like that! Full sentences! Proper grammar! Devoid of grunting!"

Mrs. Pribble scrunched up her face and snickered like a squirrel.

"What a peculiar little devil."

Oliver looked down at his lap.

"And he hasn't *once* mentioned the present sitting by his plate. Such restraint!"

"Perhaps he's only being polite."

"Is that it, Oliver? Being polite? Would you like to open your present before dessert is served?"

Oliver nodded. He hoped it was another book. He stared at the wrapping paper and saw his reflection looking back at him.

"No need to wait, then. Open it!"

Oliver ran his finger down the seam of the wrapping paper, splitting the tape and pulling it off in one swoop to reveal a familiar-looking package. He had seen boxes of them plastered across billboards and stacked high in store windows. On the front was a picture of goggles with rays of light shining from the glowing blue lenses. The words *Pribble Entertainment Co.* were laser-etched on the strap, and photos of fantastic worlds were displayed in a grid behind the image. Oliver recognized the alien monsters from *Space, Dark and Deadly* and felt a twinge of phantom pain from his ankle.

"Do you have a pair already?" Mrs. Pribble asked. Oliver shook his head.

"Very good!" Mr. Pribble said. "Well, even if you did, this one is extremely special. Our newest model. It won't be released to the general public for another year. The software is still in preproduction, with some very *unique* features. You'll be the most popular kid in school, wearing those."

"They're very nice, thank you," Oliver said.

He slid the box over and was about to put it in his backpack when Mr. Pribble jumped from his seat and yelled, "That's it? Most kids would be screaming in delight! What's wrong with you? Don't you like them?"

"I do, it's just—"

"You've never tried the goggles before, have you, dear?" Mrs. Pribble asked.

Oliver shook his head.

"I have. Once."

Mr. Pribble gasped. "Only once! Incredible! To be honest, I expected as much, considering your interest in the *written* word. Open the box."

Oliver did. The goggles sparkled inside. They had that wonderful smell that new things often do.

"These goggles are our greatest invention," Mr. Pribble said. He walked around the table and lifted them from the box, loosening the strap and sliding them onto Oliver's face. Through the blue lenses, Oliver could see the room around him as if he were underwater. The food shimmered on the table.

"When children lost the ability to imagine, I decided it was up to *me* to do it for them. This is why I read. Books are the fuel for my expansive imagination. The fantasy genre inspired *Boom, Explode, Dragon,* and of course, *stealing* some of the best elements from science fiction novels gave us the award-winning *Space, Dark and Deadly.* These experiences are my gift to the world."

"That's very nice of you," Oliver said, though he was a little uncomfortable with the way Mr. Pribble used the word *stealing* in his speech. Nervous worms began to squirm in his belly.

"This version of the goggles is truly special. It allows us to tap directly into the user's mind."

Mr. Pribble pulled the strap uncomfortably tight and wrapped his hands around Oliver's shoulders. Mrs. Pribble stood, slinking toward them. She pulled a pair of goggles from her blouse and slipped them onto her face.

"You may wonder why we invited you here," Mr. Pribble said. "The truth is, you have something I want."

Oliver felt the roast beef work its way back up his throat.

"I get everything I want, Oliver, but so far one important book has eluded my grasp. And I believe you have it."

Things always get worse, Oliver thought. He grabbed his backpack, ready to run, but Mr. Pribble's grip was too tight. Oliver looked back and saw that he, too, had slipped on a pair of goggles. Oliver wriggled, fought, kicked, but it was no use. Mrs. Pribble leapt toward him, holding his arms against his chest. Oliver screamed, and the echo bounced around the cavernous dining room.

"Are you ready, dear?" Mr. Pribble asked, and Mrs. Pribble nodded, her red lips twisting into a smile.

The goggles began to hum in Oliver's ear. The room spun, slow at first, and then faster, like the very fabric of the world was melting. The sun from the window smeared across his vision, and the large wooden table transformed into a brown blur that wrapped all around him.

He was falling, caught in a whirlwind of blue light, deeper and deeper, and the only thing he could hear was Mr. Pribble's menacing voice whispering into his ear.

The Last Remaining Copy

T he room was gone, replaced by twinkling colors and shapes that spun and spun. Oliver was still falling, deeper down, but Mr. Pribble's grip had loosened. He could kick his legs now, wiggle his arms.

"I originally designed these goggles as a quick way to create new worlds, ripping them directly from my expansive imagination. But then I discovered they may have another purpose," Mr. Pribble whispered. His voice seemed to echo across the universe, and yet felt so very close.

Oliver hit the ground. Dust rose above him in a cloud. It was very dark. He was lying by a stream in a patch of yellow grass, surrounded by forest. Fog covered the ground, and crickets sung in the night. Stars appeared in the sky as his vision came into focus.

He was wearing different clothes now—a red tunic, brown pants, and thin canvas shoes.

"You have something I want," Mr. Pribble said. His voice no longer rang from the heavens. It seemed real now, like he was on the ground with Oliver and getting closer.

"What?" Oliver asked.

He stood and began to run, passing curved trees that shimmered in the dull light of the moon.

"You remember *The Timekeeper's Children*, don't you? Written by Malcolm Bloom. Published in October of 1984."

Oliver felt like he might be sick. Of course he remembered that book. It was his favorite, and the memory of it being driven away in the back of a garbage truck replayed in his mind. By now it was likely burned or compacted or buried under tons of stinking waste.

"It wasn't a popular book, Oliver. In fact, it must have sold less than a dozen copies. Hardly more than a vanity printing. Still, it was immensely important to me as a boy, and I believe your library's copy was the last in existence. Were it not for a few unfortunate typos in the computer records, I would have found it ages ago."

Oliver continued to run, leaping over roots and curling brambles.

"There he is!" Mrs. Pribble called out.

"You can imagine my delight when I discovered it was right under my nose all this time, and I bought the entire library's collection on the spot. Oh, I'm sorry that I closed it down. I know how much that place meant to you, but you must understand that you are an anomaly. Children wear the goggles now; they don't read books. Stories and dreams are for *me* to give them."

Oliver tried to remember what the boy on the bus told him. *Place your index finger right above your left ear and hold it. Trace that finger in a straight line to the middle of your forehead. Stop right between your eyes.*

He made the motion, pressing down. The words EXIT DISABLED flashed above him.

"We searched through the collection, but the book was gone. Your name was the last on record as having borrowed it. In fact, it appears you borrowed the book *eleven* times. It must have made quite an impact on your little mind."

Oliver ran toward the trees. He could hear the distant calls of owls. The ground shook under his feet.

"I read it only once as a child, but it made a permanent mark on me. I remember some scenes from the book, random lines and vague mental pictures. The details have faded. Age does that, you know?"

If he could make it to the trees, he could hide from them, wait for the sun to rise, and avoid the Pribbles until his father grew suspicious and called for help.

Oliver came to a stream and waded through it, the water soaking through his shoes.

"More than the story, I remember how I *felt* when I read it. That electrifying tingle that races from your mind to your feet when you read a life-changing book. You understand, don't you?"

Oliver understood, but this was no time to discuss his love of stories. He arrived at the trees and entered a thin path that went through a maze of branches, ducking low to blend into the shadowy foliage. The ground continued to shake, as though bombs were exploding in the distance.

BOOM BOOM BOOM.

Where *was* he?

"You see, I've been able to acquire every other book I want except for that one, and you must understand how maddening that is for a collector of my stature."

He peered out from the branches and saw Mr. Pribble in the clearing. Mrs. Pribble waved a lantern through the fog. They were wearing brilliant blue outfits, and Mr. Pribble held an odd contraption in his arms. It was nearly as tall as he was, with a large blue canister in the middle and a white tube sticking out the front. There was a handle on the back with a trigger, and the word *CORTEXIA*™ was painted on the side. It looked a bit like a futuristic vacuum cleaner.

"I'm so very sorry to do this to you, Oliver. Since the records show that you returned the book to the library, I'm left with no other choice. It seems to have vanished and could be anywhere in the world by now. Of course, that means that the last remaining copy lives *in your mind*."

So they don't know about my stolen books, Oliver thought, but that was little relief now. He continued on, snaking through the trees, trying to get as far away from the Pribbles as possible.

"Here we are, Oliver, in the land of Dulum. Chapter one of *The Timekeeper's Children*: 'A Theft in the Land of the Giants.' The *CORTEXIA*™ is a special software tool we created—it will allow us to take the story from your mind, page by page, until the entire tome is ours. You won't miss it, will you?"

Oliver knew this place well, could close his eyes and imagine every hill and tree and—

The ground trembled, sending Oliver back on his heels. The trees parted and a tall, hooded figure appeared. It was wraithlike, taller than his father, its face hidden in the folds of its long, dark robe. Oliver certainly did not remember *this* from the book.

He let out a small scream, and a skeletal hand with long, sharp nails stuck out from the black robe, motioning for him to be silent. Oliver obeyed and turned, preparing to run away from the terrifying creature. At that moment, hands clenched around his throat.

The Kingdom of Dulum

Oliver screamed and kicked, but the grip was too tight. He looked up and saw Mrs. Pribble's sunken cheeks and wild eyes. Her hair was tied up in a bun that seemed to stretch her skin to the point of cracking, curling up her lips at a devilish angle.

"Yoo-hoo! Edmund! He's over here!"

From the clearing, Mr. Pribble hacked at branches with a stick and worked his way toward them.

Oliver's eyes raced around the forest, looking for that strange and terrifying hooded creature, but it was nowhere to be seen.

Mr. Pribble arrived in front of him and tapped his cheek, drawing his attention.

"There's no use running from us. Your best course of action is to go through the story exactly how you remember it. We'll stay close behind and slurp it up." Mr. Pribble pursed his lips and demonstrated this principle, coughing as a fly became lodged in his throat. "It's only one little story, and I *did* give you any book of your choosing from my library. Let's call it a fair trade."

Mr. Pribble pointed the *CORTEXIA*™ into the air,

his finger grazing the trigger. The tops of the trees began to bend toward the nozzle. Blades of grass twisted around Oliver's feet, stretching into long, green, noodley threads that ripped from the ground and spiraled in the air, flowing through the long tube and into the canister. It crackled with tiny blue lights, and Mr. Pribble smiled and released the trigger.

"Don't fret, little Oliver. When this is all over, we'll export the canister from your brain and you won't remember a thing. Why, you won't even remember this story ever *existed*, let alone that we stole it."

Mrs. Pribble swatted a large silver beetle from her nose.

"This forest is much bigger and darker than you described, Edmund. Are you sure we're in the right book?"

"Yes," Oliver whispered. This was indeed the outskirts of the Kingdom of Dulum, just as he had imagined. He began to recite. *"Chapter One: A Theft in the Land of the Giants."* He pictured the book lying open on his bedsheets, remembered how the faded words looked on the brittle pages.

It was a time of great darkness in the Kingdom of Dulum, and Cora and Jack found themselves lost in the Land of the Giants. The dark sorcerer Sigil had sent them here, and they were searching for something— something no human had ever held in their hands before.

Birds circled overhead, those nasty rodent eaters,
waiting for the children to drop dead on the forest floor
from hunger and thirst. They needed to solve the first
riddle, and fast.

"*Yes! Yes!* That's the one! Good work, boy," Mr. Pribble said, clapping his hands and jumping up and down. "But no reason to recite it out loud. The story lives *around* us, and any minute now, Cora and Jack should appear."

He looked around, listening for sounds, but the forest was silent save for the flapping of wings high overhead.

"Rather dark beginning, isn't it?" Mrs. Pribble asked.

"Kids like that kind of stuff," Mr. Pribble answered. "Why do you think our game *Blood, Guts, and More Blood* is so popular?"

Oliver made one last attempt to free himself, but Mrs. Pribble was deceptively strong.

"My father will wonder where I am," Oliver said.

"Nonsense. Days here equate to mere minutes in real time. We could be here for weeks and still have you back right when we said we would."

"All right," Oliver said, and small tears formed in his eyes. He felt a tingly numbness through his limbs. There was nothing he could do. He tilted his head toward the nozzle of the *CORTEXIA*™. "Just take it now. Get it over with."

Mr. Pribble laughed loudly, wheezing into his hand.

"Not that easy, boy! As I mentioned, we have to *experience* it first. Acted out through your memory, with all the pain and excitement and adventure that goes with it."

"Oh, this should be *fun!*" Mrs. Pribble said, wiggling her nose in delight.

"Now, where are those mischievous little scamps?" Mr. Pribble asked, and then was promptly hit on the head with a stone.

CHAPTER ONE

A THEFT IN THE LAND
OF THE GIANTS

Dark figures swooped from the trees, and blurred shadows spun around them. There was a howl and a thump, and Mrs. Pribble released her grip on Oliver's shoulders and fell to the ground, unconscious.

The figures continued moving, never stopping long enough for Oliver to see their faces. Still, he knew exactly who they were: Cora and Jack, the timekeeper's children, the very ones mentioned in the title of the book. Their black tunics whipped in the air as they leapt around the Pribbles, making cracking sounds that echoed through the trees.

"Heavens!" Mr. Pribble screamed. He ran toward his wife, tripping over a tree root as a kick connected with his ample posterior. "Ouchie! Stop it! *Stop it*, you two! I know who you are. Cora and Jack! Let me explain."

Cora and Jack did not allow him the privilege. They leapt upon him and, with a resounding thwack, knocked him out cold.

Oliver pressed his back against a tree and closed his eyes, waiting for them to pounce on him.

"You there. Boy," Cora said.

Oliver peeked through his eyelashes. His heart thumped in his chest.

In the moonlight, Cora stood in a warrior's pose. Her hair was long and black, and mud was smeared around her eyes. Her skin was dove white and her lips were blood-red, colored with the juice of fresh berries. She was the fiercest human being Oliver had ever seen. She was fifteen years of age, but her eyes made her seem older. Jack was a foot shorter and three years younger. His face, soft and kind, was the color of a common barn owl and framed by a nest of dirty-blond hair. He was short for his age, about two inches less than Oliver, which only meant that he tried extra hard to appear tough. He hoisted a leather satchel over his shoulder and spun a small stone in his fingers, aiming it at Oliver's head.

"Who are you?" he asked.

"I'm Oliver. Oliver Nelson."

"*Nelson?*" Cora asked. "That's a family name I've never heard before. Where are you from?"

"Far away," Oliver answered, which was quite true.

"That man said he knew who we were. How?"

Oliver shook his head. "I don't know."

Jack poked a toe at Mr. Pribble and examined his sparkling blue clothes.

"He's a weird-looking one. Who do you think he works for?"

"I don't know, but I'd bet they were looking for us."

Cora moved close to Oliver and stuck her face close to his. Her fingers walked up his chest and rested around his throat. Her other hand unsheathed a knife from her belt.

"You expect us to believe that you were just out in the

woods, alone, and have nothing to do with these people?"

Oliver nodded.

"He's not telling us something," Jack said.

"Clearly."

"Are you a member of the Gang?" Jack asked, and Cora's fingers tightened around his throat, the blade of her knife pressing hard against his belly.

Oliver weighed his options. To say *yes* would certainly be risky, but to say *no* would admit that he knew who the Gang was, which was equally dangerous in his present situation.

"I . . . um . . . what gang?" he asked.

Cora and Jack eyed him suspiciously.

"Where did you say you were from again?"

"*Very* far away?"

Cora's eyes narrowed. She smiled.

"One final question," she asked. "Are you a *good* guy, or a *bad* guy?"

There was a rustling in the woods behind her, and Oliver saw the shadow of the tall, dark figure move through the branches. Who (or what) could it be? Distracted by this ominous form, he spoke before he could properly think through the question.

"Good guy."

Cora's fingers tightened around his throat.

"Wrong answer," she said, and the world went dark.

The Horrible Hunted
Villains of Dulum

Now, had Oliver properly considered the question, he would have realized that the better answer would have been "Bad guy," for at this point of the story I must confess that Cora and Jack are not the heroes of Dulum but the *villains*.

Oh, yes. Quite a twist.

Oliver awoke several minutes later to find his arms and legs tightly tied together with thick rope. Cora and Jack whispered to each other, breathing heavy as they pulled him through the thick foliage of the forest. Brambles scraped against his arms, cutting through his thin shirt, and his head bumped over rocks. Despite the pain, he didn't move, deciding that the best course of action would be to stay silent and pretend to still be knocked out cold.

Far in the distance, he heard loud rumbles that shook the tree branches.

BOOM BOOM BOOM.

"D'ya hear that?" Jack asked.

Cora stopped and jumped onto a low tree branch, straddling the trunk as she climbed to the top.

"They're over there," she said, pointing. She leapt to the

ground, her black boots slapping on the wet stones of a small stream.

Oliver knew exactly *what* Cora was referring to. After all, they were in the Land of the Giants.

Jack dropped his satchel on the forest floor and pulled out a large, leather-bound book.

"Read it again," Cora said.

Jack opened the tome to a marked page and cleared his throat.

> *"The gears spin on jewels*
> *That are red, round, and rare.*
> *They're protected by giants*
> *And a poisonous snare."*

"Jewels," Cora said. "Where will we find jewels in a place like this?"

Jack picked at a blackberry bramble growing along the banks of the stream, and Cora slapped a berry from his hand.

"Remember. *Poisonous snare,*" she said. "It could be anything."

Jack squashed the berry with his foot and whined, "But I'm so hungry."

"I know. We'll eat as soon as we're out of this horrible place."

The children considered their options.

Oliver decided now was his chance to speak up. Perhaps

if he offered a bit of advice, he would endear himself to them and they would untie him.

He opened his eyes and motioned with his nose, saying, "You said you're looking for jewels? I saw some that way."

Cora and Jack froze.

"He was listening to us," Jack growled.

"That he was," Cora said.

"How long has he been awake?"

"Too long."

Jack bent down and picked up a rock.

"What should we do with him?"

Cora tilted back her head and laughed.

"Knock him out again? Skin him alive? Cook him for meat? Leave him for the giants?"

More *BOOM*s thundered in the distance.

"No," Jack said. "That would be too kind."

"You don't want to kill me," Oliver said. Of that he was certain.

"You know nothing about us," Cora whispered, but that wasn't true. Oliver knew a tremendous amount about them. If he let on how much he knew, it would be most surprising, so he decided it was better to say only what was absolutely necessary.

"I know you need jewels. I can show you where they are and help you get them."

"Tell us where they are and we'll get them ourselves. We don't need your help," Cora said.

"You do, actually."

"What makes you say that?"

"Because I'm a thief."

It was the first time Oliver admitted it out loud, and for some inexplicable reason, it made him feel better. *He was a thief.*

"A thief, you say? Is that why you were banished out in this forsaken forest?"

Oliver nodded. In a way, it was true.

"You must not be very good if you were caught," Jack said.

Oliver shrugged.

"But he *has* survived out here, despite the awful conditions. Perhaps he can help us."

Cora and Jack paused, eyeing him carefully. They nodded together, and Jack pulled a knife from his satchel and sliced off the ropes that bound Oliver's feet, helping him stand. He pointed the knife at Oliver's chest, which was still tightly bound.

"Lead us to jewels and we'll let you live."

"All right," Oliver said. "Cora, when you were up in the tree, did you see a canyon?"

She pointed in the direction of the North Star.

"There."

"Then that's where we need to go."

Cora swept her black cloak over her shoulder, motioning at Jack to follow.

They began to walk, passing through thorny plants and over cold, wet rocks.

Bugs swarmed around them, and birds rustled in leaves overhead.

Cora and Jack hacked at gnarled branches with their

knives, and the three children pushed through the dense forest.

Finally, they arrived at a mound of boulders overlooking a wide canyon that sloped far below. It was surrounded on all sides by slabs of craggy rocks, and a narrow stream ran through the middle, disappearing into a giant crack.

Oliver squirmed in his ropes.

"There," he said, motioning with his nose. The grass on the canyon floor was a soft blue under the starlight, and nestled beside the stream was a mound of sparkling red rocks surrounded by flowers.

Dozens of human skeletons draped with the distinctive black robes of Sigil's guard were scattered around them, most of them missing limbs or skulls.

"Jewels," Jack whispered, leaping on a bolder to get a clearer look.

Cora grabbed his shirt.

"*Poisonous snare,*" she said. "Watch for it."

Above the tops of the trees far to their left, an enormous gray hand appeared, slamming down onto the forest floor. There was a *BOOM*, followed by a scream and a crunch.

"Let's go before the giants find us," Jack said.

"The snare is the flowers," Oliver said. "See those purple ones around the jewels? One touch of their petals and your skin will burn and bubble and ooze."

Oliver shuddered. In the book, Jack had grazed one with his ankle, and the description of the resulting pain he suffered had been horrendous to read.

"How do you know that?" Jack asked.

"We have them back where I come from," Oliver lied. "They're in the woods around my house, and one time I stepped on—"

"We don't need your life story. Is there anything else you want to tell us about the jewels?" Cora asked.

Oliver thought for a moment. He knew they were supposed to go into the cave after stealing a jewel, but they didn't know that yet. He supposed there was no harm in helping them, so long as he didn't change the events of the story.

"After you steal a jewel, you'll need a plan of escape. See that crack at the far end of the canyon? Looks like that's the entrance to a cave. Go in there."

"Got it," Jack said, looking at Cora.

"And if a giant chases you, dash through its legs and stay behind it. It won't be able to see you, and they're very slow at turning."

"There are no giants in the canyon," Cora said.

"Yet," Oliver said, and the trees that surrounded the right side of the canyon rustled ominously. There was another *BOOM*—a fist hitting the ground, bones being crushed by sharp teeth, followed by a chewing sound and an ear-splitting belch.

"Let's move," Cora said. She skipped up to the top of the boulder and motioned to Jack. "Time is ticking."

Oliver wiggled his chest.

"Aren't you going to untie me first?"

"No, Oliver. We thank you for your guidance; however, you serve us better as giant bait now."

"Wait!" Oliver yelled, but it was too late. Cora and Jack

leapt from the boulder, quietly descending to the canyon floor.

He looked behind him, expecting to see the Pribbles burst through the trees at any moment, the *CORTEXIA*™ held at the ready. He couldn't follow the children with his arms bound to his sides—the canyon wall was treacherous and steep, and surely he'd fall to his death if he attempted to scale it without the use of all his limbs.

There was a rustle in the trees, and Oliver strained his neck to see.

Behind him, the tall, dark figure appeared, extending a finger toward the canyon. The figure was at least eight feet tall and moved like a shadow that had come to life.

"Who are you?" Oliver yelled, but the figure did not answer. Oliver looked in the direction it was pointing. "What do you want me to do? I'm tied up."

He heard a snap and felt the pressure around his arms and chest relax. The rope fell to the ground and slithered away.

"Did you do that?" he asked, but the tall, dark figure was gone, lost to him in the inky shadows of the forest.

Below, Cora and Jack landed on the canyon floor and began to slink over the mossy ground, hiding as best they could near roots and shrubbery, careful not to graze the small purple flowers that peppered the landscape.

Above them, the trees surrounding the canyon began to sway. The canyon walls rumbled. Dust and birds flew into the air in what should have been a very clear warning that danger was fast approaching.

"Right on cue," Oliver whispered.

Cora and Jack began to run, heading toward the sparkling, ruby-red rocks.

He had to help Cora and Jack before it was too late.

He leapt to the boulder and began to descend.

The journey to the canyon floor was long and treacherous and full of twisted tree roots and exotic flowers with sharp thorns protruding from their stems.

He touched the ground and brushed off his clothes, looking for Cora and Jack. They were far away and approaching the jewels just as a giant burst through the edge of the forest to Oliver's left, pushing off from the rocky cliff and propelling itself into the air. The massive creature fell a hundred feet to the ground, smashing its meaty hands on the canyon floor. It arched its neck and screamed to the heavens as loud as it could. A river of drool poured from its mouth. Two more giants leapt from the left side of the canyon, with a smaller giant close behind, snarling and snapping their sharp yellow teeth.

"Look out!" Oliver yelled.

Cora and Jack turned around, their eyes widening at the terrifying sight as the giants began to chase them.

A Brief Description
of the Hideous Giants

Let's pause for a moment for a brief description of the Hideous Giants, though it's quite possible that words are insufficient to describe the level of pure, unrelenting awfulness on display that night in the canyon. Feel free to use an extra dose of your twisted imagination to make them even more grotesque and wicked than the following paragraphs could ever manage.

First, as their name suggests, the giants were *huge*. Even the smallest giant was at least thirty feet tall, and the larger ones towered above it by an additional twenty feet. Their legs and arms were disproportionately long, and their hands and feet were comically bulbous. Their fingernails were sharp and cracked and absolutely perfect for removing a head from a body with minimal fuss. They wore little more than loincloths to cover their midsections, and the hides of small animals were tied in braids all along their monstrous bodies as trophies of their previous meals.

Second, they were *ugly*. Their bodies were a greenish gray, covered in bumpy gooseflesh that was wrinkled and peppered with sick-looking spots. Coarse hair ran down their backs, and scales covered their cheeks and foreheads. Feathers sprouted from the folds of their necks and armpits, leading some scholars in Dulum to deduce that they were a mixture of ancient bird, ravenous sea creature, and gorilla. None of the aforementioned species would appreciate the association, I assure you.

By far, the worst part of the Hideous Giants were their *faces*. Imagine the most grotesque thing you've ever seen in all your life, then multiply it by eleven and repeatedly bash it with a rock. They were scrunched and evil things, with small beady eyes sunk into a mass of meaty flesh. Their lips pointed down in the middle like a smushed beak, and their teeth snapped the air with a ravenous hunger.

Oliver handled his first sight of the giants remarkably well. After all, he had seen them in his imagination and was prepared for the horrible sight before him. Still, he wasn't prepared for the *stench*. It wafted off of them with every movement, surrounding them in a yellow haze. He covered his nostrils with his hand and gasped for breath.

Cora and Jack reacted to the giants the way any person of sound mind would—they screamed as loud as their little mouths could scream. The giants screamed in return, extending their arms like wings and beating them down, shaking the ground so forcefully that Jack's knees buckled and he nearly fell on top of a purple flower.

"Hey!" Oliver yelled, waving his arms to distract the giants. "Over here!"

Cora turned toward him, her black hair whipping around her shoulders.

"Leave us alone!" she yelled.

"You need to run!" Oliver replied.

The four giants grunted at one another and beat their chests. Two of them turned and ran at Oliver as the other two advanced on Cora and Jack, who were sprinting toward the pile of glowing jewels. Their lead was short-lived; their tiny legs were no match for the massive limbs of the giants, and they soon found themselves in a race for their lives.

Oliver stood in place as the giants came closer. He studied their movements, concocting a plan.

Run!

Oliver crouched, watching as the two giants advanced. His heart thumped in his chest. It had seemed so easy in the book—run through the giant's legs and stay behind them—but the reality of it was a bit different. The giants may have been slow, but they were able to jump a dozen feet in the air and land on the ground with a tremendous BOOM. Their arms could swipe from far away, making it difficult to approach, and even if one did get within throwing distance, the giant's breath was a powerful deterrent.

Oliver waited for the perfect moment, then ran through the legs of the smaller giant as fast as he could. He timed his charges, staying between the giant's legs as it howled in confusion and spun in circles, searching for its prey. The other giant pointed and growled, swiping its arm in Oliver's direction, but its aim was poor and it crashed into the smaller giant's shin, knocking it over. This caused a back-and-forth shouting match of guttural growls, and the two giants wrestled on the ground, biting the air around each other's faces.

Oliver ran away from them along the edge of the stream, teetering above a school of hungry fish that thrashed in the water below. His eyes were fixed on the jewels. He had to help

Cora and Jack, and, from the looks of things, they could use an awful lot of it.

"Through their legs!" Oliver shouted.

"Don't tell us what to do!" Cora replied. She and Jack were close to the jewels, but they were clearly ignoring his advice. Perhaps, Oliver thought, he should have let them figure out the strategy on their own, as they had in the story. They were strong-willed children and didn't like to follow suggestions, particularly from strangers. His presence was *changing* the events of the book, and not for the better.

Cora and Jack stayed in front of the giants, leading them on a zigzag path through the canyon.

"Quick! You only need one!" Oliver shouted.

Now they were five feet away from the pile, carefully tiptoeing through the deadly purple flowers. Jack wrapped his hands around a jewel, lifting it. Cora motioned at Jack to leave, but he was staring into the jewel, mesmerized by its beauty. The moon reflected on its surface, casting triangles of burning red light across his face.

"Run!" Oliver shouted.

But the children had paused long enough for the largest giant of the bunch to leap in the air and sweep its forearm across the pile, striking them hard with the back of its hand. They flew through the air, coming to a stop in the muddy bank of the stream. The jewel Jack was holding had slipped from his grip, and the giant pounced on it, cradling it in his arms and delicately placing it back on the top of the pile. Then he turned toward the children, shrieking with fury.

No one really knows why the giants are so protective of

the jewels. Some say they use them as a form of money. Others say they're attracted to shiny things. Personally, I think it's because the jewels remind them of their favorite thing in all of Dulum: fresh blood.

The two giants that were wrestling behind Oliver stood, seeing that their pile of jewels had been disturbed. They howled at the top of their lungs, racing to the children who dared touch their treasure.

"You can't leave yet!" Oliver screamed, but his cries were ignored.

Cora and Jack ran toward the opening of the cave at the end of the canyon. This most certainly did *not* happen in the book. Without the jewel, their quest was ruined.

The giants gave chase, and they howled and slapped the ground, sending tremors through the canyon and waves along the stream.

Oliver would have to help. He ran toward the jewels, staying crouched and out of the giants' line of sight. His muscles burned, and he tried to remember that this was all in his head. None of this was *actually* happening, but the pain that throbbed down his back and legs felt very real.

He slinked through the flowers. Their aroma was sweet—too sweet, actually—and his head felt fuzzy. The pile of jewels glimmered in front of him, pulsing with a beautiful light.

Cora and Jack were making good progress. Another moment and they would be in the cave, safe from the hungry mouths of the giants. But what about him? How would he make it to the cave once the jewel was in his hands and all four giants had turned their attention to him?

He would figure that out later. For now, he had to use his thieving prowess for good and take the item Jack had failed to steal.

Cora and Jack were at the entrance of the cave now, and they scaled the surrounding rocks, slipping into the opening a split second before a giant's fist slammed into the wall, creating a small avalanche of stones over the entrance.

"Help us, thief!" Cora yelled from the other side.

Her request was poorly timed. The giants spun on their heels just in time to see Oliver lift a jewel the size of a small melon from the pile. The smallest giant jumped, somersaulting high into the air. It landed with such intensity that the ground shook and Oliver was propelled upward, the jewel still clutched in his fingers. He landed on soft grass and rolled, realizing, in horror, that it wasn't grass at all but a patch of the poisonous purple flowers.

"No," Oliver whispered. The sickening smell wafted in the air, and his whole body tingled.

He pushed himself up, staggering toward the cave.

The giants were closing in, surrounding him.

"Cora! Jack! I need help!" he yelled, but the words were muffled and dull. His throat felt puffy and sore. A rash began to spread across his neck and down his arms, wrapping around his torso like a constricting snake.

The giants noticed and began to laugh, throwing their heads into the air and beating their chests. They stalked him, slower now, two circling behind and two in front.

Oliver started to run, praying that his legs would continue

to work, though the burning sensation was spreading down to his toes.

Jack had barely survived the slightest touch from the flowers in the book. He had been treated with cave mud, packed tight against his skin, but how could Oliver ever hope to live after rolling over dozens of the perilous petals? That didn't matter now. He had to get the stolen jewel to Jack and Cora, otherwise the story would be ruined.

He forced his body to move, pushing through the pain, ducking and weaving between the giants' legs. He moved closer and closer to the cave, each step more painful than the last.

"*Cuuuura! Juuuk! Huuuulp!*" he screamed again, but his tongue wouldn't move. He looked down to see that his arm had begun to swell, puffing up into a burning-red and bubbled mess. The blood under his skin seemed to pulse beneath the surface, and the rash continued to grow, spreading down his legs.

Things couldn't possibly get worse, right?

Tears formed in his eyes, either from sadness or from the poison in his blood. The world around him went blurry and dim. The giants were closer now, their bodies quivering with pre-dinner delight.

The cave was still fifty feet away, and there was no way he could make it.

He was just about to give up when he heard it: a familiar voice in the distance, calling out with a joyful lilt.

"Yoo-hoo! Oh, *giants*! Over here, you filthy, feathery monstrosities!"

It was Mrs. Pribble. She was at the other end of the canyon, having just climbed down with her husband in tow. She waved her arms in the air like the legs of a dying spider.

Mr. Pribble stood next to her, the *CORTEXIA*™ propped on his little hip and an enormous grin on his face. The canister pulsed a brilliant blue.

"You're mine now!" he yelled.

The giants froze, clearly confused by what they were seeing.

Then Mr. Pribble pulled the trigger.

CORTEXIA™

The howl of the *CORTEXIA*™ cut through the air.

"Come and get us, you hideous beasts!" Mr. Pribble screamed.

The giants tilted their heads as they searched for the source of the taunt, grunting at one another and pointing at the small silhouettes of the couple.

The ground began to shake and the canyon walls buckled. Rocks and tree stumps struggled to stay rooted before they finally released, flying through the air and melting into a thin vapor as they were sucked into the opening of the *CORTEXIA*™.

That started a fierce and irreversible chain reaction. Water from the stream lifted from the ground, twirling in the air like a giant ribbon of dull blue hues. Fish flopped in the middle of the stream, stretching out like long strands of spaghetti, their teeth still snapping for food. The water raced toward the Pribbles, and even from far away, Oliver could see the canister explode with an impossibly bright light.

The trees and grass and plants disappeared from the ground like a blanket being ripped off a bed, revealing an ashy wasteland underneath. The canyon wall that had led to the forest was gone. Indeed, the whole *forest* behind them was gone.

Mr. Pribble whooped with delight, waving the machine back and forth, his small legs propelling him toward the giants, his wife beside him.

The giants ignored Oliver now, howling in fear, unable to comprehend the villains in front of them who were stealing their home, piece by piece. Oliver limped toward the cave, tossing the jewel through the opening. He considered trying to climb up the avalanche of stones to find Cora and Jack, but what was the point? Surely he would die, and his body throbbed with pain. He fell to his knees, his swollen hands grabbing at the ground, struggling to hold on, but the *CORTEXIA*™ was too strong. Blades of green grass slipped between his fingers, twirling away from him like pieces of string.

The Pribbles were running now, getting closer and closer to the giants, the *CORTEXIA*™ squealing louder with every tree and rock and flower it slurped up.

"What are you big beasts waiting for?" Mrs. Pribble yelled, waving her hands at them. "We're awfully tasty!"

The largest giant attacked them first, its wicked face pulling and stretching, screaming from the depths of its belly as it charged. Two others followed, and their bodies seemed to melt in midair, flying toward the Pribbles like a tornado, their shapes mixing with the trees and shrubs and creating a muddy brown color that spun up and around and, finally, into the nozzle of the machine.

Above them, the stars and moon smeared, the night sky turning into an inky black fluid that spun down.

The world inverted and turned, sucked up in one quick motion, making a tiny *fwip* sound as any remaining color disappeared.

Oliver stood with the Pribbles in a world of gray dust and fog, save for the last remaining giant and the rocky entrance of the cave.

"Go on, Oliver. Inside the cave," Mr. Pribble said, wiping the sweat from his brow. "Chapter two awaits. You have the jewel, so there's no reason to delay."

The last remaining giant clutched at the air and roared.

"There's nowhere else to go." Mrs. Pribble giggled. "The Land of the Giants is gone."

Suddenly the whole world felt upside down and askew. For a moment, Oliver forgot where he was. He felt an odd sensation between his temples, like a bubble had burst.

"The Land of the—oh, my great merciful heavens, what am I saying?" Mrs. Pribble cackled. She patted the canister on her husband's vacuum. "The Land of the Giants is in *here* now."

The memory of the place was still there, but dimmer somehow, like a distant memory.

"Seven chapters left," Mr. Pribble said. "Go on, Oliver. Into the cave!"

Every inch of Oliver's flesh burned, and red clouds formed in the corners of his vision. He shook his head.

"But you must. Where else is there to go? What else is there to do?"

The lone giant roared again, looking back and forth between the Pribbles and Oliver, unsure of whom to attack first.

Cora's head appeared from the cave's entrance.

"Oliver? What's going on?" she asked, but Oliver couldn't answer. He wanted to tell them that he had thrown the jewel into the cave and that they should go on without him, but he could hardly breathe, let alone speak.

"In here!" Jack yelled. "*Quick!*"

Oliver stood and stumbled toward the giant, laying his stinging hand on a boulder to prop himself up. He wanted to go home.

"Books move in a linear fashion," Mr. Pribble said. "Onward!"

Oliver looked back at the cave, and a crazy idea came to him. He swung back his leg and kicked the giant in the toe as hard as he could.

Fingernails

It's difficult for me to describe what happened next, so I will keep my description as brief as possible and only relay the facts as I observed them.

If you're squeamish, skip ahead to the next chapter.

If not, we'll continue at the exact moment Oliver kicked the giant in the toe. The giant howled and twisted its body to observe the little creature below it. It growled in a way that made clear that it was really quite annoyed.

It lifted its massive hand and then thrust it down, its index finger and thumb forming a circle that opened and closed as its fingernails snapped.

Click clack click.

The hand swooped toward Oliver, pausing around his neck.

"No," Mr. Pribble said.

"No," Mrs. Pribble said.

The giant's index finger and thumb closed together.

The sharp fingernails made a *thwunk* sound as they pierced flesh and touched together, removing Oliver's head in one quick motion. His limp and headless body fell to the ground, and the giant tossed Oliver's small skull into the air and caught it in his mouth.

Crunch crunch crunch.

Mrs. Pribble screamed.

Mr. Pribble held his hand over his mouth, belched, and whispered, "Don't worry, love. This isn't part of the story."

And then there was blood. Oh, so very much blood.

Reset

For the briefest instant after his head was removed from his body, Oliver heard Cora and Jack scream from the cave, and then there was silence, so instant and complete that it swallowed him whole.

Only blackness remained.

Then, at the tip of where his fingers should've been, he felt *something*.

It was a peculiar sensation. He wasn't *dead* so much as he was a fine mist that floated in waves, a ghost made of particles that vibrated in the stillness.

Sounds came from around him, soft at first and then gaining volume.

"*—never should have—*"

"*—who would have thought he'd be so—*"

"*—exactly the reason I can't stand—*"

Bits of light swarmed in the distance and began to form into two figures—one tall and thin, and the other short and round.

The Pribbles.

Oliver felt his own body slowly rebuild, piece by piece, forming a hand, then arms, followed by a torso and legs and, finally—*pop!*—a head.

"Such violence," Mrs. Pribble whined. "I simply can't stand it in children's literature. Utterly unnecessary."

"As I explained, dear, young Oliver went off story. I do hope this doesn't sully your opinion of *The Timekeeper's Children*. Don't worry, we can place him right back where he belongs."

Oliver blinked. He was in a room of black that stretched as far as he could see. Long white lights blazed overhead. The floor was a shiny tile made of digital squares that glowed at the seams, blue and orange and red.

"You can't die, you know, if that was your plan," Mr. Pribble said. His shoes clicked on the floor as he walked toward Oliver.

Oliver rubbed his hands together, felt their fleshy softness.

"A very poor plan, too, getting your head ripped off like that," Mrs. Pribble said. "Disgusting! This book is meant for *children*."

"Did you think the story would be over?" Mr. Pribble asked. "That we would just . . . just . . . let you go without getting to the end?" He laughed. "We must continue, but now you will be forced to explain to Cora and Jack how you managed to survive that dreadful decapitation."

"How will I do that?" Oliver asked.

"Blast if I know! All I can say is that Cora and Jack exist in your mind, so if *you* believe it strongly enough, perhaps they will as well. I don't envy you, Oliver. It seems like a very awkward conversation."

Mr. Pribble pecked at the screen on the *CORTEXIA*™, zooming around a digital map and typing in coordinates.

"You'll reset at the exact location of your demise, right at the entrance of the cave and at the beginning of chapter two, 'A Journey Through the Cave of Horrors.' Please, try not to die again. It messes with the pacing."

"Yes, it does seems like a waste if he can just die over and over again," Mrs. Pribble said. "He can make this book such a violent experience. We need to give him some *motivation*."

Mr. Pribble tugged at his beard.

"Perhaps you're right. You know, I created the *CORTEXIA*™ so that I could remove the story from his little brain with surgical precision, but I suppose I may have been too kind." Mr. Pribble reached up and patted Oliver on the cheek. He typed more into the rectangular screen. "There. I've placed a limit on your ability to regenerate. If you die a total of five times, I'll simply remove the entire contents of your imagination with one press of a button. Every book you've read, every creation you've conjured. *Mine*."

Oliver gasped.

"You've already used one. And don't worry; if you fail, you'll be just like all the other children. Devoid of imagination, needing to use the goggles for all your dreams. If you'd like to avoid that, you should continue through the book—*alive*. Once you finish chapter eight, 'A Timely End,' the exit motion will automatically reactivate. That's a promise. You'll return to the dining room, and we'll personally escort you to the front door. You'll be without the faintest memory that this book ever existed."

"Wonderful! Now go on, dear. Send him back," Mrs. Pribble said. "I want to know what happens next!"

"Oh, darling, you haven't seen anything yet! The best is yet to come!"

Mr. Pribble glanced at his watch.

"By my estimation, your father is halfway to Burger Bistro, and we still have a tremendous amount of story to work through. Now, let's return to . . ."

The floor began to twist under Oliver's feet, and once again he felt like he was falling. He thrashed his arms about, searching for something to grab. Mr. Pribble continued his speech.

" . . . all the sights and wonders of . . ."

Dark colors smeared in the air. Chimes sounded around him.

" . . . and all the twists and turns . . ."

Wet rocks appeared underneath him, the moisture seeping through his pants. He was in the dark entrance of the cave. Lodged in the clay mud beside him was the glistening red jewel of the giants. Cora and Jack must not have seen that he had tossed it to them. Oliver pulled it out of the mud. The voice of Mr. Pribble whispered in his ear.

" . . . only have four lives left. Tick tock, Oliver."

CHAPTER TWO

A JOURNEY THROUGH
THE CAVE OF HORRORS

The Cave of Horrors glistened with the damp drippings of an ancient spring. Curved stalactites hung ominously above, like the swords of a thousand warriors waiting to plunge into pleading victims. Small pools of water formed in nooks on the floor, glowing an aquamarine. The cave's winding interior was filled with tunnels that branched off and burrowed deep into the earth. Each tunnel was narrow and full of sharp rocks and slippery descents that could plunge travelers down to a swift death, and each was full of creatures more awful than the last.

That is the opening paragraph to the second chapter of Malcolm Bloom's novel, *The Timekeeper's Children*, and, try as I might, I can't think of a better way to describe the Cave of Horrors. Yes, the cave system was a mysterious place unfit for humans, and yes, it's true that it was oh-so-very dark and spooky, but simply knowing that is not enough. It's important that you understand the despair and hollowness that visitors to this dreadful place felt—a feeling that all hope and goodness had vanished from the world.

Oliver whispered the opening paragraph of the chapter

to himself, clutching the jewel to his chest and running his free hand along a wet wall as he worked his way deeper into the cave. His head ached terribly, but at least his skin was no longer red and bubbling from the poisonous flowers.

Chapter two. Let's get this over with, he thought, feeling defeated after his previous encounter with the Pribbles and overwhelmed at their threat to steal everything from his imagination. *Go ahead and take the stupid story. What do I care?*

He felt very sorry for himself. And wasn't this whole ordeal another item to add to the list of his misfortunes? Everything that happened to him seemed to go wrong, so why should this be any different? He wanted to curl up in a ball and sleep and sleep and never wake up.

You see, even though he had just arrived, Oliver was already suffering from the stifling depression common among visitors to the Cave of Horrors. Perhaps you've felt it, too. If so, the best thing to do is carry on, and that's exactly what Oliver did.

He crawled up to a narrow opening, not much wider than his shoulders, and slipped through with his arm raised to the roof of rock. The air became stale the deeper he traveled, and shadows were playing tricks on his eyes. He felt a tightening in his chest and wanted to go outside, be in open space, raise his head and see clear blue skies above him. A soft sobbing sound came from deep inside the cave, and Oliver followed it, twisting his way over wet paths and through narrow tubes, searching for Cora and Jack.

Finally, he approached the end of the tunnel. It emptied

into a cavernous room, where thin streams snaked around the muddy floor, glowing an eerie blue. A fire flickered in the center of the room, and two hunched figures sat near it, casting long shadows. Smoke twisted up, curling around stalactites and escaping through thin cracks in the ceiling.

The sobbing sound was closer now. Cora had buried her face in her hands, and Jack was leaning against her, his arm wrapped around her shoulders.

"We'll be all right," he whispered to her, but his voice was amplified by the shape of the room.

"No," Cora answered. "Nothing will be ever be all right. We're surrounded by death."

"How do you think he knew about the jewels and the poisonous flowers?"

"I don't know. There was something special about him. Something *different*. I thought he was lying when he said he wasn't a member of the Gang, but now . . . now I don't know . . . "

"And who were those people that were with him? Sorcerers? And that strange contraption they had. The whole world seemed to—"

"It was a very wicked type of magic," Cora answered. She leaned her head on Jack's shoulder.

"We lost the jewel," Jack said, and his voice quivered.

"It will be all right. We'll find another way."

"How?" Jack asked. "Do you think another one will just appear out of nowhere?"

There was no sense in waiting. If Oliver hoped to get

through the cave and continue the story, he had to get Cora and Jack on his side. He pushed his small body out of the tunnel, sliding down a slippery, wet slope and landing in a large puddle of water.

"Hello again," he said, holding up the jewel and trying his best to look friendly.

Their screams echoed loudly.

A Very Awkward Conversation

Cora's and Jack's screams continued for three-and-a-half minutes, which is an appropriate amount of time, considering they had just seen Oliver die in a violent and bloody way.

Jack hid behind Cora's cloak, holding out his hands in self-defense. He crab-walked along the floor, searching for a rock to chuck at Oliver's ghostly form.

Cora leapt to her feet, pulling a knife from her belt and waving it in the air.

"Back, demon. *Back!*" she yelled.

The fire danced with her motion, and stray embers twirled around the ceiling. The smell of smoke was strong in the musty cave air.

"It's all right," Oliver said, pushing his body against the wall of the cavern. "I brought a gift."

He tossed the jewel toward them. Jack dashed forward, grabbed it, and ran back behind his sister.

"But . . . but . . . *how?*" Cora stammered. "And you're *alive?*"

"I have magical powers," Oliver said. "One of which is the gift of immortality."

Now it was Jack's turn to pull out his knife. The *twing* echoed around them. He advanced toward Oliver.

"Magic, you say? I didn't think that was possible for children. Do you work for Sigil?"

Oliver didn't answer. He searched his mind for the best way to respond. To say he worked for Sigil would be dangerous, for Sigil was a truly evil man, but to say he didn't would open him up to more questions. Luckily, Cora interrupted before he could stammer through an answer.

"You know who Sigil is, right? He's the wicked ruler of this land, a dark sorcerer who rules by fear and destruction."

"Oh yes. Sigil. Of course," Oliver said. "I think I've heard the name before."

"Well, we work for him," Jack growled, and now both the children were advancing, their blades sparkling in the firelight.

"Wait a minute," Oliver asked, quickly concocting a plan. "You say *Sigil* rules this land? I was always told *King Gerard* ruled over Dulum."

The children paused.

"You don't know what happened?" Jack asked.

"No. I've never been to Dulum before, but I've heard tales. I used to think it was all just something from a storybook," Oliver said.

"Well, it's not," Cora said. "And you may as well know that King Gerard is dead. Good riddance to him."

They continued advancing toward Oliver until their blades were within slicing distance of his soft throat.

"You won't hurt me," Oliver said.

"What makes you so sure?" Jack growled.

"Another of my magical abilities is being able to tell what's in someone's heart. You aren't bad, even though you're pretending to be." Oliver pushed his neck closer to their blades. "Go ahead. Prove me wrong."

There was a pause, and then Cora and Jack dropped their arms and sheathed their blades.

"Fine. We'll spare you for now, as long as you give us some answers," Jack said. "Where are you from?"

"Garden Grove," Oliver said.

"A silly name," Cora said. "I've never heard of it. And who were those two people chasing you?"

"They're called . . . *the Pribbles.*"

"Another silly name."

Oliver closed his eyes, thinking hard. What was it Mr. Pribble had said before he reset? Cora and Jack existed in his mind, so if *he* believed his story, so would they.

"The Pribbles kidnapped me from my home long ago. It's not at all like Dulum. Where I come from, *only children* possess magic. They forced me to use my powers to help them create wicked machines."

"Like that strange thing they had in the canyon?" Jack asked.

"Yes. We had been working on it for a long time. It's called the *CORTEXIA*™—"

Cora scoffed.

"—and it casts a gray fog over places, putting anything it touches under its owner's control. One day, they grabbed me in the middle of the night and we set sail from Garden

Grove. They said they'd heard of someone who wanted the *CORTEXIA*™ and would pay them richly for it. I didn't know where we were going, but when we landed on the shore and began our journey, I tried to escape in the forest. Then I met you two."

Cora glared at him, her eyes piercing through his.

"We *did* see him beheaded by a giant, and yet here he is," Jack whispered to Cora. "Maybe he's telling the truth."

"Hey," Oliver said, pretending that a thought had suddenly occurred to him. "I wonder if they mean to sell the *CORTEXIA*™ to Sigil."

"Obviously," Cora said.

Jack turned to his sister and said, "I knew his plan was more than just the clock."

Cora slapped him on the arm.

"Clock?" Oliver asked.

"Ignore him. He doesn't know when to be quiet."

"Why is it so important that you have this jewel?"

Jack and Cora looked at each other, having a silent conversation with their eyes.

"Well, we might as well tell him," Jack finally said. "It might be helpful to have an immortal magic boy on our quest."

Cora thought for a moment and waved a hand.

"Come," she said. "Let's sit beside the fire. The cold is bitter in this cave."

Oliver followed them to the fire and sat on a wet rock, warming his fingers over the blaze.

Cora's face softened in the firelight, and her smile was brighter than the flames that danced over the wood.

"What do you know about time, Oliver?" she asked.

Oliver shrugged.

"Time is all around us," Cora said, "ticking forward, impossible to stop. One minute, followed by the next."

"Yes," Oliver said. "I know that much."

"Time always moves forward at the same pace," Jack said. "Unless . . ."

He pulled a large, leather-bound book from his satchel. It was a beautiful and ancient thing, fitting several of Oliver's thieving criteria: *old*, *musty*, *ripped*, and *brittle*. The cover was smooth, and stamped on the front was an old-looking insignia of fire and lightning and rain and sunshine. At one point it must have been as white as ivory, but now it was caked in a thin film of grit.

"Do you know the history of this place?"

Oliver shook his head, and Jack began to speak, beginning the part of every book in which a tremendous amount of backstory is given in order for the rest of the plot to make sense.

Enjoy.

The Timekeeper's Children

All our lives, King Gerard has ruled over Dulum, protecting us from harm. His brother, Sigil, is an evil man, obsessed with dark magic. He was cast out of the city long ago, banished to a twisted tower in the center of a swamp to the north of the kingdom. Things were good for many years."

"That brings us to three months ago," Cora whispered. "On a dark night, Sigil snuck into Dulum and killed his brother, staking his claim over all of Dulum."

Oliver gasped, pretending to be surprised.

"With his wicked magic he could rule over the land, *except . . .*" Jack trailed off, allowing Cora to finish his thought.

"The children."

Jack nodded.

"In Dulum, only adults are affected by magic."

"Which is why we were so surprised to see you alive after . . ." Cora grabbed her skull and pretended to pull it off.

Jack carefully turned through the pages of the ancient book, laying each on top of the last. They were made of stretched animal skin, and the ink was the color of blood. Perhaps it *was* blood.

"This is a book of spells," Jack said. He stopped at a

page and traced his finger along the words. "It was written centuries ago. Sigil stole the books from King Gerard's library and studied each and every one until he found this. He may not be able to affect children, but *time* . . . well, that's a different thing altogether."

He began to read, his thin voice echoing in the cave.

> *"Time travels through Dulum*
> *With a tick and a tock.*
> *It can be only altered*
> *By building this clock.*
>
> *The gears spin on jewels*
> *That are red, round, and rare.*
> *They're protected by giants*
> *And a poisonous snare.*
>
> *The dial glows blue*
> *With the texture of skin.*
> *Their owners have teeth,*
> *And they wiggle and grin.*
>
> *Add a casing constructed*
> *With wood that is charred.*
> *It is steeped in the drink*
> *Of the Old Mountain Guard.*
>
> *In the city of Dulum*
> *Sits the crown of the king.*

By life or by death,
It must twist the mainspring.

Avoid all the troubles,
the teeth and the claws.
The lumbering fists
And the treacherous jaws.

So gather these pieces,
Assemble them fast.
Use hands that are true,
Change the future or past."

"Sigil reasons that if he can build the clock mentioned in this spell, he can alter time, speeding it up until he has . . ."

Cora and Jack whispered together:

"A kingdom without children."

"And if there are no children, then no one in all of Dulum will be impervious to the effects of his magic," Cora explained. "Sigil can rule the land with no threats to his power—namely King Gerard's son, Grayson, who's the rightful king."

Jack stood, moving to the other side of the fire, his shadows flickering along the floor.

"One night, Sigil's guards came to our house and set it on fire, destroying everything we owned. We were thrown into the night, tied up on horses, and dragged to Sigil's Twisted Tower."

"Why?" Oliver asked.

Cora nodded, as though she'd been expecting the question.

"Our father, Horace, is the city timekeeper and the most skilled clockmaker in all of Dulum. Sigil captured him to be the *hands that are true* from the spell's final verse, the one who will build the magic clock. Sigil locked us in a room at the top of his tower and told our father all the awful things he'd do to us if he didn't help with the plan. Our father agreed, waiting for the clock pieces to be delivered. We were there for weeks, cut off from the world, looking out as evil magic spread over Dulum. One day, we heard Sigil yelling at his guards. None had managed to return with any of the necessary pieces. It's their bones that litter the Land of the Giants."

"So how did you get free? And why are you helping Sigil?" Oliver asked. Of course, he already knew the answer, but he was excited to hear it from their own lips.

Cora looked at Jack.

"Should we tell him? What if those Pribble people capture him and take him to Sigil? He might reveal our plan."

"We can't let him get captured, then," Jack said, motioning at the jewel. "He's already been useful."

"And I won't tell Sigil anything. I promise," Oliver said, wishing with all his heart that they would believe it.

Cora stared into his eyes, seeming to read his thoughts, and finally nodded.

"We're not really villains," Jack said.

"Our mother died shortly before Sigil attacked," Cora said, her voice trembling. She grabbed Jack by the shoulders and pulled him close. "Our father is all we have left in the world, and to lose him would be . . ."

She was unable to continue, and Jack took over.

"We told Sigil we could get the pieces from the spell, and we swore our allegiance to him. All we asked was that, once the deed is done and all of Dulum is under his control, he lets us serve him. It was an interesting idea, because children *do* make the best thieves. So he let us leave, saying he'd kill our father if we aren't successful."

"That's why we're pretending to be bad," Cora added. "And that's why we're being hunted by the Gang of Impervious Children, led by King Gerard's son, Grayson. They don't understand our true intentions. Once the clock is made, we're going to use it to turn back time to when our mother was alive."

Oliver smiled. How many times had he wished there was a clock that would allow him to return to a time before his mother had died, to spend just one more day with her?

"I want time to turn back, too," he said, moving closer to Cora and Jack. "My . . . my mother died."

"Really? What happened?" Jack asked.

"She had a problem with her heart," Oliver answered.

"How did you survive it?"

To that, there was no easy answer. The truth was, he had turned to books. This one in particular. Reading stories gave him strength and the hope that things would get better. Perhaps, he thought, that was why he connected so strongly with Cora and Jack. They had survived the loss of their mother and had carried on, so he could, too.

"I had the help of some very good friends," Oliver said.

"We have no friends," Cora said, breaking into the

deep sobs of someone who has lost a person they love. "Not anymore, at least."

"I'm your friend," Oliver said, and had a sudden flash of sadness at the thought that he might lose them from his mind forever. This book, he realized, was far more important to him than he could ever express. The anger at what the Pribbles were doing to him boiled in his belly.

"Do you mean it?" she asked.

"I do," he said, and it was at that moment that Oliver Nelson hatched a plan of his own. He decided he was *not* going to let the Pribbles steal Cora and Jack from his mind without a fight, even if it meant departing from the original text.

But that, as you soon will learn, is a more difficult proposition than Oliver realized.

Bats!

Strange sounds filled the cavern, and the fire had reduced to a pile of ash and flickering embers.

Thump thump thump.

Oliver sat up and rubbed his eyes. Hours had passed, and his body ached. He hadn't realized he'd fallen asleep and guessed it was morning by now, though there was no way to accurately tell time in the deep darkness of the Cave of Horrors.

Thump thump thump. Louder this time.

"What was that?" Jack asked.

"Bats," Oliver answered, and goose bumps prickled his skin. He always hated this part of the book. Bats were filthy creatures, hidden in shadows, and the noises they made were pure evil, like the cries of devils resurrected from the fiery depths of the earth.

Jack held out his knife and tucked the jewel in his satchel along with his flints and other supplies. He searched the cave walls for the source of the sound.

"Where are they coming from?"

"Everywhere," Oliver said. "They're coming for us, and they're hungry for blood."

"Well, we don't have any meat. All we have is a few loaves of bread."

"I think he means *our* blood," Cora said. "Does it hurt to die in horrendous ways, Oliver?"

"Not really," Oliver lied, remembering the giant's fingernails piercing through his neck. Death hurt very much.

"We need to keep moving," Cora said.

The thumping sounds were getting louder now, a sea of clicks and beating noises that echoed in the cavernous room.

"Which way should we go?" Jack asked.

Oliver spun in place. The ground trembled, and something moved in a corner of the cavern. The tall, hooded figure stepped from the shadows. It lifted an arm, pointing to a dark crevice of the room. Oliver squinted. If they were to follow the plot of the book, they would travel through the largest opening at the far side of the cavern, track a small stream of water to an underground lagoon, and safely swim out of the cave through a narrow tunnel leading to the Green Lands.

Should he choose another route . . . why, *anything* could happen.

"That way," Oliver said, nodding at the small opening on the other side of the cavern, where the figure had pointed. It looked dark and dangerous and uninviting, but something told Oliver he should trust the figure's advice.

"Are you sure?" Jack asked. He looked back at the cave's largest opening. "That way looks like the obvious route. And it's bigger, too. Look, Oliver, the rocks in the wall are glowing, almost lighting the path. We'd hardly even need a torch."

"That's exactly why we *shouldn't* take it," Oliver said. The Pribbles would surely pick that route, too.

"What about our next item?" Cora asked. "We need to figure out the riddle. It's the only item without a clue about where to find it. It could be anywhere in Dulum."

She recited the next verse of the spell:

> *"The dial glows blue*
> *With the texture of skin.*
> *Their owners have teeth,*
> *And they wiggle and grin."*

"What could it be?" Oliver asked, rubbing his chin and pretending to think.

"It has to be something living," Jack said.

"What wiggles?" Cora asked. "A snake?"

"Snakes don't grin," Oliver said. He pointed to the pools of glowing water on the cavern floor. Loose scales floated about, shimmering with a magical blue color. "Eels do. I bet the water glows because of their scales. This cave must be full of them, so we can catch one deeper inside and get its skin. It's lucky I led you here!"

Cora eyed him suspiciously, and Jack ripped a band of cloth from his satchel, dousing it with liquid from a small vial. He wrapped the soaked fabric around one end of a stick and then rolled it in the remaining embers of the fire until it burst into flames.

A black stream of bats poured from the mouth of a side tunnel as though a faucet had been turned on, filling the room with shadowy movement. There were hundreds, perhaps thousands, of bats—some as big as dogs and some as small as squirrels. They flew in a circle, their small eyes glowing red with hate and their mouths snapping with hunger.

The bats closest to the children made a clicking sound, alerting the others of the fleshy prizes they had found.

"Follow me!" Oliver yelled, leading Cora and Jack to the small tunnel where the figure had pointed.

"Take this," Jack said, handing the torch to Oliver. "You're immortal, so you go first."

Oliver pulled himself up the side of the rocky wall and over the tunnel lip until he was lying on his belly, pushing himself forward with his elbows and waving the torch in front of him. The heat baked his face.

Cora and Jack climbed through just as a wave of bats smacked the clay around the small tunnel, hissing and flapping their wings. They were too large to fit through the narrow opening all at once. They squealed and clicked with a bloodthirsty rage, wrestling one another over who would have the honor of the first bite.

Oliver crawled faster, his body scraping against the craggy sides of the tubelike tunnel.

"Keep going, Oliver!" Cora screamed, and he pushed on, crawling forward with every ounce of strength he had.

In the cavern behind them, Mrs. Pribble's melodic voice sounded.

"Yoo-hoo! Oh, Oliver! Where are you?"

"If I remember the story correctly, they would have gone that way," Mr. Pribble said. Oliver hoped he was talking about the obvious route. Mr. Pribble revved the motor on the *CORTEXIA*™. "Let's finish up here and we'll be on our way."

The children continued to crawl as the *CORTEXIA*™ roared and began to suck up the cavernous room. Rocks slapped against walls and wings flapped and faded away. Stalactites fell from the ceiling and stalagmites ripped from the ground, spinning into mist before getting pulled into the nozzle.

From his place in the tunnel, Oliver could see just a glimpse of the cavern behind Cora and Jack. Except it wasn't really a cavern anymore; it was just an empty space full of gray dust and fog.

"We're almost through," Oliver said.

Ahead of him, an opening waited to lead them to a place outside of the story, where everything was new and different and *extra* dangerous.

PART 2

IN WHICH WE DEPART FROM THE STORY IN AN ATTEMPT TO SAVE THE TIMEKEEPER'S CHILDREN

Outside the Story

Oliver stuck his head through the opening and looked around, but there was nothing to see. This new cavern in the Cave of Horrors was so dark, he felt his eyes might burst in his skull.

He worked his arms out of the opening and rubbed his hands along the rocky wall. It went down as far as he could reach.

He pulled a small rock from the tunnel wall and threw it out into the blackness.

"Oliver, what are you doing?" Cora hissed.

"Shhh," he said, listening for a sound.

It took several seconds, but eventually it came, so soft and far away that only the sharpest ear could hear it.

Splash.

Oliver's eyes began to adjust to the darkness. The room was dim at first, and his vision was wobbly, filled with sparks of light like the ones that appear after someone's smacked you in the face. Then things came into focus, slowly, as if the room was being built in front of them, piece by piece.

Below the tunnel opening was a small ledge that wrapped around the entire room. In front of them a great underground chasm that stretched as far as Oliver could see.

Giant stalagmites rose from the darkness, their tops built up into points by thousands of years of dripping water. Many of them were so large that their points had snapped off, creating a smooth surface that would be easy to stand on. The broken stalagmites were conveniently spaced several feet apart, covering the entire length of the chasm. At the very end—far, far away—was a tiny bead of golden light.

"The Green Lands," Oliver said, pointing. He slid down to the ledge and pressed his arms against the rocky wall to steady himself. Cora and Jack followed.

"Are you sure?"

Oliver nodded. He was certain of it, though he wasn't sure why. It was as if he'd *willed* it to be true. He felt a small pain in his forehead but shook it away. He pointed at a broken stalagmite.

"Let's go."

"How will we get across?" Jack asked.

Cora rolled her eyes. "He expects us to jump, obviously."

"Jump?" Jack said. "From rock to rock? Some are too far apart. We'll never make it."

"Maybe *you* won't," Cora said. "I'm quicker and stronger, and Oliver can use his magic to . . . "

"What about the eels?" Jack said. "We can't leave without one."

"Hopefully there are some by the exit," Oliver said. He looked over the cavern. Rats scaled the sides of the stalagmites, ascending out of the darkness and squealing at the strange children in their cave. Giant spiderwebs stretched across the room, connecting the rock formations in a mesh of white silk. Spiders the size of cantaloupes crawled around, hopping from web to web and feasting on any delicious rodent unlucky enough to get tangled in their trap.

"Thank heavens there are no bats," Cora said, shivering.

"Save your thanks," Oliver whispered, holding a finger to his lips and lifting the torch up toward the ceiling. What before had looked like bumpy black rocks above them began to move and squirm, dripping with liquid that he now realized wasn't water at all—it was *drool*.

Heads turned toward the children.

Eyes glowed.

Mouths opened.

Oliver waved the torch and jumped into the abyss.

The Depths

Oliver's feet grazed the surface of the nearest stalagmite, slipping along the muddy, drool-covered top. It teetered and groaned, rocking back and forth ever so slightly before emitting a dull snap.

"Come on!" Oliver hissed. "Jump!"

The bats on the ceiling began to move, their wings uncurling. Oliver looked at the expanse of stalagmites that spread across the cavern. Even if the children moved at a tremendous rate, their survival seemed unlikely. The exit to the Green Lands was impossibly far away, and the distance between the stalagmites was uneven at best.

Cora and Jack leapt behind him, hitting the top of the stalagmite just as it teetered forward, making a loud *crack* before breaking. Slowly, it began to tip, slamming against another pillar in front of it. The children slid down the surface and Oliver pierced the handle of the torch into a cleft of the stalagmite and held on tight. Cora's fingers wrapped around the edge of the rock, and Jack grabbed his sister's ankle, dangling over the abyss.

"Oliver! Help us!" Cora screamed, her fingers slipping.

Oliver grabbed Cora's wrist with his other hand and pulled with a strength that seemed to come from the very core of his being. Inch by inch, Cora and Jack clawed their way up, digging their feet into the soft mud.

Spiders rushed around the tipped rock, wrapping it in webbing as fast as they could to stop the heavy object from falling and destroying their city of silk.

"That was fun," Jack said, wiping sweat from his brow. "Only about a hundred more to go."

Oliver scanned the room, searching for the nearest stalagmite with a broken point. The closest one was to their left, but even that seemed very far away. Could he jump that far? He wasn't sure, and the last thing he wanted was to make another one fall. That could start a chain reaction that might topple all the stalagmites and leave them with no way out of the cave. But there was no other choice.

"That's where we're jumping next," Oliver said, but his voice was drowned out by the squealing of rats. They scaled the pillars and peeked their little black rodent eyes over the edge of the rock, baring their teeth at the flaming torch and wiggling their malnourished bodies at the sight of dinner.

"Seems far," Jack said.

"You go first, Oliver, seeing as you're immortal," Cora added. "If it *is* too far and you fall to your death, you'll come back to us."

Oliver had four lives left, but what about Cora and Jack? If they died, what would happen to the story? Oliver looked down into the blackness below and his stomach wiggled at the height.

"You *will* come back to us, right?" Cora asked.

"Always," Oliver said, though he was determined not to

fall into the depths. Hitting the bottom was sure to be an unpleasant way to die.

He had backed up and was preparing to jump when Jack yelled, "Stop!"

A flapping sound came from above them, followed by shrieks and howls. Bats pushed from the ceiling and flew around the room, circling the children.

"We *really* should have taken the obvious route," Jack whined, and for a moment, Oliver agreed. Perhaps he should have waited until they'd arrived at the Green Lands to depart from the story. But it was too late to retreat now, and the bats were flying closer.

"They won't get near the fire," Jack said. He grabbed the torch from Oliver's hand and waved it back and forth, brandishing it like a sword. "I'll hang on to this."

"What about me?" Oliver protested, spinning to see the giant creatures that surrounded him. Their wingbeats sounded like the drums of ancient warriors, and their teeth scraped together like sharpening knives. He felt naked without the fire for protection.

"We'll follow right behind," Jack said.

"All right, but come quick," Oliver said. He backed up on the pillar and ran toward the edge, pushing off with all of his strength.

I'm going to make it! Oliver thought as he flew through the air, and it was true that it seemed that way at first. His legs had launched him higher than he could have ever hoped, and the pillar was easily within his grasp. But then a strange thing happened: Oliver continued to go *higher,* as if the laws of gravity had suddenly vanished. He felt a prickling pain in his back and looked up to see a bat's face above him. It beat its wings, going up, up, up, as high as the ceiling, and then dipping down to wind through a series of pillars, its giant claws clasping Oliver's shoulders.

Oliver wildly swung his fists at the bat, trying to connect with its fleshy face. Finally a blow landed and the bat released him. He fell fast, landing hard on top of a broken stalagmite and rolling. Rats scurried away and then advanced, sniffing Oliver's shins to determine if he was edible.

The short flight had moved him a good distance across the chasm. Cora and Jack were small blobs behind him, and the fire of the torch looked the size of a match head. The exit to the Green Lands was still far away, but the progress he'd made was encouraging. He cupped his hands around his mouth and screamed, "Put out the torch! Use the bats!"

Jack rolled the torch head in a small pool of drool, and the bats swooped down, snatching them from their perch and lifting them toward the ceiling of the cavern.

Oliver leapt into the air and another bat caught him at the peak of his jump, grabbing him by the midsection and wrapping him in a tight hug.

The bat breathed hot air on Oliver's neck and snapped its teeth. Drool poured from its mouth and slid down Oliver's back.

"Get . . . off!" Oliver screamed, wriggling hard to free himself from its clutches, keeping an eye on the pillars below. When one was close, he punched the bat in the nose so hard that it howled in anger and released him. He fell hard, grabbing for the nearest stalagmite. He crawled to the top and searched for Cora and Jack. They were flying close behind him, struggling with their bats and flailing their arms at the horrible creatures. Cora pulled her captor's ears, and Jack hit his in the belly, falling to a nearby pillar.

"Almost there!" Oliver yelled, and indeed, the bright entrance to the Green Lands was tantalizingly close now. The light from the ponds surrounding the exit danced on the ceiling, glowing the brilliant blue of the cave eels. A shadow moved around the ponds, waving its arms in the air. It was tall and hooded, just like the figure he had seen in the forest and earlier in the cave. It almost seemed like it was *directing* the bats.

Why does that thing keep following me? Oliver thought.

He'd worry about that later. For now, he had to get out of this place. He jumped again and felt a claw grasp his wrist, pulling him up. A cluster of lumpy pillars soon appeared below him, so he grabbed the bat's ankle with his free hand and twisted until he heard a snap. There was a series of awful clicking sounds and then Oliver was falling again, onto another stalagmite.

Ahead of him was a thin strip of ledge that formed a twisting path. It would lead him out of the Cave of Horrors. One more jump—that's all it would take. The tall, hooded figure was nowhere to be seen, if he had ever been there at all. Perhaps it was Oliver's mind playing tricks on him.

Oliver backed up, sprinting toward the edge of the pillar and pushing off with all the power left in his legs.

He heard a whooshing above him and felt the breeze from

powerful wings tousle his hair. He waited for the familiar twinge of claws against flesh, but it never came. Oliver spun his arms, desperately trying to grab on to something around him, but there was nothing to stop his plummet.

Cora screamed his name, and it echoed across the room as he fell deep, deep down, into the abyss so deep that no human could ever possibly escape on their own.

The Abyss So Deep That No Human Could Ever Possibly Escape on Their Own

The fall seemed to take forever.

Each foot farther into the abyss was dimmer than the one before, and just when Oliver thought it couldn't get any darker, it managed to turn a shade more black, as though someone had spilled a vial of ink into his eyes and then wrapped his skull with a blindfold several times.

He could hear flapping and a chorus of screeching rats around him as he continued to fall.

Will this ever end? Oliver wondered. *Maybe I'll fall to the center of the earth, right to its hot-lava core.*

But that wasn't true. There *was* a floor to the abyss, and when Oliver eventually hit it, he died in a bloody and awful and splattery way.

Let's leave it at that.

Oliver regenerated quickly, swirling with light and letters and bits of digital information. Chimes sounded around him, and he rolled into cold water and felt it rush around his ears and up his nostrils. He thrashed his hands in the darkness, searching for something solid. Now, there's nothing more unsettling than falling into dark water, and Oliver's imagination ran wild with thoughts of strange creatures surrounding him. Unfortunately, the reality was far worse.

Had he been able to see, he would have noticed that the blood from his death had chummed the water, drawing a swarm of predatory swimmers.

Every bone and muscle in Oliver's body revolted, screaming at him to get out of the water. He spun around, fighting to figure out which way was up, and his hand brushed against a wiggling creature that felt a bit like a scratchy rubber tube. It squirmed and wrapped around his wrist. Oliver broke through the surface and gasped for air. He wiped at his eyes and saw thin squiggles of blue light surround him.

The eels! he thought, just as a grinning head gummed his hand, searching for the perfect spot to crunch. He shook it away and swam about until he bumped into the base of a stalagmite. It was cool and hard, and he dug his fingers into the bumps, shimmying around, searching for a way to climb. Wet pieces of spiderweb were stuck to his hair, and he felt the cold brush of a spider's leg graze his elbow.

He pulled himself up, scaling the stalagmite, watching as the glowing eels formed a spiral around the rock. He was only a few inches out of the water—not safe from their jaws. How long could he stay here?

Something crawled up his back and he swatted it away. A chill swept through his body, and he tilted back his head and screamed for help.

"Cora! Jack! Are you up there?"

The squeal of rats was the only response.

For the squeamish among us (and, I must admit, that includes me), I assure you that our time with the rats and spiders and eels is almost complete. You may be so utterly disgusted that you're considering abandoning this book and tossing it into a waste bin. Don't. Stay with us. There is still a tremendous amount of story left, and I assure you, Oliver will not remain in the abyss for the rest of it.

Oliver screamed again for help, but the sound seemed to stop in his throat, weighed down by the heavy blackness around him. Again, there was no response, not that he expected one. For all he knew, Cora and Jack had already made it to the Green Lands and were waiting for him to appear, alive and well after his deadly fall.

Had they managed to collect an eel? He couldn't risk assuming they had.

He watched as dozens circled below him.

He needed to steal one and escape, but first he would have to survive a vicious eel attack.

A Vicious Eel Attack

All was silent for a moment, which is usually a bad sign in a dark abyss full of terrifying creatures. Then small splashes surrounded Oliver, followed by a wet scraping sound. Water lapped against the base of the stalagmite. Spiders scurried.

Oliver could see only the unearthly blue glow of the eels, which circled closer.

Suddenly there was a loud splash and something jumped from the water, smacking against Oliver's arm. Sharp teeth pierced his skin.

He cried out in pain, spinning in the direction of another explosion from the water.

Another eel leapt into the air, knocking its soft skull into his calf.

Oliver held out his arms, waiting for the next attack. When it came, he was ready. He closed his arms along the wet, wiggling creature and squeezed. The eel thrashed about, making an awful squeal that reminded him of a balloon deflating.

They're not real, he reminded himself.

Oliver squeezed harder, reaching for its head and twisting until the bones popped. The eel's squirmy body flopped against his leg. Oval-shaped scales illuminated the skin along its back, casting a soft light.

He wrapped the eel around his arm and held it close to his face. His line of vision slightly widened thanks to the glow; it was just far enough for Oliver to see another eel flying toward him, mouth agape.

Oliver ducked, grabbing the eel's tail as it passed. He whipped it into a rock. There was a dull *thump* and the creature went limp.

More light illuminated the stalagmite, and Oliver's eyes adjusted enough that he could see a shoreline ten feet away. He had to get there. No good could come from being stuck on a pillar of rock, and maybe he could find a path out of the abyss. He wrapped an eel around his arm and slid into the water.

The water glowed a soft blue, and the other eels swam around him but didn't attack, accustomed to avoiding their kind.

His kicked his feet fast, struggling to stay above the surface with his heavy, waterlogged clothes and shoes.

"Keep swimming," a voice whispered above him.

Oliver spun in the water.

"You're almost there," the voice said.

"Who said that?" Oliver asked. He lifted the eel out of the water and waved it around, but all he could see were the silhouettes of rats clawing up stalagmites.

"No time to worry about me, young Oliver," the voice said. "It isn't safe to stay in the water."

The voice was beautiful—melodic and soft, with a clipped

accent that enunciated every syllable. It echoed off the wet walls like fine music.

"Follow me. Quickly now. They won't spare you for long. Time is of the essence. Tick tock tick."

Something large passed overhead, landing in the shadows on the shoreline.

Oliver paddled his hands in the water, slowly moving in the direction of the shore. Perhaps he should have been wary of a strange voice in the abyss, but there was something soothing about the way it spoke. He was drawn to it.

"Good boy. Keep it up. Faster now."

Oliver swam farther, careful to keep the eel tight around his arm. He pulled his body onto the shore and collapsed. Blood oozed from the bite mark on his arm.

"There," the voice said from the shadows. "Come to me, Oliver. Hurry now."

Oliver obeyed. What choice did he have? He had three lives left, and if the voice belonged to another enemy intent on killing him, he would avoid it the next time he reset.

He pushed himself up from the rocks, every muscle in his body tingling. Then a thought occurred to him.

How does the voice know my name?

It was too late for second thoughts. Something moved behind him.

He spun, waving the eels in a desperate attempt to locate the source of the beautiful voice.

And then, in the shadows, he saw it.

The Nasty Rodent Eater

O liver saw the source of the voice on the rocks," the voice said. "It was a shadow that shivered at first and then hopped into the air, wings flapping in the darkness."

Oliver spun around, watching as the creature flew above him. It was a very odd thing, to have a voice talk about him as if he weren't there.

"Who's saying that?" Oliver asked.

"Perhaps a bat had followed him down into the abyss," the voice continued. "*No*, Oliver thought, *the creature is far too handsome to be a bat.*"

"What are you?" Oliver asked.

"Oliver was not a very clever boy. Clearly it was a bird talking to him, but he was too dense to realize it," the voice continued. "The bird was nearly as tall as Oliver, and his wings were wide and muscular. This was no ordinary bird— this was the most *handsome* bird in all of Dulum. He had the face of an eagle, the body of a buzzard, and the wings of a hawk. His beak was sloped as if carved by the gods. His feathers were brown, but a really nice brown, not at all like dirt. His eyes revealed a deep intelligence that—"

A rat ran down a stalagmite, and the bird landed and attacked it, snatching it with his mouth and chomping down. The rat's tail wiggled in the air before it was slurped down the bird's gullet.

The bird stepped closer, extending his wings.

"Get away from me, you . . . you . . . *nasty rodent eater*!" Oliver yelled.

"Oh, I see you know my name!" the bird boomed. "I do wish the Author hadn't been so crass in naming me. It's not very appealing, but what can one do about their name?"

The bird stepped closer still, extending a taloned foot.

"What do you want?" Oliver asked.

"To save your life, obviously." The bird shivered again and surveyed the dankness of the abyss. "Why else would I be in this horrendous place? This is not part of the story, boy, and if you don't mind my saying so, you've really made a mess of everything since you arrived. The pacing is all wrong. Now come here."

Oliver recoiled. He didn't remember such a beautiful bird in the book. Perhaps this was another of the Pribbles' ploys.

"I am offering you a one-time rescue, deus ex machina, provided you go back to the story where you belong. We're in an Abyss So Deep That No Human Could Ever Possibly Escape on Their Own, which by its very name means you will require assistance to leave. Do you hear that tapping sound? The spiders are closing in, and I do believe it's time for breakfast."

There were no other options. Oliver stepped forward,

clutching the eel, and the bird hopped into the air and flew above his head, gently grasping Oliver's shoulders with his strong talons.

"This may be difficult," the bird said. "I've never carried something so heavy that I didn't intend to eat. Please excuse a random nibble here or there. Pure habit."

With a few powerful thrusts of the bird's wings, the duo lifted into the air.

"I don't remember you from the story," Oliver said. "Did I make you up?"

The bird snorted.

"Ignorant boy! No, you did *not* make me up. I was the first thing the Author created, and the fact that you don't remember me speaks more to your limited mental faculties than I ever could," he said. They flew higher and higher until Oliver could see the tops of the stalagmites and the glowing exit of the cave. "*I* am the real star of the story. *I* have the most lines in the book. Forget those children racing to stop stupid old Sigil. *I'm* the one who carries the plot forward."

"Oh. I didn't know. I'm sorry, Nasty. Can I call you Nasty?"

"If you must," the bird said as they bobbed and weaved toward the radiant light of the Green Lands. "Or, if you prefer formalities, you *may* call me Mr. N. R. Eater, considering the fact that I am the *narrator* of this fine story."

"Oh, well . . . nice to meet you," Oliver said.

"I wish I could say likewise," the bird replied, snorting as they soared out of the cave. "It's unbecoming for a narrator to interject themselves into the story. *Dear reader* this, and *dear reader* that. It's all a bit too much for my taste."

Regardless, it's a pleasure to be formally introduced, dear reader, even if it is a third of the way through this stinking book.

CHAPTER THREE

THE GANG ATTACKS
IN THE GREEN LANDS

Sunlight hit Oliver's flesh, so bright and warm that he felt like honey had been poured all over him. It was midday, and the small birds and animals that inhabited the Green Lands chirped and scurried along the tops of the trees.

"Just a . . . bit longer . . . now," Nasty wheezed, adjusting his grip on Oliver's shoulders and taking a small bite of his hair. He coughed and spit out the strands.

The Green Lands were a gorgeous *Huckleberry Finn* dream, peppered with bridges and ladders made of rope that crossed rivers and scaled trees. There were long, rolling hills covered in fresh foliage, and an enormous mountain range stood in the distance, peaks hidden in a twirl of clouds.

"You're much heavier than you look," Nasty said, dropping Oliver on the ground and perching on a large rock in the middle of a clearing that overlooked streams and small waterfalls. He pecked at his wing and preened in the sunlight. His feathers seemed to glow as if lit by angels. His eyes were a radiant blue, intelligent and understanding.

"Thank you, Nasty," Oliver said. "I'm glad to be out of that cave."

"Yes, we're only a bit off the main path of the story. I saw Cora and Jack escape the cave before I doubled back to save you, but there were no eels around the exit—just a handful of loose scales. I'm sure they'll be happy to see that you snagged one."

Oliver lay down, extending his arms and letting the grass tickle the skin between his fingers.

"There's no time to rest," Nasty said, jumping into the air and flying over Oliver's head. He placed his talons on Oliver's shoulders and said, "Come, boy, back to the plot of the story. Cora and Jack are surely waiting. Up you go."

"No," Oliver said.

"Young man, the whole point of a narrator is to keep you on track and moving through the story at a reasonable clip, and right now you should be on the main road, heading toward the town of the Old Mountain Guard."

"How do *you* know that?" Oliver asked.

"Well, the Author provided me with vague ideas about characters and plot—just enough to give the readers some foreshadowing. I know where you're supposed to be, and approximately when, though I fear you may have ruined everything. Oh, what I wouldn't give to be omniscient, or at least omnipresent!"

"We can't go back to the story," Oliver said.

"What do you mean?"

"It's too dangerous. I'm not supposed to be here."

"On *that* we can agree."

Oliver considered his options and decided the truth was the best approach.

"This may be hard for you to understand, but you don't really exist, Nasty. This is a story."

"I *know* that!" Nasty said, scoffing. "I'm a narrator, not a nincompoop!"

"Did you see those two people chasing me? They're trying to steal the story from my mind."

Nasty looked at Oliver as though he had gone mad.

"Steal the *story*?" he asked. "You can't *steal* a story! Stories are meant to be shared! Honestly, boy, the darkness of the cave must have scrambled your brains."

Oliver continued, unfazed.

"I need to stay away from the Pribbles and get to the last chapter before they do. That's the only way I can leave. If I stick to the obvious route of the book, they'll find me and steal it, chapter by chapter, and then Dulum and everything in it will be gone forever."

"You're a horrible narrator, Oliver. That's the strangest and least cohesive thing I've ever heard. Gone forever? Why don't these Pribble people travel to the nearest bookseller and purchase another copy?" Nasty asked. "Let them read it again instead of going through the bother of stealing it from your dull little head."

"They can't. I read the last copy in the world, and now it's gone, too. There's no other way for them to get it. It wasn't a popular book. Hardly anyone bought it, and there are no copies left."

Nasty jumped back like he had been punched in the heart. He hunched beside a tree stump and covered his face with his wing.

"Just my luck," he moaned. "I always suspected the plot was derivative. A fetch quest! And those children have about as much personality as my posterior. I'm stuck in a failure of a story that no one cares about!"

"I care about it," Oliver said.

"That's no comfort to me," Nasty said. A soft sob came from his beak. "I'm the narrator of the worst story in the world."

"It's my favorite story," Oliver said. "That's why I want to save it. And you can help me. As long as we stay away from the *real* parts of the book, the Pribbles won't be able to find me, and then they can't take it from me."

"A dubious plan, Oliver. Books are meant to be linear. Point A to point B. I am solemnly bound to keep you on the proper path, just as the Author intended."

"I won't."

"You must," Nasty said. His eyes narrowed to thin, evil slits, and he clicked his talons. He approached ominously. "Forgive me for this."

The bird jumped into the air and knocked Oliver to the ground.

"Nasty! Stop!"

"Enough of this nonsense. Back to the obvious route you go," Nasty growled, gripping his shoulders, and they flew up into the sky, back to the main plot of the story, where the Pribbles would be waiting.

Birdnapped!

Up and up they went, into a brilliant blue sky full of fluffy white clouds. Below, a blanket of trees and vines covered the lush ground of the Green Lands. A rainbow arced over the forest, so bright and vibrant that it looked like it had been painted with a master's brush.

"Let me go," Oliver said, struggling against the bird's tight grip.

"Just a bit farther," Nasty said, dipping in the direction of a wide dirt road that snaked through the forest. "That's where you belong."

To his right, far away, Oliver could see a thin slice of ocean. It looked like a sheet of glass, undisturbed and peaceful except for the small, rolling waves at the coast. In front of him, the mountain range loomed, and even at their height, the tallest peak was hidden in a white haze.

Nasty tucked in his wings and they began to descend, diving toward the forest at a pace that made Oliver's stomach flutter. They could practically touch the treetops, and swabs of green and brown smeared in his vision.

"With any luck, we'll find Cora and Jack on the road," Nasty said. "They're simple characters, you know. Quite one-dimensional. If I know them as well as I think I do, they'll find their way back to the story."

"What about the Pribbles?"

"I'll have a word with them. I'm sure we can come to an understanding. As the narrator, I do hold a level of importance in this world that they'll surely respect."

Nasty extended his wings, slowly spinning onto the wide dirt road.

"Ah, such a relief to be back. Chapter thr—" Nasty lunged at a small rodent that had stuck its head out of a hole, snapped it up, and choked it down. He coughed and wiped his mouth. *"Ahem.* Chapter three. There's much to come, and we really should rest."

Nasty pointed to a hollowed-out tree stump that looked to have suffered from a severe case of wood rot. They crawled into its center, leaning their heads on the soft wood walls. The ground was covered in cushy moss that was more comfortable than any chair Oliver had ever sat in. He peeked out of a hole in the stump, watching for any sign of Cora and Jack or the Pribbles. His eyes fluttered shut, and he drifted in and out of sleep.

Hours passed, and the sun began to dip toward the horizon, igniting the Green Lands with a fiery red light.

"When will Cora and Jack come?" Oliver asked.

"Soon, I'm sure."

They waited longer, and the sun dipped farther. The world dimmed to a soft pink, and blue shadows wrapped around the trees, stretching across the path. Owls began to hoot, and nocturnal rodents stirred.

Eventually, two figures appeared in the distance, their silhouettes unmistakable against the leaves.

Cora and Jack looked tired and beaten. The ordeal with the bats had clearly taken a toll, and Oliver felt slightly ashamed at making them depart from the obvious route. Perhaps he had been selfish.

"See? As I promised," Nasty said, but the look on his face revealed that he was just as relieved as Oliver. He yanked Oliver from the tree stump, pushing him through the wall of foliage at the edge of the forest.

"Oliver!" Jack yelled. He ran, pulling his sister by the hand.

"Oh, look who's back," Cora said. "Great."

Oliver held the glowing blue creature above his head.

"I got an eel!"

Cora snatched the eel from Oliver and stared into its evil, grinning face.

"We'd have gotten it ourselves if you hadn't led us in the wrong direction."

"I know you would have," Oliver said.

"Did that fall into the abyss kill you?" Jack asked.

"What do you think?"

"Oh, I would have liked to see that one! I bet you exploded like a sack of wet slugs," Jack said, howling, and Cora smacked him lightly on the cheek.

"How did you get here before us?" she asked.

"Magic," Oliver said.

"Convenient," Cora said, raising an eyebrow. "We shouldn't stay on the path for long. The Old Mountain Guard patrols it, and the Gang could be near."

"I found a shelter," Oliver said.

He led them to the mossy stump, and Jack prepared a small fire. Smoke drifted through the trees, concealed by the mass of leaves above. Night was fully upon them, and the children were tired and hungry.

"We only need the *skin* of the eel," Jack said, pulling the book of magic from his satchel and running his fingers over the pages. He looked at Cora, and she seemed to read his mind, pulling the knife from her belt and slicing the eel down the middle. She gently removed the meat from the creature and pierced it with a stick, propping it over the flames.

The cooked eel smelled wondrous. It popped with flavors and roasted to a pleasant brown. When it was fully cooked, the children divided it evenly and gobbled up every last bite. They curled up inside the hollow stump, and Cora covered herself and Jack with her cloak. They listened to a symphony of chirps from night bugs.

Cora and Jack's mother had died, but they'd always had each other. In that moment, Oliver felt terribly alone. It was true that he missed his mother—that was a constant—but he also missed his father. He wished his father were here with him now.

Oliver peeked out of the hole in the stump and saw a shadow move through the trees. It was Nasty, keeping watch over them.

For the moment, the bird was happy. All was as it should be. The children were back in the plot of the story, and there was nothing dangerous in any direction for miles. He would have a frank conversation with the Pribbles, and that would surely put a stop to this foolishness and everything could return to normal.

The children fell asleep, and once the sun began to rise, Nasty leapt into the air, flying up and away, searching for the couple, and quite possibly, his untimely death.

A Brilliant Imagination

Nasty flew high above the Green Lands and was dismayed at what he saw.

The lands around him remained lush and beautiful and dripping with life—but that was only the half of it. In front of him, stretching as far as he could see, the world had been reduced to a field of gray dust. In the moonlight, the line that separated the gray from the green moved slowly toward him. Trees and plants bent and popped, ripping from the ground and slurping toward a single point far back on the path.

Was this the *Pribbles* whom Oliver had mentioned?

He flew down and perched on a branch, watching as a thin woman and rotund man approached. From his position, he could overhear their conversation.

"Cora and Jack should be ahead, love, which means we're in the midst of chapter three," Mr. Pribble said. His machine belched as it sucked up a particularly plump and tasty-looking rodent.

"What happened earlier, in the cave?"

"Oliver went off book, that's what. Wicked child! But I believe we're back on track."

"How many lives does he have left?"

Mr. Pribble consulted the *CORTEXIA*™'s screen.

"Three. He must have died again in the cave. It seems he went into his own imagination. A peculiar thing—I didn't think children *had* imaginations anymore, but he's a unique specimen. Quite brilliant. No matter. One way or another, I'll get the story, even if I have to take everything from him."

Mr. Pribble waved the *CORTEXIA*™ and Nasty felt the branch slip away under his feet, spinning toward the nozzle. He squawked in surprise and flew up, hopping from limb to limb on the tallest tree he could find.

"Oh dear," Nasty whispered. "That poor boy was telling the truth."

Nasty felt a rage swell inside him like the indigestion he'd once experienced after eating an army of fire ants. He jumped from the tree and torpedoed to the ground, landing on the path in front of the Pribbles.

"Good sir and madam!" Nasty yelled. He struck a menacing pose in the middle of the road. "I must implore you to stop what you are doing!"

He waved his wings in the air like a boxer's fists and kicked his feet back and forth, sending up a small cloud of dust.

"You will go no farther," he said. "You will take nothing more from this child."

"Look there! A talking bird!" Mr. Pribble exclaimed. "Do you see that, Sophelia? Another of Oliver's wondrous creations!"

"How dare you!" Nasty screamed. "Oliver didn't create me! I was hatched long ago in the loving arms of the Author.

I'm the star of the story, judging by number of words spoken, and you will listen to what I say or—"

"He seems rather insane," Mrs. Pribble whispered.

"Perhaps he's from Oliver's nightmares," Mr. Pribble said, raising the CORTEXIA™ and propping it on his hip.

"Put that down!" Nasty shouted, but Mr. Pribble pulled the trigger and a buzzing sound filled Nasty's head and made the trees around him shimmer and quake. The world seemed to melt around him, slipping between his beautiful feet like the ocean going out to tide. Trees slithered in the air and were sucked into the nozzle of the CORTEXIA™. Nasty stared down the deep black tube of the machine. He felt like a hollow egg, empty and fragile. His blood turned ice-cold, and a cluster of feathers ripped from his flesh and spun in the air before they were sucked away. He pulled back, digging his talons into the dirt, fighting with all the strength in his beautiful, muscular body.

"Why isn't this working?" Mr. Pribble yelled, slapping the side of the canister. It made a burping noise and then roared back to life. He pointed it at Nasty. "I want this talking bird!"

Nasty felt his face begin to smear. He slid toward Mr. Pribble. There was nothing but gray dust and the barren wasteland in front of him, stretching as far as he could see.

"You . . . can't take . . . me. My . . . time . . . in the . . . story . . . is not . . . complete," Nasty said, gasping at every word. He felt like a hand was gripping his neck and like his wings were being held down by giant rocks.

"You were not in the story!" Mr. Pribble yelled. He twisted a dial on the side of the CORTEXIA™, turning up the power.

"I . . . certainly . . . was."

Nasty craned his head toward the sky and lifted his wings, pushing down with a mighty flap and rising into the air.

"He's getting away!" Mrs. Pribble yelled.

"Not if I can help it!"

Mr. Pribble aimed higher and turned the dial as far as it could go.

The force pulled Nasty's legs closer and closer to the *CORTEXIA*™'s opening. His flapping made little difference. Soon he was a wingspan away from the nozzle, then half a wingspan, then a feather's length.

"Almost . . . got him," Mr. Pribble grunted, arching his back like a fisherman about to pull in a prizewinning catch.

Nasty's feet were inside the tube now, and he felt as though his very soul were slipping from his body.

"I must . . . *narrate*," he whispered, and with his last worm's worth of strength, he withdrew his feet, extended his talons, and grabbed the nozzle of the *CORTEXIA*™, yanking it from Mr. Pribble's hands.

"Stop!" Mr. Pribble yelled.

"Give that back!" Mrs. Pribble shrieked.

Nasty twisted the dial and the machine silenced. He clutched it tightly and flew upward, over the trees that remained in the Green Lands, and back in the direction of Oliver, whom he now realized he had to help and protect at any cost, for his own survival depended on it.

Below him, sounds came from the glowing blue canister— shrieks and wails followed by the deep growls of giants and the squeals of bats. The machine was hot to the touch and painful to hold, and being so close to it made Nasty feel positively awful.

"What a mess I've stepped in! I never should have gotten involved," Nasty said, spinning to the side and flying deep into the woods, where the leaves and vines of plants tangled in a mess of green colors. It was there that he dropped the machine, watching it fall toward the ground and disappear into the shadows of the thick foliage.

Good luck finding that, Nasty thought, remembering the deathly chill that went through his body when the machine had been pointed at him. He'd help save the story from this poor boy's mind, even if it meant leaving the plot and ignoring the wishes of the Author.

And, as the narrator, he knew just what to do.

A Few Introductions

Nasty scanned the path for the children.

There! Coming up the path were three small figures. Nasty dove, tucking his wings close to his body. He dipped down and landed on a tree branch that stretched over the path.

Nasty prepared himself to make his introduction and felt a stabbing pang of nerves. True, he'd been following these children since the very beginning of the story and felt he knew them better than anyone, but he had never *dreamed* of talking to them. It was a narrator's job to make an honest account of the events that occurred, and interfering with them had never crossed his mind. But he had saved Oliver from the abyss and stolen the *CORTEXIA*™, dropping it deep in the forest. He was already involved. How could he stop now?

Nasty swooped down, landing on the path and hunching his gorgeous body in the most unthreatening way.

"Hello," he whispered, trying to sound meek and humble and kind and wise. It came out sounding like none of these things.

Jack howled in surprise.

Cora jumped back, picking up a large stick and waving it back and forth before advancing like a trained fencer.

"Nasty!" Oliver yelled.

"Yes, it *is* nasty," Cora said. "Get back!"

She whacked the stick across Nasty's head, knocking him over.

"Stop it! Great wriggling worms!" Nasty yelled. "Would you help me, Oliver?"

Cora whacked him again.

"Is that bird *talking*?" Jack asked. He poked his head out from behind his sister, whom he had been using as a shield.

"I am indeed talking, and I come in peace," Nasty said. Cora lunged with the stick, but Nasty blocked it with a wing. He bowed slightly.

Cora held the stick at arm's length and circled Nasty, lunging at him anytime a single feather twitched on his body.

"Birds aren't supposed to talk," she said.

"He isn't a normal bird," Oliver said.

"He said your name. Do you know this creature?"

"I do," Oliver said.

"Explain."

"He's . . ." Oliver had to think quickly. To tell Cora and Jack the truth would mean revealing that they were characters from a story inside his mind. He decided a lie would be better. "He's my pet."

"Your *pet*?" Nasty asked with more than a hint of disgust in his voice.

"Yes. Where I come from, all child magicians are assigned a magical pet. He's sworn to protect me. Aren't you, Nasty?"

Nasty nodded.

"Is he friendly?" Jack asked, holding out his hand. "He won't bite?"

"I can't promise that," Nasty said.

"And his name is *Nasty*?" Cora asked.

"Yes," Oliver said. "Nasty Rodent Eater."

Nasty forced a smile—or as much of a smile as a beaked creature could—and leapt into the air to perch on Oliver's shoulder.

"Oh yes, I'm a pet and nothing more. *Master* Oliver, may we have a word? *In private.*"

"Go ahead," Jack said. He smiled. "We promise not to listen."

Nasty flew to an overhanging branch, searching for a secluded spot.

"I need to tell you something. It's about the Pribbles. I went to speak with them and—"

The feathers along his neck stood on end. Plants moved. A rustling came from the surrounding trees.

On the path, Cora gripped her stick to her chest and spun.

The forest was thick with broken trees and tangled weeds, and a small figure jumped to the top of a rock and launched himself near them. It was a boy, no more than twelve years of age and dressed in dirty clothing. Leaves and twigs were stuck to his shirt, and his face was caked in mud—perfect camouflage for sneaking through the Green Lands. He bared his teeth like a rabid dog and swiped at them.

"There ya are, Jack," the boy said. "We've been looking for ya."

"Morning, Rodney," Jack said. He wedged his foot under a

rock and kicked it up into the air, catching it and cocking his arm in one quick motion.

Rodney nodded toward Jack's satchel.

"What ya got in there?"

"None of your business."

"It *is* our business," another voice said from behind them.

A group of children appeared, as though materializing from the trees. There were children of all shapes and sizes—tall and short, stout and slender, dark-skinned and light-skinned, boys and girls and every type in between. Some had long hair braided with vines and twigs, and others had short hair dyed red and purple with the juice of berries. They were a scrappy bunch; some held rocks, while others held sticks fashioned with sharp thorns.

"It's the Gang of Impervious Children," Cora whispered to Oliver.

"I figured as much."

There were Adeline, daughter of the town cobbler, and Frederick, son of a butcher. There were Hazel, child of a seamstress, and Phineas, son of a shopkeeper. Rodney, who was the son of Dulum's most renowned shipwright, clapped his hands, and more children emerged from the branches. There were Rosemary and Walter, Marlowe and Arthur, Eliza and Marshall, Greta and Norris, Vera and Haydn, as well as a handful of children too covered with dirt and leaves to be recognizable. They surrounded Cora, Jack, and Oliver and began closing in, step by step.

"Who's that?" Rodney asked, nodding at Oliver.

"Just a straggler we found in the woods," Cora said.

"Where's he from?" Marlowe asked.

"None of your business," Jack growled. "But he's evil, just like us."

Oliver bared his teeth and tried to look villainous.

"Still working for Sigil, then?" Hazel asked.

"Open that bag," Phineas said, poking at them with a long and twisted branch. "Let's see what's inside."

The Gang advanced.

"Get back!" Cora yelled. She ducked to the left as Adeline lunged at her. Cora swiped Adeline's feet out from under her, then wrapped her arm around the girl's neck and squeezed.

"I'll hurt her," Cora said. "Don't think I won't."

Norris had just screamed to attack when a lone voice called, "Stop!"

The Gang froze.

A tall boy appeared from the trees. His skin was dark, but his hair was a stunning gray. He wore a purple tunic and pants stitched with an intricate pattern of gold thread. His shoes were black, made from the hide of a long-extinct creature.

"Grayson," Cora whispered, and her eyes betrayed her fear and wonder and shame and love.

"Give me the bag, Cora," Grayson said. He held out a hand. Around his wrist were gold chains that reflected the sunlight.

"We can't do that," Jack said.

"Sigil needs it," Cora said.

"Why would you help *him* after he killed my father?" Grayson spat.

At the mere mention of King Gerard, the Gang of Impervious Children bowed their heads.

"You wouldn't understand," Cora said.

"Try me." Grayson pulled a gold watch from his pocket and showed her the initials carved on the back. Even from his spot on the branch, Nasty could hear the whirring of the watch's gears. "The girl who made this for me would never betray us. I know Sigil has your father."

Cora seemed to stare through him.

"They don't care for anyone but themselves," Marshall said.

"Evil, evil, evil," Vera said, smacking a stick against her palm.

Clearly, Cora wanted to tell the truth. Nasty could practically see it fighting its way up her throat, but to admit it here would be a dangerous thing. Word might get back to Sigil and then who could say what would happen to their father? She stifled the thought, narrowing her eyes and growling, playing the part of the horrible, hunted villain once again.

"The girl you once knew is dead. You won't be impervious to Sigil's magic for long," she said, giggling madly. "Soon, he'll have you under his control, and then all of Dulum will be his to rule."

Grayson lowered his hand, staring at Cora, a deep sadness painted on his face.

"Get them," he whispered.

The attack came swiftly.

Nasty flew into the air, watching from safety as five

children leapt at Cora. She did a backflip off the path and grabbed a low-hanging branch, pulling it back. When she released it, the branch whipped through the air and whacked the children, knocking them to the ground.

Another group surrounded Jack and Oliver, leaping at them. The boys ducked and kicked and crawled, rolling on the ground as the children pulled them down and piled on top of them.

"Oh dear," Nasty said as Eliza sat on Oliver's back and pulled his arms at an unnatural angle. Jack flailed his legs wildly, connecting with anything that came near him.

"Bird, aren't you sworn to protect Oliver?" Cora called out to Nasty.

"I'm not sure how much help I'd be," Nasty said. He'd already had a difficult day and was feeling dirty and plucked.

Cora grabbed a fistful of stones and kicked off from the trunk of the tree, grabbing a limb and pulling herself up. She threw them at the attackers below, picking them off one by one.

"Then what good are you?" Cora asked, hurling more stones.

Nasty winced at the insult, smoothed his feathers, and flew to the ground in front of Oliver. He flapped his wings at Eliza and pecked at her mangy brown hair.

Two members of the Gang grabbed Nasty, and there was a whirlwind of insults and feathers and swinging fists and talons.

In the confusion, Jack and Oliver ran from the road, slipping through the trees, and Cora slid down the trunk to join them.

Nasty took to the air and watched the children assemble into a formation, then screamed, "I do believe it's time to run! Follow me!"

"Don't let them leave!" Grayson yelled, and the Gang of Impervious Children began to give chase.

Cora, Jack, and Oliver raced through the trees, leaping over rocks and stumps. Branches cut their arms as they ran into the forest of the Green Lands, the Gang of Impervious Children following close behind.

"What's the plan?" Jack yelled, but Oliver didn't answer. He continued to run, because a large boy was close behind him, tearing past plants and trees.

"This way!" Nasty called from above, leading them deeper into the thick forest.

Ahead, the ground stopped, as if it had been cut by a giant blade. A wide, ambling river ran below the ledge.

"Prepare to jump!" Nasty cried.

"Are you mad?" Jack asked, continuing to sprint toward the ledge.

"We aren't immortal like Oliver!" Cora yelled, but there was no time to consider options or the possibility of shallow water filled with large, bone-splitting rocks. The Gang was gaining on them, and the ground beneath their feet only stretched five more feet.

Three feet.

One.

Cora, Jack, and Oliver launched themselves into the air and fell into the river.

The River of Escapement

They fell and fell, not as far as Oliver's earlier plummet into the abyss but far enough that their stomachs dropped to their toes and the rushing wind stifled their screams.

Nasty watched three small splashes form in the river. None of the children surfaced.

"Oh dear," he whispered. "I do believe I've killed them all."

On the edge of the cliff, the Gang of Impervious Children stopped. Grayson appeared, holding his hand over his eyes to block the sun as he watched the ripples in the water.

"If they're alive, we'll catch them downstream," he commanded, leading the others back into the forest.

Nasty circled above, praying for signs of life. There were none.

"Where are you? Oh, where are you?" Nasty cried. He had interfered with the story, that was clear, and if he had accidentally killed the main characters, surely the Author would be furious with him. Perhaps he'd even be fired from his narration duties and reduced to a background character! Fear wriggled throughout his body.

Nasty swooped lower and landed on a rock that was poking out from the middle of the river.

"Stupid old bird, why would you help a child? Never help anyone in the story, that's the first rule of narration. Just observe and recount. Nothing more. *Observe and recount.*"

Something moved in the trees on the opposite side of the river, and he turned to see a tall, hooded figure. It wasn't human, of that Nasty was certain. It was much too tall and was dressed in a flowing black robe, and even in the bright sunlight, its face was concealed in shadows. The figure raised an arm and pointed at a small alcove of rocks jutting from the riverbank.

Nasty tilted his head. He looked where the figure was pointing and saw three small heads bobbing under the rocks.

"Oliver?" Nasty whispered.

He glanced back at the trees, but the hooded figure had vanished. He'd worry about that later.

Nasty flew to the children and perched on the small rock overhang, craning his neck to see them.

Cora held a finger to her lips and whispered, "Is the Gang gone?"

Nasty nodded, and tears of joy formed in his eyes.

"I was *so* worried you might have died in the fall! Master Oliver can come back, but you two, I believe, would be lost for good."

"You were worried about *us*?" Cora asked. "Why do you care about *us*, you ugly old bird?"

"Please don't call me ugly. Call me Nasty," Nasty said. "I care about you because you are very important children, and if you were to die, it would . . . it would just ruin everything for me."

"Have we met?" Jack said. There was something familiar about the bird's face, as though he had seen it before, following him from afar.

"No, not directly."

"What does *that* mean?" Cora asked.

"Well, I think what he meant was, um . . ." Oliver stammered.

"Look!" Nasty yelled, partly to divert their questions and partly because he saw something of great interest floating in the water. He pointed a wing.

Far on the other side of the river, a small wooden raft bobbed. It was constructed of seven tree trunks bound together by rope, and on top was a tent structure made of sticks and animal hide. Oars carved from tree limbs lay on the surface.

"Well, that's lucky," Oliver said.

"It belongs to the Old Mountain Guard," Cora said. "We must be careful."

Nasty flew over to it, settling on top of the tent and leaning through the opening. The raft drifted lazily, a slight breeze blowing the flaps of the tent open and shut.

"It's empty!" he yelled. "What good fortune! Swim over!"

The children dog-paddled toward the raft, their wet clothes feeling like heavy weights on their bodies. The current was slow but strong, and they drifted farther out into the warm water.

"Faster," Nasty said, flapping his wings in a rhythmic motion. "Wave your little arms like this. A little bit more. Kick your legs, too."

He looked over his shoulder to see if he could spot the tall, hooded figure, but there was no sign of it anywhere. Nasty was certain the raft hadn't been on the river a moment ago, and it seemed to appear just beyond where the figure had been standing. How was that possible?

The children pulled themselves up and collapsed on the raft, letting the hot sun bake their faces.

Water dripped from their clothes, and their hair stuck to their foreheads. They were silent for some time, listening to the calls of strange birds in the air and the peaceful trickle of water around them. They were exhausted, and for the moment, content to let the raft do the hard work.

"Where are we?" Jack asked, breaking the silence.

"The River of Escapement," Nasty answered. He had soared over it many times. The river twisted through the Green Lands like a serpent, passing through forests and fields of boulders toward the base of the mountains, where the sprawling cities of the Old Mountain Guard were constructed like a bad, brown fungus.

The raft drifted farther, moving faster than the Gang of Impervious Children could travel on foot. For now, the trio seemed to have lost them. They entered a tunnel of trees so tall that the tops had curved together, covering the water with a canopy of leaves. Snakes slithered along the branches, dangling down and hissing at their unwelcome guests.

Cora closed her eyes and whispered, *"Add a casing constructed with wood that is charred. It is steeped in the drink of the Old Mountain Guard."*

"Do you think our journey will get easier?" Jack asked.

"It has to," Cora answered. "I don't see how it could get any harder."

On this point, unfortunately, Cora was very, very wrong.

Nasty's Rather Ingenious Plan
(If I Do Say So Myself)

Cora and Jack quickly fell asleep, and Oliver had nearly joined them when Nasty jumped beside him and gave him a small peck on the nose.

"Not now," Oliver said, batting at the bird and covering his eyes.

"Master Oliver, may I have a word?"

"No," Oliver growled. He rolled onto his side, nearly tipping over the raft with the sudden change in weight.

"Good gracious! It's just . . . I think I have a plan, and I want to see what you think of it."

Oliver forced himself up.

"Let's go in the tent," Nasty whispered, checking that Cora and Jack were still asleep.

They crawled inside, and Nasty wrapped a wing around Oliver's shoulders, speaking as soft as he could.

"As I was about to tell you before we were so rudely interrupted, I spoke with the Pribbles."

"Really?"

"Yes, and it didn't go well. They tried to use that awful machine to slurp me up. I felt my very soul slipping away, and . . . and . . ."

"What?"

"I took it, Oliver. I took that wicked contraption and flew away with it."

Oliver's eyes widened.

"You did?"

"Oh, it was a frightening thing! Hot to the touch and full of shrieks and monsters. I flew with it as far as I could, but it burned the skin around my talons. I dropped it deep in the Green Lands."

"Well, that's good news."

"The situation is very serious, Oliver. You may not realize it from down here, but from up in the sky, you can see everything plainly: Dulum is slipping away. Nothingness as far as the eye can see. We can't go back to the main route of the story, and we certainly can't allow them to take the rest of it from your mind."

Oliver nodded, relieved that Nasty was finally on his side.

"This, Master Oliver, brings me to my plan. I am the narrator of the story, so I know a thing or two about pacing and can get us to the end as quickly as possible. Combined with your knowledge of the story, we make a formidable duo, indeed! We already have the gem and the eel skin, which means we're well on our way. And as you and I both know, the next clue refers to barrel wood from the Old Mountain Guard, so we'll get that and then cross the mountains at a different spot," Nasty said, pointing a wing at the mountain range. The peaks seemed impossibly high, as if they could touch the dusty surface of the moon. "The Gang of Impervious Children will never expect that. Then it's a quick slide down to the city of Dulum, where we'll get the crown of the king and take it north to Sigil's Twisted Tower. *The End*. If we finish this story while that awful couple is still searching for the *slurping* machine in the Green Lands, then you can leave before any more damage is done. How does that sound?"

Oliver looked out at Cora and Jack, still sleeping on the raft.

"We need to tell them the truth. It isn't fair to make them follow us into danger without knowing why."

"Absolutely not! They can never know their entire lives are fake. It would utterly destroy them. Just imagine! What would be the point of anything? Why would they care what happens?"

"I could ask you the same questions."

"Well, I care because—" Nasty paused, seeming to think deeply on this point. "Goodness! I suppose on paper there's no good reason. The simple truth is that I care because *stories* matter, and this one should remain where it is: tucked between *your* oversized ears and not stuck in some awful contraption with two old weasels." Nasty's stomach grumbled, and he rubbed it with his wings. "Oh, what I wouldn't give for a weasel right about now!"

Oliver smiled and patted the bird's head.

"I care about you, too."

"I think you missed my point entirely. Anyway, we must keep this a secret from Cora and Jack. They can never know our true plan. Agreed?"

"Agreed."

A question wiggled in Oliver's mind.

"Have you seen a tall, hooded figure following us?" Oliver asked.

"Oh, thank heavens! You've seen it, too?" Nasty asked. "I thought that machine had scrambled my brains. Yes. I saw it earlier, on the riverbank. It was there and then—*poof*—gone. Then this raft appeared, almost as though it was written into the story just for us."

"What do you think it is? I don't remember it from the book."

Nasty thought for a moment, chewing at his feathers.

"I truly have no idea. Do you?"

Oliver did. He felt it in his bones the moment he first saw the figure, but he felt silly saying it out loud.

"What if it's the author of the book?"

"The *Author*? The one and only Malcolm Bloom," Nasty said with hushed reverence. He had been just a baby when he saw Mr. Bloom last; he'd been hardly able to swallow the smallest bite of beetle. "Of course! Who else could it be? Authors *do* like to put a bit of themselves in their books, so perhaps he's here, helping us on our journey."

Oliver recalled the faded photo of Malcolm Bloom on the book jacket. It was impossible to say if it really was him—the black robe concealed his face and body—though it *felt* true. Every time the figure appeared, something seemed to help Oliver.

"But if it's true, why doesn't he zap us right to the end and finish this nonsense?" Nasty asked. He tilted his beak up and whispered, "Author! Are you there? Come help us!"

"Shh," Oliver said, pointing to the sleeping children. He looked at the banks of the river. The tall, hooded figure was nowhere to be seen. "Authors work in mysterious ways. He'll only come when he wants to."

Oliver crawled out of the tent and sat beside Cora and Jack. They were fast asleep, breathing softly, and the raft continued down the River of Escapement. At lunch, they docked on a sandy bank and scooped fish from the river and pulled fruit from the trees. They dried their clothes as the afternoon sun peaked in the sky and began its slow descent. The raft meandered on that evening, catching currents, following the river along the mountain. Oliver guided it with the oars, the world drifting further into night until everything around them dimmed to an inky black. Bugs sang a symphony in the darkness, harmonizing with the hisses of large snakes. Giant flowers covered the banks, bright white and red and gold. Vines twisted up trees and lizards ran along their stems.

They entered a cove, and tentacles of fog wrapped around them. Golden fireflies flew above them like stars that had descended from the heavens to dance in the darkness.

"Turn that way," Nasty said, guiding them far from the main path of the story.

Oliver steered them into a lagoon. The water turned purple and green and smelled like fish and sulfur. Large chunks of algae floated on the surface and stuck to the oars. Nasty bent down to taste a bit of it, but it got lodged in his gullet and he gagged it up. He hated salad anyway.

"Where are we going?" Cora asked, sitting up on the raft.

"To the city of the Old Mountain Guard," Oliver said.

"This doesn't seem right," Jack said. "The path up the mountain is the other way."

"We're taking a different route," Nasty said. "The journey may be harder, but it will all be worth it."

"That sounds like a great idea," Cora said with a smile. "Just like in the cave."

At this, she unsheathed her knife and pressed it against Oliver's throat.

Betrayal!

Cora gripped Oliver's collar, twisting it until it cut off his airway.

She pressed the knife deeper, and a small bead of blood appeared at the tip.

"Come closer and I'll slice his head off," she growled. Rage boiled in her cheeks, and her eyes darted back and forth between Nasty and her brother.

"What are you doing?" Jack asked, readying his fists.

"I was pretending to sleep earlier, and Oliver went into the tent with that bird. They were discussing something. I heard them say they had a secret and that we can never know the truth."

"What?" Jack asked.

"They're going to double-cross us."

"No, no. You must have misheard us," Nasty said. He bowed his head and extended a wing, tiptoeing closer to Cora, talon by talon, plotting a counterattack.

"What I said was—"

She pushed the knife deeper still.

"I'm serious, bird. Not an inch closer."

Nasty stopped and puffed out his feathers.

"Go ahead," he said, laughing. "Slice off his little head,

170

what do I care? You know he's immortal. Do it! See what happens."

"*Nasty*," Oliver hissed.

"He'll come back. You can't kill him."

Jack leapt from his spot on the raft and pulled a knife from his belt. He wrapped his arm around Nasty, pressing the knife below his beak.

"What about you?" Jack asked. "Are you immortal, too?"

"Goodness, no!" Nasty cried. "Please let me go! All right, children, calm yourselves. Don't do anything drastic. We can explain."

"Go ahead, then," Jack said.

Oliver looked at Nasty. Nasty looked at Oliver. They each expected the other to speak first.

"Something's wrong with them, Jack," Cora said. "I knew it the first time I laid eyes on Oliver. He's *different*. He doesn't belong here. An immortal magic boy and a talking bird? Whoever heard of such a thing? And wasn't it odd how we found him lost in the woods? He shouldn't have been there! How did he know about the flowers around the jewels? And the different route through the cave?"

"He did help us figure out the eel riddle a little too quickly," Jack added.

"Nothing he's said makes any sense."

"We're trying to help you," Nasty said. "You just have to trust us."

"We trust no one," Jack said, sliding the blade along Nasty's flesh. Feathers drifted down into the water.

"What should we do to them?" Cora asked.

Movement came from the side of the riverbank. Through the trees, a shadow emerged. Animals ran away, fearful. Insects stopped chirping. It was the tall, hooded figure. It raised a hand at the raft, and a whistling wind surrounded them.

Cora screamed as her arm stiffened. Her grip loosened on the knife, and it slipped from her fingers. Jack released his hold on Nasty and fell onto the tent, crashing through its wooden frame.

"What's happening?" Cora whispered. Suddenly her voice sounded small and scared. She was frozen in place, and Jack was held down by a strong, invisible force. "Stop it. What are you doing? *How?*"

"Oh, now you've done it!" Nasty cried, slapping his wings together. "You got the Author involved, and he isn't one to be trifled with."

Cora and Jack fell to their knees.

"The author?" Cora asked. "Is that what you called it?"

Nasty realized his mistake. "I meant to say *Arthur.*"

"You said *author,*" Jack growled through clenched teeth.

"Did not!"

"Did too!"

"We need to tell them the whole truth," Oliver said, wiping the spot of blood from his neck. He looked at Nasty for approval, but the bird shook his head. Oliver turned to Cora and Jack. "I'm sorry, but this isn't real. None of it. You're only part of a story."

Only Part of a Story

*O*nly *part of a story?* That's how Oliver chose to start his explanation? I admit, I thought it was a rather crass way to break the news, but perhaps it was best that the children hear the truth straight and unsoftened, like ripping a bandage off a particularly hairy knee.

Cora and Jack stayed frozen in place, as if the hands of the Author were still gripping them, not letting go until Oliver told them everything.

He started at the very beginning and went through each sad and miserable detail of his life. He told them about the real world he came from and how things always got worse for him. He told them the sudden and unexpected way his mother had died and how impossible it was for people to understand the grief he felt every day.

A tear trickled down Cora's face. Jack looked at her and said, "Sometimes I miss our mother so much that my whole body hurts."

"I know," Oliver said.

Nasty dabbed at his eyes, for he had been an abandoned egg, alone through life, flying above the world without anyone to talk to.

"But we're going to fix it," Cora said. "We're going to

turn back time and make everything right again."

Oliver continued, describing Ms. Fringlemeier's library and the warm loft where he would get lost in stories that took him away from his life. He told them how he would read his favorite books over and over and over until he could recite them from memory.

"In Dulum, only the wealthiest families can afford books," Jack said.

"And they're big, boring, musty old things," Cora added.

"Well, it's not like that where I'm from," Oliver said. "Books hold the best adventures, full of amazing characters and places and twists and turns."

He told them about his favorite books—ones his mother read to him and others he read a dozen times. He told them about *Charlotte's Web* and *Goodnight Moon*, about *Frog and Toad* and *Where the Wild Things Are*. He described the epic battles of the Swordflinger Saga. He summarized the plots to *The Borrowers* and *Holes* and *From the Mixed-Up Files of Mrs. Basil E. Frankweiler*. Cora and Jack listened intently, forgetting their journey, letting the raft drift farther down the River of Escapement.

That brought him to his favorite book of all: *The Timekeeper's Children* by Malcolm Bloom. The story was about a brother and sister who saved their father from an evil ruler intent on making a magical clock that would speed up time and steal the childhood of everyone in the kingdom.

"That sounds a lot like us," Jack said.

"It *is* us, obviously," Cora said, rolling her eyes. "Tell us. If this is true—"

"And we're still not sure that it is," Jack said.

"How does it all end? Are we successful?"

"I think so," Oliver said.

"You *think* so?" Cora, Jack, and Nasty asked in unison.

Oliver looked at his reflection in the water. He ran his fingers through it, disturbing the image with a trail of ripples.

"I need to tell you something. This is hard for me to admit, but . . . I'm a thief."

"You've already told us that," Cora said.

Jack nodded. "Yeah, that's literally the whole reason we brought you along."

"No, I mean I'm a thief in the *real* world. I stole books from the library. But I had a code—I only stole books that were old, musty, ripped, yellowed and brittle, and incomplete. My copy of *The Timekeeper's Children* was missing the final chapter. I don't know what happens to you, but if it helps, I always thought you were successful in your quest."

"It doesn't," Cora said. She looked at her brother. "This whole story is the biggest load of sheep manure I've ever heard. Do you really think we're stupid enough to believe it?"

"I didn't know it at the time, but the book you're in is very rare," Oliver said. "I tried to return it to the library, but it was taken from me. Now it's gone forever."

"Then why are we here?" Jack asked.

"Because you live in my mind," Oliver said, tapping his skull. "The very last copy is in here."

That brought him to the Pribbles and their obsessive desire to add the story to their collection. He described their remarkable alternative reality goggles and how they had created the *CORTEXIA*™ to suck up every detail and character in Dulum, collecting them in the glowing blue canister, until the story was complete. When Oliver was finished, Cora and Jack sat and stared into each other's eyes for a long while, thinking about everything they had just heard.

"What was that hooded *thing* on the riverbank?" Cora asked.

"Well, it's just a theory, but we believe it's the *Author* of this fine story," Nasty said.

"Maybe," Oliver said, shrugging. "It wasn't in my book."

"Creepy," Jack said.

"I don't believe a word of this," Cora said finally. "Somehow you've managed to tell a story more preposterous than your last one."

"Belief or disbelief make no difference," Nasty said. "The boy's telling the truth."

"I believe him," Jack said. "I don't know why, but for some weird reason I do."

"If it's true, then why does any of this matter?" Cora asked.

"That was my concern and exactly the reason I wanted Oliver to keep the truth from you," Nasty said. He hopped between Cora and Jack and placed his wings on their shoulders. "As a narrator, I'm a main character in the book as well, and I've given this topic considerable thought. I believe it matters because *stories* matter. You changed this young boy's life, and you need to stay right where you are, inside his thick head."

Cora thought on this for a moment and finally said, "We're going to finish our quest, save our father, and go back in time to when Mother was still alive. If you want to help, I suppose I'll allow it, but never think of lying to us again or I'll slice you."

She ran a finger across her neck.

"Wonderful!" Nasty said. "Then it's a deal!"

Jack nodded.

The group clutched hands and wing in a pact.

"With that settled, let's make a plan. I've flown over Dulum every day of my life and know it better than anyone," Nasty said. "We're moving south on the River of Escapement. Unfortunately, the main town of the Old Mountain Guard is in the other direction, and the easiest path over the mountain is right behind it. Obviously, we're not going there. I've delayed the Pribbles for a while, but we can't assume it will last forever. Perhaps a few more days. We'll go through a different town and—"

His explanation was interrupted by the chirping of three small birds in the trees. One was yellow and one was blue and one was red, and they were very loud and anxious. They flapped their little wings, hopping from limb to limb, swooping down upon the raft and ruffling the children's hair.

"What's going on?" Jack asked.

Cora swung her knife at the birds.

"Stop it, you wicked girl!" Nasty cried. "*Never* hurt a bird!"

The three birds settled on branches and continued chirping.

Nasty cocked his head, listening to them.

Chirp chirp chir-chir-chir chirp.

"Oh dear," he said.

The birds continued their chirping song, growing louder and faster.

"Oh *dear!*" Nasty moaned.

"What's going on?" Oliver asked.

"Keep paddling. As fast as possible."

Jack and Oliver grabbed the oars, working hard until they caught a current that moved them along the curves of the mountain.

"What's going on?" Oliver asked.

"The Pribbles are coming."

Bird Spies

The three little birds sat on the raft, continuing their story. Neither Cora, Jack, nor Oliver were well versed in their language, so Nasty was forced to translate.

The three little birds had been flying over the Green Lands, looking for a spot to nest for the night, when they saw a peculiar duo hacking through the undergrowth. In the forest an odd *beep beep boop* repeated, soft and far away.

"This way," Mrs. Pribble said. Her hearing must have been quite keen, because she had detected the sound from a distance and was leading her husband by the hand through the dense plant life.

The birds followed them. Dew sparkled on the colorful plants, the red bird said. Bugs and bits of dust floated through the air, illuminated in the moonlight. The couple's feet slurped in the thick mud and—

"I don't need poetic descriptions," Nasty chirped. He shook his head. "Everyone wants to be a narrator. Please get to the point!"

The yellow bird took over, explaining how the Pribbles continued walking as the *beep beep boop* got louder.

"That blasted talking bird!" Mr. Pribble had said, wiping sweat from his face and adjusting the circular glasses on his bulbous nose. "What *was* that thing? I don't remember talking birds in the book, and now we're off schedule and—"

"Quiet!" Mrs. Pribble said. She held her hand against her husband's mouth and dug her sharp fingernails into his cheeks.

Beep beep boop.

She scanned the shrubbery.

Beep beep boop.

"There!" she cried. Tucked in a bramble bush and wrapped in thorns and vines was a small plastic nozzle. A glow came from behind the branches, and the air teemed with odd roars and noises.

"Oh, I knew I should have dropped it in the sea! Didn't even delay them a day!" Nasty moaned. "Then what happened?"

The blue bird continued.

Upon finding the strange contraption, Mr. Pribble had clapped his hands and run toward the light, finding the *CORTEXIA*™ and yanking it free. The canister hummed, and the screen continued to *beep* and *boop* until Mr. Pribble poked in his password. He wiped dirt from the screen and pointed at the complex symbols of lines and circles and triangles.

"Oliver's heading in an odd direction," he'd said, tracking his finger along the screen.

"They can *track* me?" Oliver asked.

"It appears so," Nasty said. He nodded at the little bird spies and chirped, "Keep an eye on them, but don't get too close. That machine is mighty uncomfortable when pointed in your direction. Report back to me whenever you can. Thank you very much, um . . . I'm sorry, I didn't catch your names."

"Names?" the red bird said.

"We don't have no names," the blue bird said.

"The Author didn't bother to name every little creature," the yellow bird said. "It would take too long."

"Well, that's not right!" Nasty said. "I'll name you now. My name is Nasty Rodent Eater, named after my favorite food. What's your favorite food?"

"Weasel," the red bird said.

"Worm," the blue bird said.

"Walnut," the yellow bird said proudly, and then added, "I'm a vegetarian."

"There we have it! Weasel, Worm, and Walnut, I wish you safety on your journey, and thank you for your help."

The birds bowed.

"Come with me," Nasty said. He flapped his wings and flew high above the trees. It wasn't hard to locate the Pribbles; he needed only look far away, at the edge of the forest, where trees were being ripped from the ground, spiraling into the *CORTEXIA*™ and leaving a massive gray expanse.

The three little bird spies headed toward the shrinking Green Lands.

"Good luck to you," Nasty whispered. He turned back to the mountain range. It spanned ahead, so wide and tall that it filled his vision. He flew higher, passing through thin wisps of clouds. Far in the distance, Nasty saw the faint shapes of a town of the Old Mountain Guard. There were large wooden structures built on stilts, one on top of the other, hundreds of feet tall. Wooden pathways and rope bridges stretched from building to building. Torches lit every corner of the complicated wooden structure, and large beams were screwed high into the sides of the mountain. Perhaps if they could make it through *that* town, they could steal the wood they needed and start their ascent up the mountain.

Nasty tucked in his wings and flew back to the raft.

"I know where we need to go," Nasty said. "Start paddling!"

Jack and Oliver picked up the oars. Nasty supervised from above, directing them.

"What if the Gang of Impervious Children follows us?" Cora yelled to him.

"Let's only worry about one adversary for now," Nasty said. "Besides, I doubt very much that they will track us this far from the plot."

They turned onto a different branch of the river and continued on a current for another hour until they reached a thin bank of wet mud and docked their raft.

Ahead, the lights from the Old Mountain Guard's town flickered.

"Now, we need to make it through undetected, steal some wood from their ale barrels, and then it's just a quick climb up the tallest mountain peak before the Pribbles catch up to us. Easy peasy."

In hindsight, it was a preposterous statement, but in the absence of a better idea, the children followed Nasty through the wooded bank and toward the town, where things were about to get a bit sketchy.

CHAPTER FOUR

A SNEAKY ROUTE PAST
THE OLD MOUNTAIN GUARD

T he Old Mountain Guard were a thick breed, muscular and hairy, as were their husbands. It was mostly women who guarded the base of the mountain, protecting the villages from attacks by nearby lands. The men, or anyone who didn't want to be a warrior, largely drank and fished and cooked over fires. Because of their distance from the Kingdom of Dulum, the Old Mountain Guard ruled themselves. They distrusted anyone from the other side of the mountain and were rumored to throw intruders into their stews, cooking them in the juices of their animal prey.

All that to say visiting their town was very dangerous.

Cora, Jack, and Oliver crept toward it, and Nasty perched on Oliver's shoulders, watching for any sign of danger.

Something is wrong *about this place*, Nasty thought as they got closer, though he couldn't pinpoint the root cause—merely the symptoms.

First of all, there was no sound. There wasn't a peep from the people who walked along the bases of the stilted structures, nor the slightest squeal from the children climbing the rope ladders and running along the connecting bridges.

The sun was beginning to rise and the town was waking up. The whole place seemed to be covered in a shimmering gray haze, so thick that you could almost eat it. Nasty rubbed his eyes to make sure bugs hadn't flown into them.

"OMG," Jack said.

"What?" Oliver asked.

"Look—it's a member of the Old Mountain Guard."

A mountain woman walked down the path, beginning her guard shift, and a man followed, walking toward the river and dragging a coil of rope.

"Get down," Cora hissed. She pulled Jack off the path and Oliver followed, crouching at the edge of the forest.

The children stared in wonder as the people walked past. Something wasn't right. They had *no faces*.

"What in all creation?" Nasty whispered.

Their heads looked a bit like if you squint and cross your eyes while staring at your thumb. There was a swab of brown color where hair should be, and their flesh-toned faces blended with their necks, which were attached to wide, blurry torsos. Their shirts squirmed in the air as they walked and looked almost transparent at the edges. Their pants appeared as two large strokes of brown.

"I can't see right," Cora said. She rubbed her eyes with her fingers and blinked rapidly.

"I can't either," Jack said. "What's happening?"

The town was a mass of crisscrossing blobs, smeared in the air like streaks of mud.

"Oliver, how well do you remember the chapter describing the mountain town?" Nasty asked.

"I don't know. It was a short chapter, only a few paragraphs, and—"

"Oh dear. I suspect we're in a Loosely Rendered Town."

"A what?" Jack asked.

"When the Author wrote about the mountain town, he only bothered to describe the town you were *meant* to pass through. The rest were described in quick strokes and sweeping generalities. A word here and a word there. Just enough to add quick dots of color to the mental image. That's what we're seeing now, being so far away from the story."

"That didn't happen when we went off route in the cave," Oliver said.

"Yes, but you were still very close to the main plot of the story, and the Author spent a good amount of time describing the cave. Anyway, perhaps he was there, helping you. If my suspicions are correct about the tall, hooded figure, then maybe . . . "

"What are you talking about?" Cora asked, still skeptical of the fact that they were in a story.

"Oh, Author!" Nasty hissed into the forest. "Author, are you here? Will you help us?"

As if on cue, a rustling came from the bushes and a figure appeared, tall and dark and menacing.

"Him again!" Jack yelled, grabbing his sister and pushing her behind a stump.

"I didn't think that would work," Nasty said. "Dear Author, I do hope you will be so kind as to assist us. We need to make it through this town, you see, and it appears . . . well, it appears you didn't give it much attention in your book."

The figure growled and waved its arms.

"Not that you needed to! No, no, as far as I'm concerned,

it was merely background scenery, sketched far off in the distance. The story hardly needed it, and I understand your reasoning for being brief with the world-building considering the word count, but please, we need to make it through this Loosely Rendered Town and steal something for the spell. What was it again, young Cora?"

Cora recited the next verse of the spell, her voice wavering in the shadow of the Author.

"Add a casing constructed
With wood that is charred.
It is steeped in the drink
Of the Old Mountain Guard."

"Very good! Yes, that's all we need! Once we get one of the barrels of the Old Mountain Guard's drink, we'll continue up and over the mountain and move into the city of Dulum. We promise we'll stay closer to the plot from here on, dear Author, but . . ."

The figure slunk back into the trees and vanished. Nasty continued babbling for a few moments before he noticed.

A whoosh of air surrounded them, and soft noises began to come from the town.

Oliver closed his eyes and felt that same tingle in his head. Pressure formed behind his nose.

"Look!" Jack whispered.

The Loosely Rendered Town came into focus, the details solidifying, one after another. Slight sounds swept through the air. Gray beasts with tusks and pointy tails lumbered around in the mud, snorting and drinking from troughs of slop. Parents leaned from their windows, yelling at dirt-covered children who squealed and climbed down long rope ladders hanging from their homes. Men carried buckets of bait to their boats. There was a lively marketplace at the base of the mountain, full of the nastiest thieves, drunkards, and fighters you've ever seen. Large donkeys snorted and slogged through the mud, carrying heavy packs of food and supplies on their backs.

"It's working!" Nasty cried. "Oh, thank you, Author. *Thank you!*"

"Yeah, thanks so much," Cora said. "Not like you could just *give* us a piece of wood. Never mind, we'll get it ourselves."

Cora led Jack and Oliver from rock to rock until they were within throwing distance of the wide, wooden stilt legs of the city. Nasty flew above, circling the town and examining every beam and plank. There was still a slight haze over the Loosely Rendered Town—a thin, glimmering cloud—but Nasty could make out a group of children playing on the ground underneath a swaying, wood plank rope bridge. They threw mud balls at one another and wrapped their small arms around the legs of the structure, seeing how high they could climb before sliding back down.

Nasty returned to Oliver, settling on a rock.

"Good news," he said. "The inhabitants of the town seem to be quite distracted by their work. Bad news: There's an awful lot of them. We need to find an empty spot to enter."

"Over there," Cora said, pointing to a great wooden cylinder that was high up and to her right. Underneath it was a fenced-in pen lined with feeding troughs and buckets of brown water. Dirt and hay was piled in every corner, and shelves stacked with tools were drilled into the craggy side of the mountain. A few monstrous pigs moved about, slurping up food and rolling in sludge.

"What is that?" Jack asked, eyeing the wooden cylinder.

"It appears to be a grain storage structure of some kind," Nasty answered. "They store the fresh food for themselves and dump the older stuff for the animals."

"It's really high up," Oliver said.

"Well, they're wise to store their food above the ground, lest the"—Nasty's stomach rumbled—"*rodents* contaminate it with their . . . delicious little toes and tails and noses and—"

"You're an odd bird," Cora said.

"Quite. Look!"

Nasty pointed a wing. Tucked in the corner of the animal pen was a ladder that led all the way up to the wooden cylinder.

"The grain storage structure should be unoccupied, mostly, which makes it a perfect start to our sneaky route."

"Are you able to climb ladders, Nasty?" Jack asked.

"Why would *I* climb ladders, you nincompoop? I'm a bird. I'll fly, thank you very much, and I'll send signals from above if danger is approaching. Can I climb ladders! Honestly!"

Jack blushed at this, realizing the stupidity of his question.

"One squawk means *move forward*, two squawks means *watch out*," Nasty said. "Now look here."

Nasty waved a wing at the far side of the structure, where a long and narrow rope bridge led to a cluster of square

188

homes. Each one had a single window covered in thin animal hide, and from time to time a mountain dweller would poke out their head and scan the forest for intruders.

"Getting through there may be tricky, but it's part two of our sneaky route. I'll alert you if I see any danger."

Past the small group of houses was another rope bridge—this one short and wide—that led to a small set of stairs. At the top was an enormous rectangular building.

"Now, part three—I believe *that's* the tavern, and *that* is where you will find some barrels of ale."

Fire flickered inside, and hulking silhouettes moved about, throwing fists at one another and pouring jugs of dark liquid down their throats.

"Bit early to be drinking, isn't it?" Jack asked.

"One would think. On the bright side, ale clouds the vision and fogs the mind. Perhaps that will make it easier to take what you need. With any luck, you'll leave that room with the wood in your possession. Then it'll just be a matter of making it to the mountain."

Nasty pointed to the left side of the tavern, where an enormous pole jutted into the air. Wooden beams fanned out around it, creating a spiraling Great Staircase that went to the highest point of the Loosely Rendered Town.

"The Great Staircase will take you as high as possible. Be careful not to be seen by the guard on the Wooden Watchtower. When you reach the top, you'll find a structural pole bolted into the mountainside. Tiptoe across it and you'll be safe and sound. Then we can begin our little climb."

As Nasty described it, it all seemed very easy, but Oliver

sensed it would not go that smoothly. Still, he felt a dash of excitement mixed with an undercurrent of dread and fear and sickness.

"It will be all right, Master Oliver," Nasty said, noticing the complicated emotions on the boy's face. "I'll be watching from above, and I won't let anything bad happen to you."

"Shouldn't we wait till it's nighttime?" Oliver asked. In the book, this chapter had taken place under cover of darkness. Still, it was a foolish question, because the morning sun was still low in the sky and it would be many hours until nightfall. Nasty didn't answer. Rather, he pointed at Cora and Jack, who had already begun running to the animal pen.

Blumpf!

Oliver crouched as he ran, staying in the shadows along the edge of the forest as he approached the wooden Loosely Rendered Town of the mountain people. The closer he got, the bigger it all seemed—tall and complicated and fraught with danger.

"Wait for me," Oliver hissed, following Cora and Jack into a small dirt ditch surrounded by felled branches and leaves. From here, they could see the feeding troughs stacked in a line under the grain storage structure. Bugs flew over the dark and slimy water, and brown pigs lay in the mud, little more than smudges of pink at this distance.

They scanned the area for any mountain people, but none were near. Nasty flew high overhead and squawked once to confirm.

"Let's go," Jack whispered.

They stood and ran to the animals, hopping over the short fence and tucking themselves into a corner of the pen. To the side, kids played and squealed, and they could hear loud songs and shouts from the tavern high above them.

Oliver's heart beat in his chest. He closed his eyes to calm himself. When he opened them, everything seemed a bit clearer, and he could now see the knots in the wood and the splatter pattern of mud.

Another single squawk sounded above, quieter this time.

"The storage structure's empty," Cora said, wrapping her hands around the ladder and beginning to climb, her black hair whipping her back like the tail of a wolf. "Let's go."

Another squawk sounded.

"Stop," Jack said. "Was that a second squawk?"

"No, I think that was a single squawk again. Your bird is very impatient, Oliver."

She was halfway to the top now, taking the ladder three rungs at a time.

"Maybe we should wait," Oliver said. "I think Nasty's trying to warn us of something."

"He could be right," Jack said, but his sister wouldn't listen.

Cora reached the top of the ladder and pushed her hand against a rectangular trapdoor, crawling through and waving at them to follow.

Jack and Oliver scaled the ladder, moving as fast as they could and pulling themselves up through the trapdoor and into the room. Around the edges of the circular structure were mounds of hay and grain, piled up to the ceiling.

A *psst* sound came from a small window near the ceiling. Nasty was flapping outside, furiously bobbing his head in the direction of the door and the rope bridge.

"I squawked twice," he whispered.

"There was a pause between them," Cora said.

"It was a bit confusing," Oliver said.

"Oh for heaven's sake! *Look!*"

Oliver cracked open the door of the storage structure and saw an enormous person approaching. The rope bridge swayed with the motion, groaning under the weight.

"Someone's coming," he whispered.

There was a bang on the door that nearly knocked him over, followed by a confused grunt. Oliver pressed his back hard against the door, bracing for another impact.

"We have to hide," Jack said. He dove into a pile of grain, sinking down until only a tuft of hair was visible.

Cora tiptoed around the room, looking for something to use as a weapon. "I'm not hiding in that. I can fight them."

"Hogwash!" Nasty cried.

"It is not!" she said. Her foot accidentally caught a metal handle, and she knocked over a bucket of putrid-smelling liquid. It soaked her ankles and dripped into her boots.

"Oh, gross! What is that?" Cora asked, pinching her nose.

"Hogwash," Nasty answered. "I think they use it to make their ale. Anyway, I tried to warn you. Will you stop being so difficult and *listen?*"

There was another forceful bang on the door and an indistinguishable sound from the mountain dweller.

"Hide and I'll distract them," Nasty said. "Quickly now!"

Cora jumped into the grain beside her brother, holding her breath and blending in. Oliver slid into a shallow pile near the door and used his hands to shovel grain over his face and chest just as the door to the room burst open. Oliver cleared a space over his left eye just large enough to see the foggy shape of a giant man enter the room.

"Blumpf!" the mountain man bellowed, looking around for whatever had been blocking the door a moment ago. He held a large iron mug of ale in one hand, and he staggered as he walked. Deep, unnatural sounds came from his throat—a mixture of grunts and belches. He bent down, scooped up a handful of grain, and tossed it into his mouth. He chewed, scratching his tan belly before washing the food down with a long swig of ale.

Cora gagged.

The mountain man turned at the noise and sniffed the air. He began to move, searching for the sound, his free hand curling into a fist.

"Blumpf?" he whispered.

A loud crashing sound came from below. The trapdoor quivered up and down as Nasty beat his wings against it, trying to lure the man away from the children.

"Blumpf!" the man yelled. He pulled the trapdoor open and gazed down at the muddy ground far beneath him. All fell silent.

He grunted in confusion and bent down, sticking his head through the opening. His large posterior was facing Cora and Jack, and it wiggled about as he searched for the source of the sound.

Slowly, Cora rose from the grain. It trickled out of her hair and over her face. She braced herself, swinging back her leg and then connecting it to the man's rump with a definitive *"Hi-yah!"*

The mountain man lost his balance and slipped through the trap door, howling as he fell. He made a wet slurping sound when he impacted the mud below and yelled, "Blumpf!"

Nasty reappeared at the window, his feathers wet and caked with mud.

"Oh dear, part one of our sneaky route went rather poorly. No matter. On to part two. Move, move, move!"

Cora, Jack, and Oliver jumped from the grain, brushing the disgusting stuff from their clothes and opening the door that led to the long and narrow rope bridge. It was constructed from a row of boards tied together with tough rope, and it had a thin handrail made from braided animal sinew. The bridge swayed precariously as they walked, and the ground below seemed bone-shatteringly far away.

"Stay down," Cora hissed. She led Jack and Oliver across, looking for guards stationed on high rooftops and for the wandering eyes of any mountain people leaning out from their homes.

Nasty flew above, perching at the top of the cluster of houses before them. He watched from above as the mountain people moved about. A woman leaned out of the home closest to the children and cupped a hand around her eyes to block the morning sun. She scanned left to right and then retreated inside.

Nasty squawked once and pointed, and the children snuck under her window, keeping their backs pressed to the side of the building. They entered a small alley between houses and waited for another signal.

Nasty watched for an opportunity, and when he was sure the path was clear, he squawked once and the children ran. Nasty pointed a wing at a small platform to the left of the walkway and they slipped onto it, waiting for the next signal.

He waited and observed, squawking at the next opportunity.

The children ran to the next location. He squawked again, but judging by the look on Oliver's face, something was wrong.

He leaned over. No one had seen the children, so what could—

Thunk.

A chamberpot smacked him in the head.

A woman leaned from her third-floor window, howling with laughter. She barked something unintelligible.

"Ruff habble glee doo!" she said.

What in the heavens did that—

Someone else leaned from a window, lobbing a large metal spoon at him. It hit his wing and he took to the air, looking for a safe place to perch.

Pain shot through his body, and with every flap he felt a surge of hot lighting in his chest.

Perhaps he should have found a better way of communicating than squawking. It seemed to have annoyed the townspeople, and—

A plate knocked him in the chest.

More people stuck their heads from their homes, tossing objects at him and yelling as he fought against the barrage.

"Higga loo!" the crowd shouted. "Higga loo!"

Underneath, the man from the grain storage structure ran along the ground, pointing at Nasty and shouting, "Blumpf! *Blumpf!*"

As Nasty watched, the man started climbing back up to their level. He was covered in mud and looked positively determined to catch them.

Jack and Oliver watched with some concern as Nasty was pelted with stray objects. Cora giggled, clearly enjoying the senseless assault on the poor bird. She grabbed her brother's hand and motioned to Oliver, and they zigzagged back and forth through the alleyways between houses while the mountain people were distracted with their squawking target. The townspeople lobbed cups and clothes and spittoons and candles through the air. The items smacked into Nasty, each hit more painful than the last, and rained onto the walkway below.

"Stop it!" Nasty cried. *"Squawk!* Stop it!"

The man continued to point at Nasty. He noticed the children and began to jump up and down, yelling, "Blumpf! Blumpf! *Blumpf!"*

"You're on your own for now," Nasty cried, swooping over the Loosely Rendered Town and disappearing into the trees, where he perched on a branch to tend his wounds.

Part two of the sneaky route had been a disaster, but Nasty hoped part three, in the tavern, would go smoother.

It wouldn't.

The Mountain Tavern

Cora led Jack and Oliver to the large, square building at the center of the wooden town, climbing ever higher. Oliver looked down the tall, stilted legs and felt a wave of dizziness pass over him. From this height, the people and animals below looked as small as roaches.

"Are you ready?" Jack asked.

Oliver nodded.

The commotion from the houses had died down after Nasty flew away, though they could still hear faint cries of "Blumpf! Blumpf!" behind them.

"You're clear on what we need?" Cora asked.

Jack nodded, quickly reciting the next verse of the spell:

> *"Add a casing constructed*
> *With wood that is charred.*
> *It is steeped in the drink*
> *Of the Old Mountain Guard."*

"Simple," Cora said.

They ducked onto a thin porch outside the tavern entrance, pressing their backs against the building. A blanket of animal hide was nailed to the doorframe, and Cora pushed it aside with a finger to peer inside the room.

It was dim. Thick window shades cut out all the sunlight, and firelight flickered from chandeliers and torches. Beams intersected along the ceiling, and the heads of giant animals were mounted along the walls, boasting teeth and tusks and scowls. Large tables and benches made from split logs were placed throughout the room, occupied by hazy mountain people. Together, they made a deafening chorus of indistinguishable shrieks and grunts and laughs, almost as if they were speaking a newly invented language.

"Guff babble doo!" a man yelled, which was followed by loud laughing.

"Higga loo!" the crowd shouted. "Higga loo!"

There was more laughing. On the far side of the room, a mug of ale flew through the air and connected with a mountain man's jaw. A raucous fight began.

"Follow me," Cora said. She used the distraction to run into the room, ducking behind a long wooden bench. Jack and Oliver followed her, creeping through the shadows.

A group surrounded the fighters, chanting and hollering as fists and hair flew.

"There!" Oliver whispered. He pointed at the bar. Tucked in a corner of the room was a stack of dark wooden barrels, each the size of a plump watermelon.

The bartender ambled over, grabbed one from the top of the pile, and held it over a brass mug, squeezing it between his thick hands until the iron hoops bent and the wood snapped.

Thick brown liquid poured over his fingers and dripped into a mug. He hurled the wooden remains into a fireplace behind the bar, then slid the drink to a woman at the end of the counter.

Jack nodded to the pile of discarded wood around the fireplace.

"Let's get it," Cora said. She pulled her cloak over her head and ran from her hiding spot to the next table, ducking into the shadows. Jack and Oliver followed, curling into the space behind the bench and waiting to hear whether anyone noticed them.

Silence.

Cora ran to the next table with Jack at her heels. Oliver trailed behind them, and he looked over at just the right moment to make eye contact with the bartender.

Time seemed to freeze. His heart fluttered in his chest. Oliver ran into the shadows and whispered, "I think he saw me."

A grunting sound came from their right. The bartender ambled around the bar, heading directly to the table the children were hiding under. He pounded his fist on the tabletop and kicked one of the table legs, then scratched his head and hocked a wad of green phlegm out the window.

A horrified squawk came from outside. Oliver looked over to see Nasty perched on the windowsill, wiping something from his chest. He poked his head into the room and squawked again.

The mountain people stopped what they were doing and

looked at the gorgeous bird. Sunlight poured in around him, and the mountain people squinted at the glare.

"Flup blurd a loo?" one asked, standing up.

Nasty squawked again and did a little dance in the window, shaking his wings and kicking his feet in a very demeaning cha-cha.

"Ah, glurp be sittle grappy!" the bartender shouted.

The mountain people began to laugh uproariously, clapping their hands at the bird and chanting, "Higga loo! Higga loo!"

"Quickly now, I can't stall them for long," Nasty said.

"Now's our chance. Go, thief," Cora said.

Oliver crawled behind the empty bar and toward the freshly discarded pile of broken wood on top of the fire. He slid along the ground, moving over sticky ale stains, heaps of animal bones, and other discarded food. He needed only one barrel's worth of wood, and he'd need to get it quick, before the bartender returned.

He began to sweat, and his hands trembled. He was a book thief, not a barrel thief, and Ms. Fringlemeier was never this close to him when he committed his crimes.

You still have three lives left, he reminded himself. *What's the worst that can happen?*

Nasty was still dancing in the window, but the crowd had begun to turn on him. Their cheers slowly turned to taunts and jeers. They demanded a more entertaining dance, one that Nasty was not willing to provide.

A cup struck Nasty in the beak and he spun in place before crashing to the floor.

The crowd erupted, clapping and hollering, and then more plates and food flew through the air.

Oliver seized the opportunity, using a stick to slide a barrel's worth of wood from the top of the pile and discarding the two metal hoops that once held it together. Embers glowed at the edges of the wood, so he dunked them, piece by piece, into a bucket of suspicious brown liquid sitting nearby.

The wood sizzled and smoked, revealing a dark, marbled grain that looked like the rolling waves of the ocean. The pieces were heavier than he expected, but he hoisted them to his chest and slipped back into the shadows just as the bartender returned to his spot. The heel of the bartender's boot grazed the side of a metal hoop, and it slid across the wet floor, making a *clang* as it hit a chair leg.

"Grunk?" the bartender said. He bent down and picked up the hoop, then saw the second hoop on the floor, separated from the pile of wood. He held them up to his head like earrings and laughed.

Oliver slunk farther away, back in the direction of Cora and Jack. Jack took the pieces of barrel wood from Oliver and stuffed them in his satchel. The bag was becoming quite heavy and certainly would be a burden for the climb up the mountain.

The bartender clanked the hoops together and furrowed his brow, as though he was thinking deeply. He knelt down and looked under the bar. He sniffed at the floor, and just as he was about to stand, he tilted his head and saw the children.

"Grunk?" he said again. He jumped up and whacked the underside of the bar, shouting a string of horrible-sounding words that were probably naughty. He jumped on top of the bar and screamed again, pointing at the spot where the children were hiding.

"Heavens, I'm beginning to think we aren't very good at being sneaky," Nasty said. He watched as the mountain people walked toward the children with evil expressions pasted on their faces.

The man from the grain storage structure ran into the tavern and waved his arms, jumping up and down and yelling, "Blumpf! Blumpf!"

"Higga loo!" the crowd began to chant. "Higga loo!"

"Blumpf! Blumpf!" the man said again. He hopped on the bar and clapped his hands, pointing wildly.

"Run!" Nasty yelled, somewhat relieved that the attention was off him for the moment. He leapt into the air and flew through the window, journeying upward to circle the Wooden Watchtower that stood beside the Great Staircase.

Cora, Jack, and Oliver obeyed, running out of the tavern and toward part four of their sneaky route as a mob of slightly blurry people followed, grabbing torches and axes and other sharp things that would hurt very much if struck with.

The Wooden Watchtower

The beams of the walkway creaked as the children ran for their lives. The Great Staircase was in front of them: a spiraling structure that looked like an arrow that had been shot into the sky, piercing a fluffy expanse of clouds. Bells rang around them in the Loosely Rendered Town, alarms and screams and curses that demanded capture and blood. At the top of the nearby Wooden Watchtower, a dozing guard blinked and looked around before resting her head back on her arms.

"Faster!" Nasty screamed. "Put those scrawny legs to work!"

"You're one to talk, bird thighs!" Cora yelled.

"How *dare* you!" Nasty cried. He flew in front of them, directing them to the Great Staircase. He had to help Jack and Oliver survive this. Cora . . . well, at the moment, he wasn't so sure he wanted to help her.

The town was fully awake now. Firelight lit the corners of buildings, and the screams of small children echoed across the mountainside.

A mob of people chased them from the tavern. The bartender led the charge, waving the bent metal hoops of the barrel and screaming, "Gee blogulous!"

"This is not ideal," Nasty whispered.

Another mob of people appeared, blocking the entrance to the Great Staircase.

"What do we do?" Jack asked.

Dangling from the top of the Wooden Watchtower was a thick strand of braided fibers that softly swayed in the morning breeze.

"Climb the rope!" Nasty yelled. "You can swing over to the staircase!"

"We'll surely die!" Cora screamed.

"I'm willing to risk it."

Jack reached the rope first and stretched out his arms, leaping as high as he could. He grabbed the rope and twisted his legs around it, then began to pull himself up, one arm's length at a time.

The rope slithered in the air and the Wooden Watchtower creaked. Nasty flew to the top. He could hear the rumbling snores of the guard.

"Oh, be quiet. Please be quiet," he whispered, which was a rather stupid thing to say considering how a large mob was forming on the bridge below.

Oliver grabbed the rope next, pushing off from the ground and holding on tightly, each pull burning the palms of his hands. Cora was close behind, growling at him to climb faster.

They ascended five feet, then ten, then twenty.

"Don't look down!" Nasty said, swooping from his perch and flying around the children. "Don't *ever* look down."

Below, a person had lit a torch and was touching it to the

base of the rope. It smoked and burst into flames, traveling up the rope's braid like a lit fuse.

"Fire!" Cora yelled.

"I told you not to look."

The girl is clearly trouble, Nasty thought.

The flames continued to rise, moving faster than the children could climb. They were halfway to the top, and Nasty spiraled around the fire, trying to blow it out with the force of his powerful wings.

"You're high enough!" Nasty shouted. "Swing over to the Great Staircase! Go on!"

"How do you expect us to do that?" Cora asked.

"Use your bodies to create momentum. All together now! Kick your legs and *swing*!"

Cora, Jack, and Oliver kicked out their legs, swinging back and forth in unison, aiming for the Great Staircase that would lead them to the mountain.

Below, people grabbed at the burning rope, shaking it and barking in anger.

"Come on now! Jump! You can do it!"

From her spot at the bottom of the rope, Cora swung hard and released at the optimal moment, arching her back and soaring through the air. She seemed to move in slow motion, a majestic bird girl, her dark hair waving behind her like the wings of an eagle. Her fingers caught the edge of the staircase and she pulled herself up, watching as Jack and Oliver continued to swing.

The guard at the top of the Wooden Watchtower had been stirred awake due to the commotion, and she observed the scene below in confusion. She yelled down to the mountain people, and they screamed a reply, pointing their fingers at the swinging children. In a flash, the guard understood. She roared and began reeling in the rope, wrapping it around her thick arms as she lifted the children higher.

"Now's your only chance!" Nasty shouted. "Jump!"

"It's too far," Jack said. Cora was much better at these things, and to miss the jump would mean certain death. He kicked his legs harder, creating momentum, moving back and forth like a pendulum.

"Think positive!" Nasty yelled. "Take your time. You can do it!"

The rope was yanked up again, and the guard's teeth glistened in the morning light. She pulled a knife from her belt and began hacking at the rope.

"Actually, don't take too much time!"

Nasty flew to the top of the Wooden Watchtower and flapped his wings in the guard's face, pummeling her with his mighty talons. Feathers flew, and the guard shook her head and snapped her teeth.

"Watch the wings! Oh heavens! Ouch!" Nasty yelled. He gave one final scrape at the guard's face and then tucked his body into a tight, bulletlike shape, soaring from the Wooden Watchtower to the Great Staircase.

Below, the crowd grew in size. Torches flickered and weapons shook. Everything was twisting into focus now—Oliver could see the individual faces of the crowd, each one sharp and furious.

"What are you waiting for?" Cora yelled.

The flame was moving higher up the rope, leaving behind a truly awful smell.

"On the count of three, we go," Jack said.

Together Oliver and Jack swung back and forth, counting, "One . . . two . . ."

Fire touched Oliver's feet, and he yipped as it burned the hem of his pants.

"Three!" Jack yelled. At that exact moment, the guard's hacking was successful and the rope snapped, disrupting the arch of their jump.

Cora screamed as they flew through the air.

They screamed in reply.

The guard screamed above, and the townspeople screamed below.

Overall, there was an awful lot of screaming.

They began to fall, lower in the air than anticipated, several rotations below Cora on the Great Staircase.

Jack reached forward, grabbed a board of the Great Staircase, and clung for his life with one hand, the other holding the strand of burned rope. Oliver dangled on the rope below.

"Can I let you go, Oliver?" Jack gasped. "You'll die and come back, right?"

Oliver looked at the fire and pitchforks and knives below.

"I'd really prefer if you didn't," he said.

Nasty began to fly toward them, yelling, "Climb up! Hand over hand! That's the way!"

Oliver obeyed, pulling himself up. The charred rope between the boys began to fray.

"Just a little bit more, Oliver!" Nasty called. "You can do it!"

With a *twang*, the final charred strands of the rope snapped.

Oliver began to fall.

The Great Staircase

Nasty flew with all the might in his body, pumping his wings and ignoring the pain, talons extended. The wind blew his feathers majestically. Oliver fell toward the base of the Great Staircase, four stories down, where the mob of mountain people had congregated.

He hit the pitchforks like a piece of soft meat—*thwunk*—and screamed in a way that was appropriate considering he'd been impaled in about seven places. The mountain people roared with delight and closed in on him, their torches burning him from head to toe.

With a *pop*, Oliver disappeared, and chimes rang out from the heavens. A glowing swirl of blue light came from the clouds, twisting down toward the mob. Nasty followed the light, batting the crowd with his wings, moving them away from the spot of the boy's death.

"Make way! Shoo! Shoo!"

The light formed together into the shape of a boy, and the moment Oliver was a solid mass of flesh again, Nasty squeezed his shoulders in his talons and lifted him. Nasty's whole body hurt, but he tried to forget it, flying higher.

"Two lives left, Oliver. That's not so bad," he wheezed.

Oliver didn't reply. He rubbed at his chest, feeling for any holes left in his body.

Below, the mountain people shoved their way onto the Great Staircase. It trembled under the weight of the mob, and the orange flames of their torches glowed in their hands. Heat radiated up, and black smoke formed a cloud that danced in the air like a dragon's breath.

Jack, who'd managed to pull himself up, sprinted along the Great Staircase to join his sister. On each level, pathways jutted out from the sides of the staircase, leading to bridges that snaked around clusters of houses.

By now, the entire mountain town was awake, and people peered from their homes, shaking their fists and yelling, despite not having the slightest idea of *why* they were yelling.

Nasty dropped Oliver beside Cora and took a wide turn over the Loosely Rendered Town. The townspeople were continuing their push up the spiraling stairs and were two rotations below the children. The man leading the charge waved his muddy fists in the air and shouted, "Blumpf! *Blumpf!*"

"You again?" Nasty whined.

The children continued to run, looping around the staircase's center pole, going higher and higher.

The crowd was gaining on them, and the fire below heated their toes and made them quicken their pace.

Finally, the wooden support beam leading to the side of the mountain was just ahead.

"One at a time now," Nasty said. "Climb across and keep your eyes forward. Maintain balance and *never* look down. Especially you, Cora."

He flew to the mountainside and perched on a large iron screw fastened into the rock.

Cora went first, leaping onto the beam and running to the other side on her tiptoes. She rolled onto a small landing of dirt and moss, ducking behind a brown mountain plant.

Jack was next. He stopped halfway across, glancing down at the muddy ground, which was at least several hundred feet below, and began to sway.

"Why does no one listen to me?" Nasty moaned.

"You can do it!" Cora yelled. "Hurry!"

The crowd was closer, within smelling distance. Jack crouched to regain his balance, wrapping his hands around the beam and crawling the remainder of the way across.

"One more! Go, Oliver, go!" Nasty cried.

Oliver closed his eyes and crawled onto the beam. He could hear the rumble of the crowd behind him. The beam shook.

Don't look down, he told himself. *Don't look down.*

He moved forward.

One foot. Then two.

The mob arrived. They shook the beam back and forth, and the wood groaned and cracked.

Oliver tried to move faster, but his body would not obey. He felt frozen at this great height, like every muscle was fighting him.

Glancing down, he caught a glimpse of the ground and felt the entire world spin.

A woman stepped onto the beam behind him, brandishing a fiery torch and whispering threats in deep gibberish.

"Come on, Oliver!" Jack yelled. "You're almost here!"

But Oliver was unable to move, no matter how short the distance.

The woman moved closer. She waved the torch and snapped her teeth, her nest of greasy black hair flowing down her shoulders.

"Oliver, what are you waiting for?" Nasty cried.

The crowd was growing larger—all the town's adults were on the Great Staircase now—and they cheered the warrior woman on, begging her to attack. She'd lifted the torch, preparing to bring it down on Oliver, when a large man jumped on the beam and shoved her aside.

"*Blumpf,*" the man growled.

Oliver recognized him as the man from the grain storage structure, the very one whom Cora had kicked into the pigpen. "I'm really sorry. We didn't mean to hurt you, it's just—"

The man turned and roared at the mob. They screamed in return, pointing their torches and weapons at him.

"BLUMPF!" the man screamed. He wrapped his arms around Oliver and held him over his head, shaking him so hard that Oliver felt like his internal organs were bumping against his ribs.

"Put me down!" Oliver yelled, and instantly the man lowered him, cradling him in his arms. Through the mud,

Oliver saw his face. It was plain and wide, with two large brown eyes and a pair of sloping eyebrows. Below his eyes was an unremarkable human nose, and his mouth was a large circle with tiny lips, as if someone had punched a hole in a mound of dough. It twisted up at the ends, *almost* as if the man was trying to smile.

"Blumpf," the man whispered.

"Are you . . . are you trying to *help* me?" Oliver asked.

The man smiled and nodded, jumping on the beam like an excited toddler. The wood creaked and splintered.

"Blumpf!" he yelled. "Blumpf! Blumpf!" He turned to a man waving a torch and ripped it from his hand. He hurled the torch into the middle of the mob, and a roar erupted as the planks of the Great Staircase were set on fire. The flames traveled to the center pole and quickly spread. The mob dispersed, screaming as fire licked around them and spread across the wooden structure.

"Who are you?" Oliver asked.

"Blumpf," the man answered, and it was now apparent that *blumpf* was the only sound he was capable of making. Blumpf threw Oliver on his back and lumbered across the beam to the rocky ledge of the mountain, where he gently set down Oliver beside Cora and Jack.

Blumpf wrapped his arms around the support beam and began to pull. His bulging muscles popped with veins and rippled with sweat. The screws that held the beam to the mountainside began to groan until the beam broke free with a tremendous *CUH-RUNK*.

"Such strength!" Nasty said, flying over to perch

214

near the man. "And such stench! It appears the Author has sent us more assistance! Thank you, dear Author, wherever you are!"

Blumpf howled his name once again and pushed the beam away from the mountainside. The Great Staircase was engulfed in fire now, and black smoke exploded from the top. The entire structure had weakened, the wood glowing a deep orange. Lacking its top support beam, the Great Staircase teetered with Blumpf's push—slow at first, until the whole thing cracked in half and fell onto the town below. Fire spread along the rope bridges and up the cubed clusters of homes. Families fled, sliding down the stilts and watching as their Loosely Rendered Town was destroyed in the fast-traveling blaze. The tavern exploded into a large fireball, likely due to the large quantities of flammable ale, and from there it was just a few moments until the whole town had joined the inferno.

The group watched as the final structure fell, joining the smoldering heap of burning timber on the ground.

"Well, I suppose that marks the end of our sneaky route," Nasty said, clapping his wings together. "I think we can call that a success."

"We destroyed the entire town," Jack said.

"Oh, they made it out safely, and they'll rebuild quickly. They're very resourceful, aren't they, Blumpf?"

Blumpf shrugged.

"This way, children! I think I see a path to travel," Nasty said. He rubbed at his sore wing. "Unfortunately, I won't be flying with anyone else for some time, but we have just a quick climb up this mountain and then it's a straight shot to Dulum proper. Come, come." He jumped in the air, kicking his talons in delight.

Yes, at that moment, Nasty was convinced that everything was going perfectly perfect, blissfully unaware that the easy part of their journey was over.

CHAPTER FIVE

AN UNEXPECTED ENCOUNTER AT THE TOP OF THE MOUNTAIN

Oliver looked up. The mountain peak was hidden in clouds, and the whole thing was so massive that he felt dizzy looking at it.

Blumpf grabbed Jack's satchel, strapping it to his meaty back. He pounded his chest and pointed up the mountain.

"Blumpf," he said.

"Oh goodness," Nasty said. "Well, I guess he's coming with us. Who am I to argue with the Author? Perhaps he'll be of some assistance."

Cora led the charge up the mountain, and Nasty flew ahead. He settled on a spiked rock and called out directions to the children and to Blumpf. From time to time, they reached chasms too wide to jump across, and Blumpf would pick the children up and toss them over. Considering his size, he was surprisingly balanced, able to tiptoe across narrow passages.

The higher they climbed, the more of the Green Lands were visible, and Cora and Jack's faces went pale as they watched the horrible plague of gray ash spread across the land. It was simple to deduce the location of the Pribbles from this height; one needed only to look for the edge of the forest, where trees stretched and spun, fading out of existence as they were ripped from poor Oliver's mind.

"I'm *really* starting to think Oliver's telling us the truth," Jack said. He wedged his foot around a tree root and hoisted himself up to another small ledge, then helped Oliver, who was behind him.

"It doesn't matter to me one way or the other," Cora said. "As long as we save our parents, he can tell us whatever he wants."

"And save them you will!" Nasty said. "This is a children's book, after all. I'm sure everything will work out fine."

"If only Oliver hadn't stolen an incomplete book, he could tell us how it ended," Cora growled.

Oliver grabbed a tree root and looked out over what had once been the Green Lands. He hoped they would all have a happy ending. The wind blew his hair, and his body shivered.

They continued to climb, slowly working their way up the mountain as the sun crested in the sky and began to descend. They crossed narrow rock bridges and used rotted vines to swing over holes that vented hot steam from the mountain's core.

Hidden in the cracks of rock were small rodents that squeaked and gnashed their teeth, their eyes glowing in the darkness. Nasty stuck his beak into the rock face and pecked at them, pulling them out by their tails and slurping them down.

Despite the rodents' ugly appearance—thin and mangy and bald around the head—their meat was quite flavorful. By evening, hunger had sprouted in the children's bellies, and Blumpf ripped a twisted tree from the mountainside and snapped it in half. Jack doused it in liquid from his vial and struck knife to flint while Nasty went hunting—flinging rodents from their hiding places and tossing them to the fire.

The group warmed themselves around the flames, and Blumpf turned the muscly meat on a spit. The moon hung overhead, and the peak of the mountain still loomed far above them.

"Why are you helping us?" Cora asked Blumpf for the eighth time, and for the eighth time she was answered with "Blumpf."

"We'll never make it to the top," Jack said. He rubbed at his feet. They were raw and blistered, and his shoes were nearly worn through.

"Quiet," Cora said, biting into a rodent. "We'll make it."

From his spot, Jack could see all the way to the ocean. He studied the spreading gray dust that was left in the Pribbles' wake. He turned to Oliver. "Tell us about some other books."

Oliver thought of the twentieth-anniversary special edition of *The Swordflinger Saga* that Mr. Pribble had given him. He began to share with them the story of the village of Cromwell and the dragon that attacked it. He told of the brave band of knights sent to fight the dragon and the adventures they encountered. Soon Blumpf's snores filled the air, and Cora and Jack drifted to sleep.

Nasty tucked his wings over his eyes, bracing himself against the cold, dark night as the young boy continued the story until sleep caught him, too. Snow began to fall, and ice became caked on the edges of the rocks. When the rays of morning light hit Nasty, he felt as if arrows of fire were shooting through his chest.

He looked down and saw that the Pribbles were heading toward them, walking along the banks of the River of Escapement.

"We need to keep moving," Nasty said, waking the children and Blumpf.

They continued on and by midmorning arrived at a fork in the path.

One side led to a great crevasse sliced into the side of the mountain. If they could cross it, they would reach a wide and inviting path that snaked up the mountain at a walkable angle.

The other side led to a thin ledge that would require quite a bit of climbing and balancing oneself atop a perilous cliff.

"Clearly the route across the crevasse is the safer bet, if only we could find a way to cross it," Nasty said.

Blumpf shook his head and grunted, pointing at the narrow and difficult path.

"Blumpf!" he said.

Nasty ignored him.

"Oh, look at that tree!" he said, pointing at the near side of the crevasse. A gnarled tree twisted from the ground. It was barely wider than a sapling but appeared adequate to support their weight.

"If our thick-armed friend here can knock it down, I believe it will be a suitable bridge to the other side."

"Blumpf!" Blumpf yelled, flapping his arms like a bird.

"Good sir, if you are suggesting these children can fly

across, than you have much to learn about human anatomy and abilities!"

Blumpf continued to flap his arms.

"You know full well that I can't fly them across. Cora and Jack are much too heavy, and with my injured wing—"

Blumpf pecked at the air, sticking out his nose like a beak and chomping imaginary worms.

Jack laughed at this.

"Are you *mocking* me?" Nasty yelled. He smacked Blumpf with his good wing and said, "We are taking the crevasse route, and that is the end of this discussion. I am the narrator, and I get the final say on decisions such as these! I don't enjoy arguing, particularly with a character of no real importance to the story!"

Blumpf whined and looked at his feet, clearly hurt by Nasty's nasty comment.

"That's not nice," Oliver said. "He's part of our team."

"*Barely*," Nasty said. "That's enough discussion. Come here, Blumpf. Be a good boy and knock over the tree."

Nasty flew on, perching on a tall rock and preening his feathers.

Blumpf shook his head and ran to the tree. He wrapped his large arms around the trunk and rocked it back and forth until the wood began to creak and splinter. He gritted his teeth, straining with the effort. The trunk snapped and fell, slow at first and then gaining speed, until the top struck the other side of the crevasse.

"Hoo-ray!" Nasty cried. He flew across the crevasse and waved at the children. "Come, children. One at a time."

Oliver rubbed his eyes. Something moved behind Nasty, and a long shadow stretched across the path and then disappeared. Was it the tall, dark figure? Perhaps, but it seemed much too big. Maybe he had imagined it.

Cora went first, holding out her arms as she balanced over the great height. The tree bent in the middle and groaned, but she ran on, diving to the other side. Jack followed, swaying in the harsh mountain winds.

"What's that?" Jack asked, pointing to an enormous bundle of twigs and branches tucked in a nook of rock on the other side. Three large blue eggs sat in the middle.

"It's a nest!" Nasty chuckled. "My word, Blumpf, you weren't mocking me! You were pointing out a nest. Blumpf?"

Blumpf hadn't crossed the crevasse, and neither had Oliver. Blumpf lifted the boy and ran away, tucking him into a shelter of rocks.

"Where are you going?" Nasty asked. "It's just a nest. The eggs won't hurt you, silly man, and there's no sign of their . . ."

A shadow passed overhead. A bird swooped down, its wingspan five times wider than Nasty's. Its small black eyes were filled with a blind rage, and its beak snapped viciously.

"*Mother,*" Nasty whimpered.

The giant bird swooped, bending her body so her talons pointed at Cora and Jack. She flapped her wings and descended upon them.

"Run, children!" Nasty screamed. He lifted into the air but flew lopsided due to the throbbing pain in his wing.

Cora and Jack ran behind boulders and braced themselves.

Blumpf wedged himself next to Oliver, wrapping his large arms around the boy's body.

"We have to help them," Oliver said.

"*Blumpf,*" Blumpf pleaded.

"If you want to protect me, you have to protect *them.*"

Blumpf nodded and looked to the sky, tracking the giant adversary as she dove and struck the ground around the children.

"You couldn't have warned us about the giant murderous bird, Oliver?" Cora yelled.

"This wasn't in my story!"

The bird let out a ravenous *"CA-CAAWWW!"* and swooped toward Cora, her eyes lit with a motherly rage. Blumpf leapt onto the fallen tree, running to its middle as the limbs swayed and buckled. He jumped to the other side, sprinting toward the nest.

"Oh, don't touch the eggs!" Nasty screamed. "Birds really don't like that!"

But that's exactly what Blumpf did. He rubbed his meaty hands along their smooth blue shells, calling out *"Blumpf blumpf blumpf"* in a melodic taunt.

The bird's attention diverted from the others, allowing Cora and Jack to cross back to the other side of the crevasse. They ran to Oliver's shelter and tucked in beside him.

The bird screamed another deafening *"CA-CAAWWW!"* and swooped at Blumpf, her talons pinching the air. Blumpf ducked, rolling on the ground as the bird passed by, missing him by several inches, and then soared up, preparing to attack again.

Nasty flew in circles high above, watching the horrible scene, unable to help. What could he do, anyway? He was vastly outsized, and his talons were hardly more than needles compared to those of the massive mother bird.

Blumpf jumped to his feet and wrapped his fingers around an egg, lifting it high above his head.

From this distance, it appeared to Nasty that Blumpf kissed the egg and rubbed its shell, then gently arched back his body and lobbed the egg far away from the nest, screaming, "BLUMPF!"

"Oh my," Nasty whispered.

The egg sailed through the air, descending down the side of the mountain. The mother bird shrieked, changing course to pursue her falling offspring. She pumped her massive wings and prepared her talons to grab.

Blumpf peered over the mountain's edge, hopping from foot to foot, watching as the bird closed in on the egg. Just before it hit the ground, she clutched it, twirling her body in a corkscrew movement before launching back into the air on a powerful updraft.

"Well done, Blumpf!" Nasty cried.

"Blumpf," Blumpf whispered, wiping sweat from his forehead. It appeared that even though he was a simple character, he still had compassion for the little egg, and he smiled and bounced across the tree to the other side of the crevasse, pointing at the thin ledge that led to the more challenging route up the mountain.

The mother bird surely would be back, and the path that

Blumpf had first suggested now looked much more appealing.

"Well," Nasty said, smoothing his feathers with his wings, "perhaps you *should* lead the way from here on, dearest Blumpf. I'm sorry to have doubted you."

"Blumpf," Blumpf said, nodding.

The Climb

They ran to the narrow and difficult path, keeping a frequent lookout for the bird's return. Blumpf pushed Oliver up, and Cora and Jack followed. Jagged rocks stuck from the rock face, and vines jutted from the cracks, threatening to wrap around the children's ankles with each small shimmy above the cliff. They ascended, foot by foot, until they reached a small plateau to rest.

They watched as, below, the mother bird set her egg back in the middle of the nest and then perched on top, ready to protect them from other intruders.

"So the giant bird wasn't in your story," Cora said. "What happens in the other version?"

"You and Jack cross the mountain by following the shortest path, but then have an unexpected encounter at the top," Oliver said

"The Gang," Jack says.

"Yes. They scale the mountain at a different point, then ambush you and try to take all your items."

"How do we defeat them?"

"There's a big battle, and it seems like they're going to capture you, but you escape by sledding on chunks of ice down the other side of the mountain and into the outskirts of Dulum."

"That sounds fun!" Jack said.

"It's not. You barely survive."

"Well, I'm glad we don't have to deal with any of that unpleasantness. The climb up this higher part of the mountain will be difficult enough as it is," Nasty said, and indeed it was.

The next few days were a tedious routine of climbing, sleeping, climbing, hunting for rodents, sleeping, climbing, and more climbing. Snow pelted them in thick flakes, sticking to their thin clothes. Each time Oliver looked up, the peak of the mountain seemed higher than before, always so far out of reach.

Ice formations clung to the mountainside, trembling in the wind, preparing to fall. They heard the distant booms of faraway snow releasing in great sheets, starting massive avalanches that sent clouds of white mist into the air. Animals howled at the sky, and the cries of other strange birds echoed around them.

Sometimes, when the journey proved too difficult, Oliver would ride on Blumpf's back, clutching the monstrous man's shoulders and watching the edge of gray dust spread across the forests of Dulum. The Pribbles were moving slowly on foot, and with any luck, Oliver thought, he and his companions would be over the peak before they reached the base of the mountain.

There were no longer any easy-to-follow paths. The mountain had twisted into great shards of snow-covered rock that jutted out at impossible angles. They ventured on, sweat pouring from their bodies and freezing on their skin. Whenever one child felt unable to carry on, they would stop and huddle together for warmth, and Oliver would continue the story of the Swordflinger Saga to take their minds off the climb ahead. Then they would press on, ever upward, going higher and higher.

At one point, Blumpf ripped large thorns from a black, petrified bramble. He gave two to each child and kept two for himself, showing them how to hold the daggerlike thorns in their hands and strike at the icy side of the mountain, creating handholds for pulling themselves up, foot by treacherous foot.

Hours passed, and the children soldiered on. Every muscle in their bodies hurt, right down to their bones. The air was getting thinner, and Nasty wheezed. He was only able to fly short distances, from one rock to another, and his strength was failing. There were no signs of life at this height—not a single mangy rodent to be found—and he shook with hunger.

Finally, the peak was almost visible through a ceiling of cottony clouds, painted with the golden red light of sunset. Tears streamed down Cora's face at the sight and instantly froze.

"Look!" Jack cried. He pointed to the shorter section of the mountain, miles away, where they *would* have gone had Oliver not interfered with the story. Small shapes scaled the snowy ridge, waiting to ambush the children at the peak.

"It's the Gang of Impervious Children. Just like Oliver said!"

Cora laughed, throwing back her head and screaming, "You'll never catch us from over there! Come and get me, Grayson!"

"You'd like that, wouldn't you?" Jack said.

Cora shoved her brother, and he slid a few feet down the slippery rock, stopping his fall by digging his thorns into a crevice filled with ice.

"What? You would!" he yelled, giggling.

"Blumpf?" Blumpf asked.

"Ignore them, Blumpf, it's just adolescent drama," Nasty said. He hopped to a thin rock bed and pecked at a few brown weeds. "It's been a long day; perhaps we should rest for the night before making our final push to the peak."

The group agreed.

There was no wood for a fire, so Oliver curled into Blumpf's arms and Cora draped her cloak over her brother. Oliver closed his eyes and slept deeply, dreaming about how everything would soon be fixed; he would reach "A Timely End" long before the Pribbles arrived. There was no possible way they could catch him now. The mountain would see to that.

Hours passed. Night turned to dawn, and the sun appeared on the horizon. Long rays of yellow burst around them. Oliver looked out, squinting in the blinding light.

That's when he saw them.

Bird Spies, Part II

Three small birds flew toward them and circled above in a tight formation. The lead bird chirped a singsong melody, and Nasty croaked a reply.

"Weasel? Worm? Walnut?" he asked. "Is that you?"

The birds tucked in their wings and landed beside the children, shivering in the cold and exhausted from the flight.

"Ah, our little bird spies have returned!" Nasty said, half delirious from the long days on the mountain. "What news do you bring from the ground? All is good, I hope."

The children sat up, and Blumpf tilted his head in the way a curious puppy does when you say its name near dinnertime.

The birds looked at one another, nodding toward Weasel.

"Go on," Nasty said, and he translated between each verse of the bird's song.

Weasel told how they had flown over the Green Lands, looking for the Pribbles at the edge of the forest, where trees and rocks and plants sucked together to a fine point, slurping into the *CORTEXIA*™. They stayed far enough away from the nozzle of the terrifying machine to be safe from its pull but were close enough to eavesdrop.

"It's slow work, but we're making progress," Mr. Pribble had said. There was no boat for them to take, no river current to carry them, and the journey by foot along the rocky bank had been long and tedious. He switched off the machine and wiped dirt from the screen. "The other side of the mountain is where the story picks up, love. I'm sorry for the diversions, but—"

"I feel that we're losing the plot," Mrs. Pribble said. She swatted a branch with her hand and a long strand of spiderweb twisted around her arm. "Is this *one* little book worth it?"

"You don't understand," Mr. Pribble whined. He had already explained this to her several times and was getting rather discouraged. "It is, but Oliver's left the main plot of the story. We need to get him back on track and then you'll see."

"I hope you're right," Mrs. Pribble said.

Mr. Pribble consulted the screen of the *CORTEXIA*™ and pointed around a curve in the river.

"He seems to have gone that way," he said, pressing his finger down on the *CORTEXIA*™'s trigger. The water at the river's edge twisted in the air and funneled into the nozzle. As the water disappeared, Mr. and Mrs. Pribble walked to the middle of the riverbed. They followed its snaking path, giant waves forming to either side as the *CORTEXIA*™ drank up the river, until they arrived at a bank where the lush forest melted into the burned remains of the Loosely Rendered Town.

"When was this?" Nasty interrupted.

"Yesterday afternoon," Weasel replied.

"Oh dear."

"It gets worse," Worm said. She continued the story.

The town was a flurry of activity as the Pribbles

approached. The toppled Great Staircase and tavern lay at the base of the mountain in a giant pile of charred, blackened wood. All around them, mountain people cut down trees and used ropes to hoist them up the layers of the structure, rebuilding their Loosely Rendered Town beam by beam.

Mrs. Pribble clapped her hands and called out to the townspeople. *"Hello!* You there! Has anyone seen a small boy and two other children? Short and rather dirty? Does anyone remember them?"

The people of the mountain town had turned their heads in unison and began descending the newly woven rope ladders, yelling curses and threats. They pointed at the remnants of their town, whooping and hollering at the strange intruders. Of course they remembered the children.

"I think they're responsible for this," Mrs. Pribble said.

"Well, it appears we've underestimated little Oliver once again. No matter." Mr. Pribble pulled the trigger on the *CORTEXIA*™ and waved it around, sucking up the entire mountain town in a sloppy swoop until there was nothing left but a handful of pigs and a pile of felled trees.

Mrs. Pribble leaned over to look at the screen and then tilted her head to the heavens.

"He's trying to climb that mountain," she said, pointing.

Mr. Pribble double-checked the screen and nodded.

"Yes, you're right," he said. He hoisted up his trousers and swung the *CORTEXIA*™ onto his back. Inside the blue canister, there were muffled screams and growls from the Old Mountain Guard. "I suppose we should follow them up."

Worm ducked her head at this, as if she were ashamed to deliver such bad news.

"Well, they can't be too close," Nasty said. "We had a head start, and I doubt they're skilled at climbing."

"Wait, it gets even worse," Walnut said. He took over narration.

At the base of the mountain, the bird spies had watched with amusement as Mr. Pribble struggled to hoist his small legs up a large pile of rocks. The couple had hardly made it twenty feet up the mountain, and every inch was more laborious than the last.

"Why'd he have to climb the highest part?" Mr. Pribble grumbled. "A little help?"

Mrs. Pribble squished her thin hands into his backside and leaned forward. Her arms shook under the weight, and Mr. Pribble kicked his legs to propel himself up as he clutched at a small branch. He wiped ash from his clothing and grabbed the *CORTEXIA*™, pointing it at the rocks below him.

He pulled the trigger and sucked them up in a quick burst, accidentally ripping up the ground from underneath their feet.

The Pribbles had slid all the way down the mountain, landing on the gray soot where the town of the Old Mountain Guard used to be.

The three little bird spies laughed hysterically at this, rolling around on the snowy mountain and reenacting the scene.

"Why, that's not worse at all, Walnut!" Nasty said. "I

suppose there's little chance of them catching us now! Thank you for help, friends, now we really should be—"

"We didn't get to the bad part yet," Weasel said.

Nasty sighed.

Walnut puffed out his chest and continued to chirp.

The Pribbles had rolled on the ground.

"Let's wait until we're at the top of the mountain to use the *CORTEXIA*™," Mrs. Pribble said. She pointed at the snowy peak. "We wouldn't want to start an avalanche, would we?"

"No, I suppose not," Mr. Pribble said.

They started to climb again, this time making it about forty feet up the mountain by nightfall. They settled in a small nook carved into the mountainside. Mrs. Pribble went to look for food. Mr. Pribble tried to make a fire but was hardly able to conjure the tiniest spark.

Finally, he quit, resigning himself to the cold. He sat with the *CORTEXIA*™ and fiddled with the buttons, watching the dots on the screen pulse and swirl.

"Oliver's making good time," he whispered to himself. "He'll cross the mountain long before we will. And then . . . *hmm . . .*"

Mrs. Pribble appeared and held up a bundle of puny weeds and three small rodents.

"Salad and steak," she said, her face falling when she saw that the tiny piles of twigs at her husband's feet had not transformed into roaring flames. "What have you been *doing*?"

"Thinking," Mr. Pribble said. "We're in great danger, love. We could be eaten, or we could freeze on this mountain.

Oliver's taking an unknown route, *goodness knows why*, and this world is full of obstacles that we are unprepared for."

"You mean . . . we could *die*?"

"In the story, yes, but we would be reset indefinitely, returning to the same spot of our demise. That's how we designed it. Should an avalanche take us, we'd be reset back *inside* the avalanche, over and over and over until someone on our staff wises up and rips the goggles from our faces. Who knows how long *that* could be."

"It seems you were rather lazy in your planning."

"Well, I never expected Oliver to be so feisty, did I?"

He continued to poke at the screen.

"Take his whole imagination. We'll sort through it later," Mrs. Pribble said. She placed her finger on her temple and began to trace a line to the center of her forehead. "Come, let's exit."

"No," Mr. Pribble growled. "I'm a man of my word. A deal is a deal, and Oliver still has two lives left. Besides, do you know how difficult it would be to find this story inside his mind and sort it out? Nearly impossible! He's a very odd child. Look at how detailed this world is. Goodness knows how many books he's read. His head is full of dreams and vivid creations, things I didn't think children were capable of producing. We need another plan."

"Like what?" Mrs. Pribble asked.

"If I knew that, love, we wouldn't be stuck on the side of a mountain."

They settled in, sleeping restlessly through the night. When the sun rose, Mrs. Pribble jumped to her feet.

235

"What is it?" Mr. Pribble asked.

Mrs. Pribble grabbed the *CORTEXIA*™ and ripped off the screen to fiddle with the wires underneath.

"I had a thought! If I can hack this system, I can try to relocate us to their general location," she said. "No more climbing, no more freezing, and no more rodent steaks— we can be within five hundred feet of them in a matter of seconds."

"But you haven't programmed in years!" Mr. Pribble said, and Mrs. Pribble glared at him.

He slunk back into his corner.

She continued to work, tapping at the screen and splicing wires together with her long, cracked fingernails. The bird spies had watched this, unsure of what was happening but concerned by the joy on the Pribbles' faces.

Sparks flew. Mrs. Pribble twisted a red and green wire together. The *CORTEXIA*™ smoked, and strange sounds echoed in the glowing blue canister.

Snow had begun to fall, piling up at the nook's entrance, and the birds perched just beyond, doing their best to spy without being seen.

Mrs. Pribble pulled out a yellow cord and threw it on the ground. It smoked and twisted like a decapitated snake.

"There," she said. "I've successfully reconfigured our position indicators. Now I need to calculate their position in three-dimensional space, relative to the geometry of the surrounding terrain."

She bit her lip and touched the screen. Mr. and Mrs. Pribble began to flicker, covered in square pixelation.

"Something's happening!" Mr. Pribble screamed.

"That was the easy part. Now I need to decouple our primary axis points from our current location. Then it's simply a matter of plotting a landing spot, being careful not to place us in some dangerous topography, and—"

Walnut stopped his story and asked, "What does *topography* mean?"

"Basically, the ground," Nasty said.

"Ah, we thought it was an animal," Worm added. "Anyway, that's when we decided this was important information for you to know."

"What are they saying?" Oliver asked.

"We're saying they could be here at any moment!" Weasel, Worm, and Walnut sang.

"I really wish you had started with that," Nasty said. He looked at Blumpf and the children and pointed up the mountain. "We need to move."

The Peak

Oliver poked his head through the clouds. All he could see around him was a sea of white, rolling clouds that stretched on forever.

Blumpf's head appeared next to his. Mist twirled around his skull, and snow caked his black stubble. He blinked his eyes lazily, looking at the remarkable scene around him. He arched his neck and pointed at the top of the mountain, grabbing Oliver's shoulder and howling with delight.

"That's right, Blumpf, we're almost at the peak," Oliver said.

Nasty flew through the clouds, drops of condensation beading on his beak. He wheezed in exhaustion, landing in front of Oliver and looking out at the wondrous expanse. From this high up, they could no longer see the ashy gray disease spreading across Dulum.

"It's beautiful," Nasty said. "It's as if the mountain below was all a dream and we're the only ones left in a world covered in the softest snow."

Cora and Jack climbed through the clouds. They looked haggard and thin. The climb had been rough on everyone, but they had insisted on climbing the whole way, refusing to take turns riding on Blumpf's back.

"The top," Cora whispered. Above the mountain, the sky was a dark blue that faded to black, and the faint outline of the moon was still visible, hanging large among sparkling stars.

"Well, I guess that's over with," Nasty said. "The way down should be quicker."

He had no sooner said the words when a strange humming sound filled the air around them.

A tornado of blue pixels spun on the ledge below them, several hundred feet away, and the shadows of two figures appeared in the midst of letters and drawings and strange shapes.

The Pribbles' torsos and limbs snapped together, transparent, until they were fully formed and opaque.

"What's going on?" Cora asked, frantically watching the strange aura filling her vision.

Mr. Pribble blinked, his eyes adjusting to the brightness of the clouds.

"Ah, dear Cora and Jack, it's so good to see you again," Mr. Pribble yelled to them. "And who are *you*, man?"

"Blumpf," Blumpf answered. He made a fist and hit his chest, jumping in front of the children.

Mr. Pribble pointed the *CORTEXIA*™ at Blumpf and rested his finger on the trigger.

"Nobody move."

The children obeyed, and Nasty perched beside them. If this was the end for him, he would not face it alone.

Mr. and Mrs. Pribble climbed the ledge until they reached Blumpf. Mrs. Pribble eyed him up, running her nails along his shoulder.

"Is he not part of the story, love?" she asked.

"He is not."

"He looks an awful lot like the people from that dreadful mountain town."

Blumpf growled at this.

"Indeed," Mr. Pribble said. "He's nothing but a background character. Doesn't belong here. Stand back."

His finger brushed against the trigger, enough that Blumpf felt a sickness shoot throughout his body.

Jack bent down, slowly picking up a loose stone and holding it behind his back.

"This was not the peak you were meant to climb," Mr. Pribble said, pointing to a gap in the clouds where the other, shorter peak jutted up in a sharp point. "Why would you subject yourself to this monstrosity instead of sticking to the path of the story?"

"To stay away from you and that awful story-stealing machine," Cora snapped, and at this Mr. Pribble laughed and pulled harder on the trigger.

"Ah, so Oliver's told you?" Mr. Pribble said. "I really wish he hadn't."

Wisps of color began to bleed from Blumpf's clothes, and he felt a numbness that started at his fingers and went all the way to his heart.

"Please don't hurt us," Jack said.

"My dear children, we would never hurt *you*. I love you and your sister, and I desperately want you to finish your quest. It's *Oliver* you should be afraid of. He's taken you places you weren't meant to go and put you in great danger."

Blumpf arched his back and roared into the air.

"Stand still, you beast!"

Blumpf wouldn't obey.

"Stop it!" Jack yelled at the Pribbles. He lobbed the stone and it smacked the side of the *CORTEXIA*™, ricocheting into the air, where it stretched and spiraled into the nozzle.

Mr. Pribble laughed and released the trigger.

"Please understand that none of this is personal," he yelled over the vicious whine of the motor, "but you've wasted a tremendous amount of time, and I really need to get to work."

He pointed the *CORTEXIA*™ at the peak of the mountain and squeezed the trigger. Rocks liquefied and spun toward him. He continued one swipe at a time, gulping up the top of the mountain until there was nothing above Cora, Jack, Oliver, Nasty, the three little birds, and Blumpf but air.

"You only need one more thing for the spell, yes?"

Jack looked at Cora for approval to answer. She didn't give it.

"What was it again?" Mr. Pribble asked, and he aimed the *CORTEXIA*™ at Jack, who whispered the next lines of the spell:

> *"In the city of Dulum*
> *Sits the crown of the king*
> *By life or by death,*
> *It must twist the mainspring."*

"That's it! A difficult one, if I remember correctly, considering kings of Dulum don't wear crowns. Very good! You should be on your way. I'll make it easier by getting rid of this mountain."

"Let's start with that stupid bird," Mrs. Pribble said. "He's the one who delayed us."

"Right you are, love."

The nozzle moved down, and the trigger was squeezed. Nasty felt his feathers rip from his skin and melt with the snow. Color drained from the world, and every inch of his body ached.

"Author," Nasty whispered. "Help us."

He had no sooner said the words when a shadow moved below them on the mountain, breaking through the clouds. It seemed to glide up, as if its feet were hovering above the snow.

The tall, dark figure stopped and stood on a rock. It pointed a long arm at them, and the Pribbles turned to look at this strange new character.

"Who in *blazes* is that?" Mr. Pribble asked. He swung the *CORTEXIA*™ around and aimed it at the figure, but before he could place his finger on the trigger, his arm stiffened and the nozzle lifted, pointing at the moon.

The tall, hooded figure waved its arm and the *CORTEXIA*™ flew from Mr. Pribble's hands, crashing on the side of the mountain. It bounced down, smashing against rocks and ice, and a high-pitched sound filled the air as something became lodged in the trigger guard, activating the machine.

The mountain shook as boulders and swaths of snow were sucked inside.

"Oh dear," Nasty said. "I believe our journey down will be *much* quicker than our journey up."

Avalanche

The *CORTEXIA*™ fell, spinning down the mountain, bouncing over rocky spikes and sheets of snow. It swiped back and forth, taking huge chunks of mountain with it.

"No!" Mrs. Pribble screamed.

The ground under their feet shook with a violent rhythm. Rocks fell. Cora held out her arms to balance herself on the tilting mountaintop. Jack wrapped his arms around her.

"If this is the end, I love you," he said, and she turned and kissed his cheek.

Nasty flapped his wings, searching for the tall, hooded figure, but it had disappeared in the commotion.

The *CORTEXIA*™ continued to fall, slurping up chunks from the middle of the mountain, unsettling its delicate balance.

A deep rumble came right from the base, and the rock they were standing on began to slide down the side of the collapsing mountain.

"Hold on tight!" Nasty screamed. He flew through the dust, coughing and shielding his eyes. The pain in his wing was strong, but he pressed on, staying near the children.

Mrs. Pribble slipped. She made a horrible sound, her arms

flailing like a windmill as she staggered over the edge of the rock, launching into the air and falling through the layer of clouds.

"Darling!" Mr. Pribble screamed. "I'll meet you at the bottom!"

Blumpf wrapped his body around the children, shielding them with his meaty arms. He dug his fingers into cracks in the rock and moaned as stones pelted his back.

They slalomed down, clinging to the rock as it accelerated and bounced over spikes of disintegrating mountain. All around them was dust and dirt and ice in a blur of colors.

They hit a ramp of ice and went airborne.

Mr. Pribble clutched the rock and screamed a series of words not suitable for children. When they landed, the rock cracked in two and he lost his grip, sailing through the air and rolling down the mountain to join his wife at the bottom.

"Whatever you do," Nasty screamed from overhead, watching as the Pribbles turned into small specks above the expanse of gray dust. "Stay away from that machine!"

The *CORTEXIA*™ was far below them, continuing its work. The mountain could no longer be called a mountain—it was more a collection of rocks loosely suspended in the air, waiting for gravity to bring them down to earth. Everything began to fall, and the children were no longer sliding so much as plunging to the ground.

Oliver dislodged from his location under Blumpf's armpit. Air rushed around his face. He could hardly breathe. His fingers slipped along the ice. There was nothing to grab on to, and he lifted his arms, free-falling beside the slab of rock where Blumpf protected Cora and Jack, who were holding on for their lives.

Blumpf let go, soaring to Oliver and wrapping his large arms around the boy. Boulders and stones rained around them. They were halfway to the ground now, and on one side Oliver could see an endless expanse of gray. On the other was a patchwork of green and brown land that led into the city of Dulum.

"You have to save *them*," Oliver said, pointing at Cora and Jack. He still had two lives left, and if anyone was going to die in this avalanche, it should be him. Mr. Pribble had been right: This was his fault. He had placed Cora and Jack in danger, but he had never meant to hurt them.

Blumpf seemed to recognize the earnestness in Oliver's face and did as he was told. He shielded his eyes from the dust and located the rock that Cora and Jack were clutching. He charted a route, jumping from falling rock to falling rock until he was back to them. He lifted them in his arms and protected their heads.

"Oh, Author, where are you *now*?" Nasty called out. He searched the sky, but the tall, hooded figure was gone. He had called for assistance too soon, and now he'd have to save Oliver himself.

Birds swarmed about, and one cast a particularly large shadow on the ground as she tried desperately to save her eggs from the fall. A massive nest twisted behind the mother bird, floating in an updraft of snow and wind.

"Look there!" Nasty yelled. "Grab the nest! You can use it to soften the impact!"

Pop pop pop! The mother bird's three eggs were sucked into the pull of the *CORTEXIA*™, and the great bird's shrieks echoed across the rocks as she chased the eggs into the nozzle the moment before it hit the ground. Whatever had been lodged in the trigger guard broke free, and finally the machine stopped.

Blumpf grabbed the massive nest out of the air, returning to Cora and Jack and cradling them inside it, hoping the bed of soft twigs would break their fall. He closed his eyes, waiting for the moment of impact.

It would be soon.

Nasty pressed on, flying as fast as could, dodging his way through the maze of tumbling rubble. He was getting closer to Oliver, fighting his way through the avalanche. He held out his talons, preparing to grab Oliver by the shirt and whisk him to safety. *Closer now. A little bit closer.* He tried to ignore the pain in his wing, but it sent jabs of red heat through his body.

"Help the others!" Oliver yelled. "I have two lives left!"

"You'll need them!" Nasty replied. He flew faster. *Faster.*

Rocks beat Nasty's flesh. Feathers ripped from his body, and the cloud of dust and debris blinded him. Every muscle in his body screamed, and he screamed, too, sticking his feet out as far as he could.

The nest slammed into a sharp decline of rock and ice. The twigs flexed and cushioned Blumpf, Cora, and Jack's fall, and then they were sledding down what was left of the mountain. They flipped in the air and Blumpf tucked the children tight against his chest, landing on the ground, battered but alive.

Above, Nasty's talons snapped together. He couldn't see anything, but he could *feel*, and he felt his claws close around Oliver's thin arm. He pulled back, flying up just as the mountaintop smashed into the ground, erupting in a cloud of dust and dirt and snow.

"That was close, wasn't it, Oliver?" Nasty yelled.

There was no reply.

"Oliver?"

Nasty looked down. The limb he had grabbed wasn't one of Oliver's—it was a branch, approximately human-arm-sized.

"Oh no," Nasty whispered. He dropped the branch and changed course, dipping down to the mutilated remains of the mountain.

"Oliver! *Oliver!*"

There was no way Oliver had survived. Surely he had burst apart, spilling blood and guts and bones all over the ground. Nasty searched through the rocks, calling his name over and over.

"Do you see him?" Cora yelled, but Nasty ignored her. He continued to yell.

A chorus of hums came from deep within the remains of the mountains. Three chimes sounded above the group, harmonizing at different octaves, and a light rain began to fall. Blue light twisted down from the heavens, snaking through the cracks in the rocks, swirling with light and letters.

"I believe he died," Nasty said.

Jack nodded. "Then *they* must have, too."

Nasty tried to stay positive. The other two blue twirls of

light went deeper into the mountain, where the Pribbles were buried under tons of rock. With any luck it would take them a considerable amount of time to dig themselves out, and if Nasty could find Oliver first, they would have a head start to the end.

"Oliver!" Cora yelled, hopping from boulder to boulder. "Oliver, where are you?"

"Quiet," Nasty said. He landed and laid his head against a smooth stone. "Do you hear that?"

A coughing sound came from the rocks.

"This way!" Jack said, motioning at Blumpf. "He's over here! Dig!"

Blumpf lifted rocks over his head and hurled them far away, digging through the layers until a small tuft of dark hair emerged.

"Oliver!" Cora cried.

Oliver's face appeared, covered in mud, his cheeks scraped and bloody.

"Are you all right?" Jack asked.

Oliver nodded, though that had been the worst death of them all. The crashing rocks had crushed his bones and squeezed his head until it popped, splattering pieces of him everywhere.

Blumpf pulled him from the pile, and Oliver steadied himself on the rocks, wiping dirt from his clothes.

Weasel, Worm, and Walnut flew overhead, circling the group.

"Oh, good, you survived!" Weasel said.

"Didn't think it was possible," Worm said.

"I really don't like blood," Walnut said, looking judgmentally at Oliver.

"Yes, for the moment we're all alive," Nasty chirped back. "But this won't stop the Pribbles. It would help greatly if you continue to keep an eye on them for us."

The three bird spies nodded and settled on a rock, waiting for any sign of those wicked villains and their awful machine.

"We need to go," Oliver said. He tried to sound brave, but his voice wavered. He looked around for any sign of the Pribbles, then looked ahead at the faint silhouette of the city of Dulum, a series of pale gray shapes painted against the horizon. One shape stood taller than the rest: the castle where King Gerard once lived with his son, Grayson.

Grayson, Oliver thought. *The last piece we need.*

The rain continued to fall, and the sun disappeared behind dark clouds. Oliver watched Cora skip down the rocks ahead of her brother, helping him traverse their slippery tops to reach the far grassy field. Surely she knew what was coming.

He would do anything to help her, but he'd have to be careful. He only had one life left, and he'd need to survive the city of Dulum, and beyond that, the final chapter in the Twisted Tower, which he had never read.

Tick tock, Oliver.

Stay alive.

PART 3

A DARK AND TWISTED END

CHAPTER SIX

AN EVIL LURKS
IN THE CITY OF DULUM

Rain fell hard across the outskirts of Dulum, and the stone buildings in the distance glistened against the fields of dirt and dull green plants. Small streams snaked through the land, joining together to form a river that cut through farms and hills, all the way to the city.

The city of Dulum was protected by a massive iron gate, and the castle stood in the center, a proud structure with two towers jutting into the sky and a large white clock on the front. Even from miles away, Oliver could see light glinting off of two golden hands.

"That's our father's masterpiece," Cora said, pointing with one hand and using the other to wipe a tear from her cheek. It was the biggest clock her father had ever made, and she remembered how happy he'd been when he was summoned to the castle, how proud he was to be selected as the king's timekeeper. She remembered visiting the castle with him, spending long hours in the courtyard as he assembled the pieces, his tools laid out on a short stone wall where ivy and flowers grew from the cracks. Sometimes King Gerard came to watch him work, and Grayson would stand beside his father, mesmerized by the spinning gears. Grayson would stay, too, watching for hours as the face of the clock was painted, the hour markers set, and the hands attached, until the glorious thing was finished and finally hoisted to the top of the castle, where it was proudly displayed for everyone in the city to see.

On that day, the town had gathered, faces lifted to the sky, watching as the seconds ticked past and then the minutes and hours.

"It's beautiful," Grayson had said, and Cora had reached into her pocket and given him a gift: a pocket watch made of gold that she'd constructed in the evenings, taking everything she'd learned in the day and building it with her nimble fingers until every detail was perfect.

"When I'm king, you'll be my timekeeper?" he had asked, and Cora had nodded. Of course she would.

But how things had changed in a few short years. Now her mother was dead, and somewhere deep in the forest and swampland beyond the castle was Sigil's Twisted Tower, where her father was being held captive, forced to construct a wicked clock that could change time to create *a kingdom without children.*

Jack seemed to know what his sister was thinking and took her hand in his.

"We'll tell Father our true plan," Jack said. "As soon as we can, we'll tell him everything. He'll understand why we did it."

"I hope so," Cora said.

Nasty looked back, scanning the few trees peppered around the base of the mountain. How quickly it had fallen, almost as if it had never been there at all. He felt nauseated at how fast the land was disappearing and angry that anyone would dare to take things that didn't belong to them. The Pribbles would surely find their way out of the rubble, but would Oliver be able to get to the end in time?

He doubted it. And even if they did, what would be left of Dulum? Perhaps getting Oliver out of here with just a notion of the characters and the story would be enough. If Oliver remembered they existed, he could force the Pribbles to return all of the story to his mind. It was all Nasty could hope for.

"Master Oliver, may I have a word?" Nasty asked. He was resting on Blumpf's shoulder, stretching his wing, hoping a bone would click into place and the pain would subside.

"You don't have to call me 'master' anymore," Oliver said, but Nasty didn't agree. What had started as sarcasm had morphed into respect, and now he would do anything to protect this young boy.

"The Pribbles will be back," Nasty said, nodding to the collapsed mountain, "once they find that awful machine."

"I know."

"I'm sorry things have turned out this way. It seems the more I try to help, the more things get ruined."

"It isn't your fault, Nasty."

"Thank you, but I disagree. We'll need a better plan for the next item on our quest."

Jack, overhearing their conversation, chimed in.

"*The crown of the king*," he quoted. "It never made any sense to me. King Gerard would never wear something like that."

"Perhaps Sigil made one since taking power," Cora said.

"That doesn't make sense, either," Jack said. "The spell was written long before he overthrew King Gerard."

"Maybe it's hidden in the castle," Cora said.

Nasty rubbed a wing over his face, and Oliver stopped.

"Should you tell them, or should I?" Nasty asked.

"Tell us what?" Jack asked.

"*By life or by death, it must twist the mainspring*," Oliver recalled. "The crown isn't what you're thinking."

The children paused.

"What is it?" Jack asked.

Cora's face had gone pale, and she was unusually silent.

"*Crown* is another word for head," she whispered. "Grayson is the rightful king, and he needs to turn the mainspring, dead or alive. He's the final piece."

Nasty nodded.

"Then we'll have to capture him and turn him over," Jack said. "Maybe Sigil won't hurt him—"

"Of course he'll hurt him! He'll probably kill Grayson just for the fun of it," Cora yelled. "We need to tell Grayson the truth, too. He'd help us if he knew."

"He won't!" Jack snapped. "No one would believe us."

"He can't die thinking that I—"

Cora's voice broke off into a deep sob.

"Children," Nasty said. "It seems to me that all these details will be unimportant if you are successful. Even if Grayson dies, by turning back the clock, he and his father will be alive once again, as will your mother. Still, our efforts should be focused on a plan to capture Grayson *alive*. Whatever Sigil does to him after is out of our hands."

It was at this moment that Cora voiced the fear that had gripped her from the start, the thought she had tried to push down each time it bubbled to the surface:

"But what if the clock doesn't work?"

To that there came no answer.

"I wish you knew how this all ended," Jack said, and Oliver nodded.

"I may not know how it ends, but I know where Grayson will be. After they cross the mountain, the Gang of Impervious Children returns to the City of Dulum. You arrive the next morning, and Cora tracks the Gang to the center of the city, behind the fountain. While Jack distracts the others with a chase through the market, Cora corners Grayson in an alley and convinces him of your plan."

"I bet you'll like that," Jack said.

Cora wrinkled her nose at him.

"We should rest first," she said. "We can sneak into an inn and get something to eat."

"Blumpf," Blumpf said, for no other reason than that he felt he should contribute to the conversation.

Oliver considered protesting. That didn't happen in the book. They were meant to go directly to the fountain before anyone knew they had returned, but it would be dark by the time they arrived in the city, and the thought of a warm bed and food in his belly was too tempting.

They followed the river, creeping across patchwork fields of farmland and over short wooden fences, crouching through long, tangled weeds tipped with blue flowers that swayed in the wind. Wooden windmills stood along the edges of the farms, their blades spinning in lazy circles, pumping out milled grain to the workers below.

The rain continued throughout the day, a steady fall that soaked them to the bone. By the time they reached the city gate that evening, the sun had set and the air was chilled.

Sounds of life came from inside—hooves over cobblestone streets and barking dogs, footsteps through muddy alleyways and whispered conversations. Shops were closing, and the people of the city were settling in for the evening, lighting the torches attached to the edges of slate roofs.

Normally, the city was alive with laughter, but no longer. Sigil's guard barked commands to adults under the spell of evil magic, their heavy footsteps echoing through the streets.

"We'll need to disguise Blumpf," Nasty said. "He'll look most out of place in the city, and we don't want to raise suspicion."

"You're worried about him? What about us?" Jack said. "We're the most-wanted villains."

"You're small and quick and can sneak through town," Nasty said, and then remembered their previous attempt at sneaking. "At least, you can try. You'll avoid the main entrance and stay in the shadows."

"We need to make a disguise that will hide both Blumpf and Oliver," Cora said. The children pulled long strands of grass and fashioned a sort of wig, positioning it over Blumpf's head to conceal most of his face. Cora removed her cloak and draped it over Blumpf's shoulders, though it only properly covered him to the waist. They found Blumpf a long and gnarled stick, and he hobbled with it, trying to pass as an old woman. Blumpf scooped Oliver into his arms and hunched over.

"Oh dear. Perhaps in the shadows it will be convincing," Nasty said. "You'll win no awards for beauty, Blumpf, but it's our only hope." To Oliver, who was successfully hidden in the folds of Cora's cloak, Nasty said, "Stay with Blumpf, Master Oliver. You can be his voice."

Jack craned his neck and looked for the outlines of familiar buildings, then pointed to a spot on the city wall.

"Over this section is an entry to an alley. Go straight through it and then take a left. Follow it until you cross a bridge with three arches. Turn right, and follow the road past the market. There is an inn where we can stay the night."

Jack opened his satchel and removed the giants' jewel. He held it above his head and struck it on a sharp rock, hard enough that a small piece cracked from the side.

"Take this," he said. "Use it to rent a room. Don't talk to anyone. Light two candles in the window as a sign, and we'll climb the building and join you. Tomorrow, we'll capture Grayson."

Cora looked positively sick at the thought but offered no alternatives.

"Good thinking, my boy," Nasty said. "I'll keep a watch from the rooftops and signal when it's safe."

Content with their plan, Cora and Jack dipped their fingers in the fresh mud and smeared it around their eyes and over their cheeks. They waded into the river and let the current drift them past the iron bars of an aqueduct that led inside the city.

Blumpf clenched the walking stick in his mouth and began to climb the wall, digging his toes and fingers into cracks in the mortar and pulling Oliver and himself to the top. They peered over the edge, looking for any signs of Sigil's guards, and then slipped to the other side, descending to the ground of the city.

Blumpf adjusted his disguise, sweeping the strands of the wig over his face. He tucked Oliver in his right arm and used his left hand to hold the stick.

They entered the alleyway, staying to the shadows and following it through the wet cobblestone streets. The whole city had an odd aroma, like fish and death and sweat.

A shadow moved overhead as Nasty soared above them, perching on a roof at the end of the alley. He poked his beak to the left, signaling when it was safe to move.

Blumpf slipped out of the alley, surprisingly fast for such a lumbering creature, and tiptoed toward the bridge with three arches. It was a carved stone creation, extending over the river that ran through the center of the city. Whenever Blumpf was within view of a person, he would poke the stick to the ground and hobble along, playing the part of an old woman with impressive skill. They crossed the bridge and Blumpf adjusted his wig.

"Turn right," Oliver whispered, and Blumpf obeyed, following a street lined with the empty tents of merchants who had gone home for the night.

They followed the road until a squawking sound came

from above, which was followed by a rhythmic beat of footsteps against the stone road.

"Stop!" Oliver whispered, and Blumpf moved behind a pillar, leaning out to see a procession pass by.

Six members of Sigil's guard appeared on the street, patrolling the city for any signs of disobedience. There were three men and three women, each with hair pulled back and braided into a long strand that hung down their back like the tail of a wet rat. They were dressed in dark clothing, with the crimson symbol of Sigil's guard stitched on the front, and they held long, black rods that crackled with white lightning at the tips, full of their leader's evil magic.

Adults in Dulum walked along the curbs, their eyes glazed and their heads bowed in obedience. As they passed the guards, they would hold out their hands, placing money they had earned from the day's work into the guards' hands. If one of them dared to look a guard in the eyes, the guard would aim their rod at them and whip it around, conjuring a strand of energy around their feet until they fell back in line.

"Get going!" one of the guards shouted.

"Bedtime for you all!" another yelled.

The guards' steps on the stones echoed throughout the city, and the light from their rods glowed against the rain-soaked streets all the way to the hill that led to the citadel and the castle.

In the homes and shops, children peered out the windows, watching darkness descend upon Dulum. They stared as the guards patrolled the city with magic that had no effect on them. But what could they do to stop it? Who would lead the charge against Sigil?

Grayson, of course. Oliver was nervous at the prospect of catching him tomorrow.

They were changing the events of the book again, and that always seemed to make things more difficult. Still, Oliver was hopeful that this one time would be different.

"Follow them," Oliver said, pointing to a line of adults shuffling past the market.

Blumpf obeyed, waiting for the guards to turn the corner before crossing the street, staying hunched behind the line and resting his weight on the walking stick. He limped along, trying his best to blend in despite his size. Blumpf was an odd sight, and from above Nasty watched as the strange shape walked by the market, toward a three-story square building with a sign hanging from a curved iron pole that read INN.

"Safety at last," Nasty whispered to himself, which should have been an obvious indication that things were about to get worse.

The Inn

Blumpf hobbled toward the inn as another group of guards turned the corner, stomping down the middle of the road. One guard looked at the strange old woman and raised an arm, holding up the black rod. Lightning from the tip illuminated the street, and she squinted at the old woman's grasslike hair, then raised the rod above her head, preparing to attack with magic.

"Go," Oliver whispered, and Blumpf leaned his meaty shoulder against the inn's door and stumbled inside.

Oliver poked his head out of the cloak and watched the guard stop in her tracks, squinting through the dirty window. The rest of the guards continued their patrol, stomping along, before she scowled and ran to catch up.

The inn was large and empty, save for a few wooden tables and chairs made with stretched animal hide. There were paintings on the wall of Dulum and the surrounding countryside, and a blank square free from smoke discoloration that probably once held a picture of King Gerard.

An innkeeper leaned against a wooden bar, his fingers wrapped around the edge and his head drifting up and down, nearing the point of sleep. A smaller person moved in the corner of the room, wrapped in a hooded robe. Oliver assumed she was the innkeeper's wife, and she stirred a pot of stew that simmered over a fire. Smoke traveled up the narrow chimney, and the smell that filled the room was delicious.

"You lookin' for a room?" the innkeeper whispered from behind the counter, his voice barely audible above the steady downpour of rain.

"Yes," Oliver croaked, trying his best to sound like how he imagined the large woman of their disguise would talk.

Blumpf walked to the counter, and Oliver watched through the folds in the cloak as the innkeeper eyed him from head to toe, with glazed eyes and an open mouth, clearly deep under the spell of Sigil's magic.

"And where are you from, ma'am?" the innkeeper asked.

"Out in the country," Oliver said, and the man sleepily nodded.

"Ah, yes. Beautiful place, that. Ain't been in ages. It'll be three pieces of silver for the night."

"Don't have silver," Oliver replied.

"Quarter piece of gold then. I don't set the price, ya see. It all goes to *him*," the innkeeper said, motioning in the direction of the castle on top of the hill.

"No gold, either. Just this," Oliver said. He slid the small piece of giants' jewel down Blumpf's arm and into his palm. Blumpf placed it on the bar in between the innkeeper's brown hands. The light from the fire hit the sides of the jewel and sent a dazzling red light across his face.

"Oooh," the man said. He held the jewel between his fingers, and the sparkling colors seemed to momentarily wake him from his spell. He smiled, then shouted "Blankets!" to the figure at the hearth.

"You say you found this in the country?" he asked, turning back to Blumpf.

"Didn't say where I found it," Oliver whispered. Surely the guards would find out about this on their patrol tomorrow, but by then Oliver and Blumpf would have left the inn.

The figure in the corner moved to see what they were discussing, but the innkeeper yelled, "Get our guest some stew, dearest! Quickly now!"

She obeyed, scooping a large helping of boiled meat and vegetables into an iron bowl and placing it on top of a pile of folded blankets.

"Thank you," Oliver said. "I'll eat this in my room."

The figure waved an arm and pointed to a narrow staircase in the corner of the entry room, then led them up the creaking steps, cradling the soup and blankets in her arms. Blumpf continued his act, groaning with each step and using the walking stick to move his massive body up to the top floor.

"Here," the figure said, setting down the blankets and soup. She unlocked a door and placed a skeleton key in Blumpf's calloused hand. "I'll be downstairs if you need anything."

The room was small but cozy. It was largely made of wood—the floors and walls were constructed of uneven beams stuck together with white mortar. There was a furry rug on the floor, and a single window looked out over the city, distorting the other buildings through a pane of wavy glass. Torches flickered at the corners of spires and smoke pumped from chimneys, as though an army of dragons was sleeping in the streets.

Oliver lit two candles and placed them on the windowsill, then moved the blankets and soup to the bed.

Soon, a rapping sound came at the window and Jack's eyes appeared. He'd scaled the side of the building, clinging on to bricks and ivy, and hoisted himself inside with Cora close behind.

"Something smells good," Jack said, eyeing the bowl of soup. Blumpf was already scooping it down in large spoonfuls.

"Hey, slow down!" Jack shouted, and Blumpf growled, then laughed and held out the spoon to him.

The children ate, passing the spoon back and forth between them, hunting for cubes of meat and slices of carrots and potatoes.

Nasty flew to the window and watched them, content for the moment that they were all together, safe and warm, if only for a night.

"Would you like some, too?" Oliver asked, but the look on Cora and Jack's faces told him they didn't want to divide their portions any more.

"Goodness, no!" Nasty said. He laughed and patted his belly. "This city is a smorgasbord of rodents. Plump rats and sweet mice around every corner. I've had my fill already."

This wasn't entirely true. The rodents were average at best, with a slightly chewy texture, but he supposed the children wouldn't be interested in those details.

"Sleep well tonight, children," Nasty said. "Don't worry about a thing—I will keep watch from the roof, and tomorrow we'll devise our plan to capture Grayson."

They all agreed to this. When the soup was gone and the bowl had been licked clean, Blumpf and the children piled into bed, draping the blankets across them.

Nasty perched on the roof and watched boats lull in the river, their motion rocking back and forth, up and down. He'd promised to be the lookout, but he was so tired, and a little rest would do him good. Hadn't he earned it? After the climb up the mountain and the avalanche and the journey to the city, surely he deserved a little sleep. He closed his eyes, just for a moment, and may have drifted off for one or thirty minutes, unaware that, on the ground floor of the inn, the small figure had removed her hood, revealing the face of a young girl.

She wasn't the innkeeper's wife; she was his *daughter*, and she moved behind the counter and stood on her toes, looking at the sparkling red jewel.

The girl held the shard between her fingers, considering the strange person who had paid with it. Where would such a thing come from? It wasn't from the city, and it wasn't from the countryside, either, of that she was certain.

She had heard of such jewels, long ago, in a child's story about giants far away. And hadn't she just recently heard that Sigil was sending leagues of his guard to meet their deaths in the Land of the Giants? Could it be that this old woman knew about the children the Gang was searching for?

She placed the jewel back where she found it and returned to the fire, throwing another log on the flame—an unusual act for such a late hour. Normally she'd let it extinguish, but the fire roared back to life now, sending a fresh trail of smoke through the chimney.

The girl pulled a blanket from the pile and stretched it between her hands, then waved it over the fire—*whoosh whoosh whoosh*—sending out a signal to alert the Gang of Impervious Children of her strange guest.

They would know what to do.

On the roof, Nasty continued to sleep as the shadows of children surrounded the inn.

The Gang of
Impervious Children

Oliver woke, and in the darkness, something moved around the room. All was silent, and at first he considered that his eyes might be playing tricks on him.

Could it be Nasty? Or had the bird spies returned with news of the Pribbles?

He sat up and felt something cold and sharp press against the soft flesh of his neck.

"Shh," a voice whispered, and when Oliver's eyes adjusted, he saw familiar dark skin and gray hair.

Grayson! he realized, but it was too late to warn Cora and Jack of the intruder.

Grayson pushed his hand against Oliver's mouth and whispered, "Don't say a word."

He slid Oliver off the bed and pulled him to his feet, dragging him to the door of the small room.

A pair of eyes appeared through the glass of the window, and then another and another.

"You're surrounded," Grayson said. He opened the bedroom door, where more children were waiting at the top of the stairs. They slipped into the room, pulling out knives and standing guard over Cora, Jack, and Blumpf.

"Come with me."

From above, Oliver could hear Nasty's faint, wheezy snores, and from below, the quiet rhythm of the river's water.

He had no choice but to obey.

Grayson led Oliver into the hallway and down to the bottom floor of the inn. The innkeeper's daughter, who introduced herself as Marian, stood by the fire and absentmindedly stirred the pot of soup.

"Well done," Grayson said, and her cheeks darkened. "You've led us right to these villainous children. I can never thank you enough."

He pulled a rope from the corner and tied Oliver to a pole in the center of the room, so tight that it burned his skin and made it difficult to breathe.

"I didn't know it was them," Marian gushed. "I just thought something was *strange* about that old woman and the jewel she had and—"

Grayson held a finger to his lips and pointed to the back room.

The innkeeper snored loudly on his cot, and Marian bowed her head to Grayson and unlocked the front door of the inn. More than a dozen children streamed in, filling the bottom floor. They eyed the soup hungrily, and Marian passed out spoons, ignoring the formality of bowls and allowing them to eat directly from the pot. They all looked so thin and hungry, and Grayson waited until each had a spoonful before scraping along the bottom for the last bits of carrot and mush.

"What do you want from me?" Oliver asked. In an instant, several knives came out and were pressed against him, and he thought of his final life and how all this would be over and his imagination wiped clean if one of the children pressed their blade into his body at a fatal spot.

"Who are you?" Grayson asked. "I know of the timekeeper's children, but you . . . *you* are most strange."

"I'm Oliver," Oliver said, but that didn't really answer his question.

Grayson's eyes narrowed.

"Are you from the city?"

"No."

"The country, then?"

"No. I'm not from Dulum."

"I don't understand."

What could Oliver possibly say that would explain this? He decided to change the topic.

"Cora and Jack are not the villains you think they are. They're trying to help you. And I'm trying to help them."

"Rubbish," one of the boys said.

"Another trick," a girl said.

Grayson smiled and waved a hand at them.

"Tell me more, Oliver."

Grayson waited. Oliver considered telling him the whole truth. Should he tell Grayson that he was merely a character in a story? Cora and Jack had barely believed his story and might have stabbed him themselves if the tall, dark figure hadn't arrived to help him. How could he hope to convince a room full of skeptical children?

"We already know that they're working for Sigil," Grayson said. "What we don't know is *why*."

"Sigil took their father," Oliver said.

"Sigil took *all* our fathers. Our mothers, too," a girl said, pressing her knife deeper so that a drop of blood appeared on Oliver's arm. "Maybe not to his Twisted Tower, but they ain't right anymore. They're under his spell, so that's no excuse for Cora and Jack to betray us."

Oliver closed his eyes.

"I know it's not. And they haven't betrayed you. They think they can—"

Before he could tell them about the spell and the clock that could alter time, there came a vicious squawk from the floor above. Nasty had finally stirred from his sleep, seen the situation, and deduced what was happening. He squawked again, beating his wings against the bedroom window. There was a deep roar that shook the inn as Blumpf jumped to his feet, followed by the howls of children.

Footsteps sounded and fists made impact, and the fight made the entire inn tremble. Oliver now feared that the whole building might come crashing down upon him. What a terrible way to die!

The innkeeper stirred in his cot, sitting up and rubbing his red, bleary eyes.

"I'll take care of him," Grayson said, nodding to the other children. "You help upstairs."

"What's goin' on?" the innkeeper yelled. He leapt to his feet and moved around the counter. Marian ran in front of Grayson, holding out her arms to protect him.

"Father, wait, I can—"

"King Gerard's boy?" he asked, then spat on the ground. "What are *you* doin' here?"

He pushed his daughter and lunged at Grayson, his fists aimed at the boy's skull.

Grayson dodged the attack and spun in place, pushing the man over a table. The innkeeper landed hard on the floor and moaned, crawling to the door and yelling for Sigil's guards.

"Help me!" he screamed. "They're here! The children are here!"

He managed to push the door open just a crack, enough that his screams traveled far in the silent night.

Grayson jumped on the innkeeper and pulled him back, but it was too late. Doors and windows opened, and people leaned out to see what the commotion was about.

"Help me. *Help me*," the innkeeper continued to blubber. Grayson pulled a cloth napkin from the table and tied it around his mouth.

Crashing came from above as the rest of the Gang of Impervious Children arrived at the rented room on the top floor, and Blumpf roared, pounding his fists into the walls.

Other visitors to the inn ran from their rooms, streaming down the stairs and out into the dark night, trying to escape the awful scene.

"Stop!" Oliver yelled to Grayson. "Tell them to stop!"

Blumpf would do anything to protect him, but that didn't mean he wanted any of the children to get hurt. They were all on the same side, and if they could only stop long enough to *listen* to each other—

A thumping sound came from the courtyard, and through the window Oliver could see six members of Sigil's guard marching along the street, heading in the direction of the inn. Their rods crackled with light, and they spun and whipped them at anyone who dared look out their window.

"Get back inside!" one yelled.

"Lights out!" another yelled.

Blumpf continued to roar above. Glass shattered and rained on the street. Children poured from the window like confetti, slamming onto wooden carts and falling through canopies.

The guards were running up the street now, and if they weren't stopped, things were destined to get much worse.

"Wait!" Oliver yelled, but it was no use. The fight continued, and three children spilled down the staircase and rolled along the floor, their faces bruised and their clothing ripped.

"They have a giant," one of the children said, and Oliver didn't bother to correct her. Blumpf was no giant. If they truly had a giant, then the entire inn would be destroyed and the children's heads would be ripped unceremoniously from their bodies.

Blumpf came bounding down the stairs, taking them four at a time. He held two children above his head while one clung to his midsection, trying unsuccessfully to bring him to his knees.

Cora and Jack were close behind, pushing their way through the throng of children, slashing their knives in the air and dodging similar attacks.

"Everyone stop!" Oliver yelled, but Blumpf could hardly hear him above the screaming children. He leaned back and threw one of the children clear across the room, behind the counter where the innkeeper had stood and rented them their room less than an hour ago. Blumpf grabbed another child by an ankle and spun him around, launching him into the empty stewpot.

Outside, children rose to their feet, limping, clutching their arms and sides and heads. They kicked the door of the inn from its hinges and ran inside, ready to continue the fight.

Cora and Jack kicked and dodged their way through the room. Nasty flew through an open window and heroically circled above, watching it all and flapping his wings at anyone who dared approach Oliver, who was still tied to the center pole, utterly unable to help himself.

"We could use some assistance, Author!" Nasty cried. "Now is the time!"

Sigil's guards had clear sight of the inn now, as well as all the children. They looked at one another, perplexed by what was happening and unsure how to proceed.

"Help me," the innkeeper screamed through the gag, which sounded more like "*Huupppp muhhh.*"

The children saw the guards with a certain mixture of fear and excitement, and for a moment the fighting stopped. The guards ran inside, and Grayson ducked behind the children to hide his identity.

"What's going on?" one guard shouted.

The innkeeper continued his muffled groans, and the lead

guard bent down and pulled the gag from his face. "What did you *do*?" he asked.

The innkeeper shook his head, clearly unsure of what to say now that the guards had come to his rescue.

"I . . . I called for help as soon as I—"

"You let the Gang of Impervious Children stay here?" another guard asked.

"Not on purpose. They tricked me, see? Dressed like an old woman and—"

"You're helping them," the lead guard said, and he raised the long black rod above his head. A spark of white light appeared.

"I'm not, please believe it. May Sigil's name be praised! They came in darkness, and I wasn't—"

"You weren't prepared," the guard said. "And which is worse? Working with the children, or being fooled by them?"

He brought the rod down and a swirl of lightning hit the innkeeper. The innkeeper screamed as the light twisted around his neck and wrists and pulled him to his feet. His bleary eyes were wide open now, and his face contorted in agony.

"Stop it!" Marian said. She held up a hand and walked through the chaos of light as if it weren't there at all. She was impervious to its effects, and the light passed through her body, flickering on her face. She held her father tight.

"I'll never be fooled again!" the innkeeper screamed. "I promise! Sigil be praised! May he rule Dulum forever! What do you ask of me? Anything!"

Marian swatted the rod, but the guard held tight,

laughing at her attempts. She smacked the guard's chest and arms, but still the lightning controlled her father, holding his arms as though they were on puppet strings.

"Let him go," Grayson commanded. He emerged from behind the children, his piercing eyes staring down the guards. In the light from the rod, the golden stitching on his clothes seemed to vibrate.

"Never thought I'd see *you* tonight," the lead guard said. He lowered his rod and the lightning stopped. The innkeeper fell to the ground, tears streaming down his cheeks. "What do you think Sigil would give me if I brought you to the castle myself?"

The guard whipped the rod and sent a massive line of lightning through Grayson. It had no effect, but it was loud and bright. Grayson may have been impervious to their magic, but he wasn't impervious to their fists, and the light provided just enough distraction for the other guards to leap toward him. A punch landed on his cheek and knocked him to his knees.

Cora lunged forward to protect him, but the Gang of Impervious Children arrived first, pushing her away, their attention momentarily shifting to the guards.

The fighting started again, as quickly as it had stopped, and now the guards were slinging their fists and whipping around their rods. The children were dodging and rolling along the wooden floor and on top of the tables.

Despite the guard's best efforts, they were horribly outnumbered, and soon the Gang of Impervious Children had them surrounded in the center of the room, where they stood back to back, along with Cora, Jack, Oliver, Nasty, and Blumpf.

"We have you now," a girl said.

Knives glimmered in the light from the fire.

The floorboards groaned. Something moved in the streets. Oliver squinted. Could it be?

"Did you get everything Sigil needs?" a guard asked, glancing at Cora as he dodged a punch from a small girl with leaves braided through her hair.

"Almost," Cora said. Grayson jumped at her, trying to grab her before she kicked him in the side. "We're only missing one item, but I'll have it soon."

"Good," the guard said. "Sigil will be most pleased."

"You tried to protect me earlier," Grayson said, just as he swung a fist at her face.

"I didn't," Cora said, but her eyes disagreed. She blocked the blow and returned another.

"You *did*," Grayson said. "Surrender. You'll never escape now. There are too many of us."

The Gang tightened around them.

Cora lowered her arms and dropped her knife.

"What are you doing?" Jack asked. He was still making a valiant attempt at defending himself from a group of four boys.

"I'm going to tell them," Cora answered.

"Which part?" Oliver asked. Perhaps they would believe the part about the spell and the clock, but how would they ever understand that they were only characters in a story?

"Everything."

"You can't," Jack said, and Cora was just about to speak when the tall, hooded figure stepped through the tendrils of fog on the street and approached the inn.

Some Help

The figure was too tall to enter the room without ducking, so it bent in the middle and softly stepped over the broken door that lay in the entrance.

The children and guards froze.

"Thank goodness you're here, Author!" Nasty gushed. "It sure took you long enough!"

Nasty flew and landed in front of the figure, pointing a wing at the fold in the dark hood where the face should be.

"And where, may I ask, were you when we were dealing with those Pribbles and that awful avalanche? I called for you then, but you were nowhere to be—"

The figure raised its arms and Nasty twirled in place, rising to the rafters, his beak clamped shut by an invisible force.

The figure waved its arms and Sigil's guards rose from the floor, hovering several feet above the ground. Their rods dropped to the ground and rolled under the tables.

"Stop it!" one of the guards yelled.

Another guard wiggled her body and swiped at the figure.

"Let us go, you stupid—"

The guards' jaws clicked shut, as if all the muscles in their faces had tensed, and silently they continued to float around the inn's ceiling.

The Gang of Impervious Children stood up straight, their arms pointed upward. Their weapons flew from their hands, joining together to form a swarm of shiny metal that slithered out the doorway and dropped to the street.

The tall, hooded figure spun in place, arms extended, and the children's feet slid out from under them. They landed on their bottoms, sitting in neat rows, their hands folded and stuck to their laps. They looked to their leader, unaccustomed to being controlled by strange magic.

Grayson's eyes darted back and forth, and it was now obvious to Oliver that he also was unable to move.

"How is that *thing* doing this?" Grayson asked through gritted teeth. "We're impervious to magic."

"This isn't magic," Cora said.

"Then what is it?"

The rope that was wrapped around Oliver uncurled and slithered down his legs. It shot into the air and bound Sigil's floating guards, constricting like a snake and tying off into a tight bow.

Oliver stretched and rubbed the raw spots on his arms and legs. He looked at Blumpf and pointed to the guards.

"Take them to our room," he said, and Blumpf snatched them from the air like a bunch of balloons and led them up the stairs.

Cora, Jack, and Oliver were the only children unaffected by the hooded figure's motions, and they stood awkwardly in front of their audience, each waiting for someone else to speak.

"Well?" Jack finally asked. "I guess we should tell them."

Cora slid over to Grayson and lifted a small pocket flap on the front of his tunic, pulling out the gold pocket watch she had built him a lifetime ago. She looked at the small hands and markers on the dial.

"Do you ever wish things could go back to how they were?" Cora asked.

Grayson looked at his feet and whispered, "All the time."

"Sigil found a spell that can alter time." She pointed at Jack's satchel. "With our father's skill and the items in the bag, he wants to build a clock that will speed up time. He'll steal your youth in a flash, and there will be no children left in the Kingdom of Dulum. No one to threaten his reign."

Grayson's nostrils flared.

"How can you help him?"

"Don't you see?" Cora asked. She turned to address the room now. "We needed to play the part of villains. No one else was successful in getting the pieces needed for the spell, but they didn't have our motivation."

"Our mother," Jack said, nodding.

"If the clock is created, it can alter time," Cora said. "It can speed up time, but it can also *reverse* it. We can put things back the way they're supposed to be, with King Gerard alive and your parents free from Sigil's magic."

There was a long pause, finally interrupted by Blumpf bounding down the stairs, singing cheerfully, *"Blumpf blumpf blumpf."*

"It's a trick," one of the children shouted, but Grayson shook his head.

He stared deep into Cora's eyes, and his face softened. "You told the guards you still needed one item. What is it?"

Cora did not answer.

"The crown of the king," Jack said. "But you don't wear a *crown*, so we figure it means your *head*, which means *you* have to turn the mainspring, either by choice . . . or Sigil can use the bones of your skull. It's up to you which you prefer."

"That's rather dark," Grayson said, but there was a lightness to his voice that Cora hadn't heard for a long time, and she rested a hand on his shoulder. He stood, released from the hooded figure's hold.

"I'm so sorry for betraying you, Grayson. We had to play the part of the villains. If word gets back to Sigil that we plan on double-crossing him, he'll kill our father, and then—"

"I understand."

"Even telling you now is a risk, but there's no other choice. Will you help us?" Cora asked, and he nodded.

"I will. But how do you explain *that*?" Grayson asked, looking to an empty spot in the room. At some point during Cora's explanation of the spell, the tall, hooded figure had disappeared without being noticed.

Nasty flapped his wings and flexed his beak, flying out the doorway to see if he could spot the figure, but it was gone. The children unfolded their hands and stood, realizing for the first time that they were no longer being held in place.

"That's a different story altogether, one that I'm not sure you'll believe," Cora answered. "Oliver will tell it."

A Final Plan

A nd so Oliver told his story, starting at the beginning, with his thefts from Garden Grove Library, and continuing to the day when the Pribbles visited the library, bought all the books, and then invited him to their mansion to *pick his brain*. He told them about his favorite book, *The Timekeeper's Children*, and how every person here was merely a character inside his mind. He told them how the world of Dulum was being stolen, chapter by chapter, until there was nothing left. He told them about the tall, hooded figure who had been following them along their journey, helping them at crucial points.

"All authors leave a piece of themselves in a book," Nasty interjected. "And we presume the tall, hooded figure is the one and only Malcolm Bloom, who is altering the plot to help us reach a successful conclusion."

"I see," Grayson said, though his face had the expression of someone who was horribly confused.

Oliver continued, telling them about Blumpf, the background character who had joined their group. He described the climb up the mountain, followed by the avalanche that trapped the Pribbles under tons of rocks. He told them he wouldn't be able to exit Dulum until he reached the last chapter of the book, "A Timely End," when the clock was made and the story was completed. He was rather sloppy in his narration, jumping back and forth between topics, adding details that weren't the least bit relevant, and omitting facts that would have made it easier for the children to understand. It was painful to observe.

The Gang of Impervious Children watched him with a mixture of humor and confusion, for they were largely unfamiliar with the concept of libraries and completely clueless when it came to alternative reality goggles and strange contraptions that could steal things directly from the imagination. It was as if an alien had dropped down from space and was trying to explain the meaning of scrumbledyglunk to them.

"That's quite a tale," Grayson said when it was over. He ran his fingers through his hair and sat on top of a table, staring at Oliver.

"I didn't believe him, either, and I'm still not sure I do," Cora said. "It's quite possible Oliver is mad, but I've seen the Pribbles with my own eyes and I've seen the world around us disappear into their machine. Whatever is happening, it's a powerfully wicked thing."

"All part of a story," Grayson whispered. "How do you like that?"

"If I may," Nasty said. "Do not dwell on the fact that you're only a character. *Everyone* is merely a character in a story in some way, and it shouldn't change the way you view yourself or others. What we're doing is still important, because stories are important, and the things you do and feel are very real. We must keep moving forward."

Grayson nodded, then turned to Oliver.

"If what you say is true, how does the story end?"

"He doesn't know," Jack said. "The copy he stole was missing the final chapter."

"*Conveniently*," Cora added.

"I know just enough to get us to the Twisted Tower," Oliver said. "After that, I assume we'll be successful."

Grayson leapt to his feet at this.

"You assume?" he asked, motioning for the Gang to join him around the tables. "That's good. It means we can shape our own ending."

"Precisely my thought," Nasty said. "We need to make a plan and follow through. If we can reach the end before the Pribbles catch us, then Oliver can go back home with all of you right where you belong and everyone can get what they want."

Not everyone, Oliver thought, in a sudden painful flash. No matter what happened, his mother would still be gone.

They spent the next hour concocting a plan. Three children would keep watch over the guards in the upstairs room, while the six tallest children would take their uniforms and continue patrolling throughout the night, just long enough so that their absence would not raise suspicion.

The following morning, Jack and Cora would tie Grayson and lead him up the hill, through the citadel, and to the castle, surrendering him to Sigil along with the other items needed for the spell.

"Father won't build the clock unless we're alive," Jack said. "He'd sooner die. We're safe until it's complete."

Cora looked at Grayson. "And he won't kill *you* unless you resist. He'll take too much pleasure in torturing you."

"Right. Then Sigil will take us all to the Twisted Tower," Grayson said. "He'll keep me bound while your father works. The Gang will follow us there, and as soon as the task is complete, we'll make our attack, using the clock to turn time back to before any of this happened, just as it was meant to be."

Cora smiled at Grayson and nodded her head. "What could go wrong?" she asked, and the children settled in for the night, sleeping in the inn until the sun rose and birds began to chirp.

CHAPTER SEVEN

THE TWISTED PATH
TO THE TWISTED TOWER

Grayson struggled in his ropes. He bit the gag in his mouth and thrashed his arms as he watched the crowds that had gathered in the streets. He was a spectacle to the city of Dulum, a shadow that had hung for months over the shops and courtyards, homes and alleyways. He had been a threat to the adults and the last piece of hope for the children, but now that he was here, in plain view, he seemed small and broken.

Cora pushed him by his collar and steered him through the crowds, up the sloping roads to the citadel. Jack clutched his satchel. It was packed with the leather-bound book, the jewel of the giants, the skin of the cave eel, and the planks of wood from the barrels of the Old Mountain Guard. With Grayson in tow, all the pieces for the spell were here, ready for their father's hands to build into a clock.

"Traitor!" a young girl yelled from the window, and Cora bared her teeth and continued to push. They were the villains once again, and Cora seemed to delight in playing the role a final time. She tilted back her head and howled. She grimaced, sneered, and frothed.

"Let him go!" another boy yelled, and a nearby guard waved a rod at him.

Normally, Sigil's guards would have yelled at everyone to go back inside, but today they allowed the people to watch their once-future king be led toward the castle. It was worth it for the pure humiliation.

Grayson stumbled on an uneven rock in the road, and Jack kicked him in the leg, knocking him over. He laughed and clapped his hands, whispering, "Sorry," as Grayson struggled to his feet.

Nasty observed this all from the rooftops, perching in the shadows of sloping roofs. The morning sun was warm and painted long shadows through pink light. He did his best to stay hidden as he watched the children's slow march to Sigil.

Soon everyone in the town was awake and watching, and the distraction proved beneficial for Blumpf, Oliver, and the Gang of Impervious Children. They crept through back alleys all the way to the city's outer wall, where Oliver directed them to a cracked spot with easy footholds and Blumpf provided a boost to the top. When all the children had made it over, Blumpf tossed Oliver on his shoulders and then climbed, straddling the stone wall and cupping a hand over his eyes to see the throng of people gathered near the citadel.

"Blumpf," he whispered, and then hoisted his meaty leg over and slid to the ground.

Blumpf waved at Nasty and then slipped into the trees. The journey to the Twisted Tower in the middle of the swamp would take all day and night and would lead them through the Dark Forest.

"Best of luck," Nasty whispered to himself, lifting a wing in reply.

Back on the streets of Dulum, Cora and Jack had reached the stairs of the citadel and were climbing them to a wide, stone bridge that spanned the river. Cora pushed Grayson's back, and Jack held out his knife, poking it between Grayson's shoulder blades, being careful not to pierce flesh.

The castle guards stepped aside when they saw them, and the crowd parted to let them through.

The doors to the castle were made of large wooden planks, held together with black metal bars and gold rivets. The stone walls were covered in dying ivy, as if everything that touched this place had become sick and wilted. It didn't use to be like this. Above, the hands of the clock displayed the time, ticking forward at a predictable pace.

"We're here!" Cora shouted to no one in particular. The words hung in the air.

Jack threw down his satchel and put his hands on his hips.

Nasty flew to a parapet and tucked in his wings, hoping to blend in with the shapes of the roofline. He saw movement through a window high in the castle wall, and the whole city seemed to hold its breath in unison, waiting to see what would happen next.

There was an echoing laugh, and the doors slowly opened. A shadow appeared in the doorframe, stepping into the light.

Sigil.

One look at him made clear that he was a bad character, as if built from a collection of stock parts from a villain handbook. Nasty shuddered.

Sigil wore leather sandals on his feet and seemed to glide as he walked, almost as if he could float above the ground. He was tall and thin, wrapped in a black hooded tunic. A red symbol was stitched in the front like a smear of blood—some ancient marking of evil magic. His white hands, streaked with blue veins, were folded across his stomach. His face was narrow and unpleasant, full of sharp angles that gave him the appearance of a piranha. The sockets around his eyes were deep and dark. A widow's peak poked down on his forehead, and his long, greasy black hair was tied in the back.

"Your highness," Cora said, and she and her brother bowed their heads. Grayson stood, defiant.

Sigil smiled, revealing silver teeth that sparkled in the sun, and began to cross the bridge. He squinted in the light and raised his hands.

"Well," he hissed, his voice tight and high-pitched. "You've returned to me."

He approached Grayson and held out a hand. It sparkled with evil magic.

"Bow to me, boy."

"Never," Grayson said.

"BOW!"

Rays of light shot from Sigil's hands, passing through Grayson's torso and wrapping around his legs with no effect.

Sigil tucked his hands back into his tunic.

"That will be so much more satisfying to watch when you're wriggling in pain, *begging* me for mercy. Soon. You'll see."

He bent down to examine the bag, pulling out the jewel and the eel skin.

"Everything is there," Cora said.

"We'll see about that once the clock is built," Sigil sneered. "This could be a trick."

"It's not," Jack said.

"For your sake—*and your father's*—I hope that is the truth."

He sniffed a piece of the barrel wood and grimaced at the smell.

"How is it you children managed to succeed when none of my guards could?"

Cora and Jack didn't answer. What was there to say?

Sigil spun on his heels and examined the line of his guards. Their backs stiffened, and fear flashed in their eyes. They stared ahead, trying not to look directly at their leader.

"You're useless," he said, addressing the guards, despite the fact that none of the guards who were present in the city had attempted nor failed in the quest. "Dozens were sent to the far reaches of Dulum, and not one returned with a single object, let alone with their life."

He waved his hands, sending rays of evil magic through the guards. They collapsed, falling to their knees, screaming in pain.

"These children were able to deliver because they had proper *motivation*: Fear. Fear for their father. Fear for what I would do to them. Fear is the only thing that works. I've been too kind to you."

He closed his hands and the magic stopped. The guards stood, still shaking.

Sigil turned to the crowd and raised his hands again,

throwing them back as if preparing to strike. The adults in the crowd gasped and hid behind their children. Sigil laughed, spinning on his heels and motioning to his guards.

"Take us to the tower. *Now.*"

Three guards swooped in, gathering the pieces for the spell and leading Cora and Jack to a carriage. Grayson was held by the torso and feet by two guards and swung into the back. Horses were hitched, and Sigil pulled his thin body inside the carriage, pointing a long finger to a gate at the rear of the city that would take them to the woods, through the Dark Forest, and back to his tower in the swamp.

With a flick of the reins, the driver steered the carriage around the castle, and the entire city finally exhaled and returned to their homes and shops, waiting for the guards to begin their patrols. The children stayed in their rooms, huddled under blankets, unsure of what would happen next but certain it would be unpleasant. With Grayson gone, what hope was left?

Nasty hopped from rooftop to rooftop, watching as the carriage left the city. He was just about to fly when three small shadows surrounded him, and he looked to the sky to see Weasel, Worm, and Walnut, chirping madly.

"Ah, my dear friends. What news do you bring?" he chirped back.

The birds didn't answer. Rather, Weasel pointed a wing back at the main entrance of the city, where two small shapes approached the iron gate. The ground behind them was an ashy gray, and with a quick swipe, the stones around the gate melted and twirled into the *CORTEXIA*™ and the bars of the gate bent and swam through the air like cave eels through water.

A merchant pushing a cart of melons was next to swirl into the nozzle, followed by a dog and a row of small tents by the river. The Pribbles stepped forward, starting on the cobblestone streets and continuing their work on the wall of the city.

"Oh dear," Nasty said. He had been so distracted by the business with the Gang of Impervious Children and Sigil that he'd neglected to think of the Pribbles. It was one bad thing after another, it seemed.

"There's no time to talk," Nasty said. "We're done with the city. Fly with me."

He flapped his wings and flew above the thin clouds, high enough to see that fields of gray nothingness had replaced all of the outskirts of Dulum, reaching far back to where the mountain once stood. Ahead, he could see the black trees of the Dark Forest, and the large swatches of bubbling swamp. Miles away, in the center of a massive swamp, standing as though it had grown there, was a tower. The sides were splintered, and spikes of sharp wood shot from the top. Even from this far away, Nasty could see torches burning all along the path leading to its entrance. It was a wicked place, where only the most treacherous person would ever think to live.

Weasel, Worm, and Walnut followed behind, their wings vibrating fast to keep up with him.

"Now," Nasty said, turning to the three little bird spies, "tell me everything."

And they did.

Bird Spies, Part III

After the avalanche, Walnut told him, it seemed as if the Pribbles had died, smushed by the massive, collapsing mountain.

"They can't die," Nasty said. "Not really."

Indeed, after the mountain's destruction, the sound of chimes had cut through the air and an odd, sparkling blue light had slithered through the cracks in the massive pile.

Weasel, Worm, and Walnut had watched this happen several times, and each time, the couple regenerated exactly where they had died. Then there were a few moments of grunting and struggle, the quiet hum of the *CORTEXIA*™, the slurping of rocks, and then a loud collapse—*squish!* Then chimes would sound again.

Inch by inch they worked their way out from under the mountain, and the bird spies perched on a broken branch and waited. Hours passed, and still the couple worked.

They must have died six dozen times, Worm explained, and Weasel swore on her mother's nest that it was more. The Pribbles crawled their way out until finally Mrs. Pribble's pinkie poked through the wreckage, and then her whole hand appeared, followed by her arm and the rest of her.

She brushed off her clothes, looking disheveled and deranged, and then bent down to roll a large boulder down the mound. She clawed through the debris and pulled out her husband, then promptly slapped him across the face.

"Using the CORTEXIA™ on a mountain! How stupid can you be?"

Mr. Pribble was in no mood to argue. He knelt by the hole he had crawled from and lifted out the contraption. The nozzle was bent and the trigger guard had been destroyed. A web of cracks wrapped around the sparkling blue canister, which held the earlier chapters of the book.

"I protected it with my stomach," Mr. Pribble said. He wiped sweat from his brow and tried to bend the nozzle back into shape. "We're lucky this thing didn't break."

"*Lucky*," Mrs. Pribble replied with a snort. "We haven't had a bit of good luck since arriving in this awful place. I'm sick to death of this stupid story. Now find where they are and transport us to them."

Unfortunately, that request revealed more bad luck. The screen was completely gone, ripped from the top of the CORTEXIA™ when it made impact with the ground. It was likely still buried somewhere under tons of rock, and neither of the Pribbles felt like crawling back into the labyrinth to find it.

"That's fine," Mr. Pribble said, trying to put a cheery spin on their predicament. He pointed to the small silhouette of shapes in the distance. "We don't need to use it to zap to Oliver's location, anyway. The city of Dulum is right ahead—I can see it clearly. A day's journey and we'll be there. After that, it's on to the Twisted Tower, and then we can finish this thing."

Mrs. Pribble sighed dramatically. They crawled down the rubble to the ground and began to walk. Weasel, Worm, and Walnut followed at a safe distance. By now the sun was setting, and the river provided peaceful sounds to accompany the night. They walked past farms where sheep bleated and pigs snorted in their pens. The Pribbles were exhausted, and Mr. Pribble engaged the *CORTEXIA*™ from time to time, just enough to grab a few details from the surrounding countryside.

"Not much happens here," he explained. "It's more of a transitional location. I'll be more thorough in the city. "

As evening wore on, they settled at the wooden base of a windmill and fell fast asleep. It was at this precise time that the Gang of Impervious Children were surrounding the inn in the city, miles away.

Weasel, Worm, and Walnut had rested in a small hexagonal window behind the spinning windmill blades and watched them.

"Awful snores," Worm recounted. "Louder than the milling grain. Just terrible."

The Pribbles rose early in the morning, before the sun appeared, and continued their journey. The *CORTEXIA*™ hummed as they walked, sucking up whatever crossed their path.

Hours later, they arrived at Dulum's gates just as Sigil

was loading Cora, Jack, and Grayson into his carriage and exiting through the rear of the city, returning to his swamp.

"That's when we found you," Walnut said. "Good timing, too, by the looks of things."

"Indeed," Nasty said. He flew faster, leading the spies behind them. The pain in his wing had lessened to a twinge, so he paid it no mind. Below, the small shapes of the Gang of Impervious Children cut through the forest, leaping over twisted vines and rotten tree stumps, scaling small cliffs, and balancing on fallen trees that lay over mushy marshland. Animals howled and birds rustled the tops of the trees. Somewhere down there were Oliver and Blumpf. Cora, Jack, and Grayson were with Sigil, and who knew what he would do to them? Nasty closed his eyes and wished the Author would grant them safety.

The end was near. Nasty could feel it all the way down in his talons. If they were lucky, they'd finish the story together, all of them in one place again. Oliver would leave, and though Nasty would miss the dear boy terribly, at least he would forever live in Oliver's mind, instead of inside that horrible machine. He looked back, hoping the city of Dulum would distract the Pribbles for most of the morning, long enough that the children could arrive at the tower and the clock could be finished before they were able to make their way to the end.

"Keep watching the Pribbles," Nasty commanded the bird spies. "Find me if they reach the edge of the swamp."

He saw a large shape running through trees. That had to be Blumpf, he thought, and he dove toward it.

Weasel, Worm, and Walnut tucked their heads and swooped back to the city. Nasty hoped he would not need to see them again.

This, I'm sad to say, would not be the case.

Through the Dark Forest

Sigil's carriage raced through the Dark Forest on a thin path lined with weeds and brambles. No sun could get through the canopy of leaves, and the deeper they traveled, the colder it became. A cloud of fog hung over the trees. Water dripped from above, and strange rodents scaled the branches.

Oliver hid in the trees, Blumpf beside him, and watched the carriage pass. He could see the shapes of Cora, Jack, and Grayson through the window, bound and unmoving. Sigil sat before them, screaming at the driver to go faster. Reins were whipped, and the poor horses struggled on, over the uneven path and toward the Twisted Tower, where the spell could be completed.

"Blumpf," Blumpf whispered, pointing to the silent shapes slinking around them. The Gang of Impervious Children were skilled at moving through difficult terrain, but they were no match for the speed of a pair of horses on a path. Sigil would arrive at the Twisted Tower long before they made it on foot, but with any luck the clock would not be completed until the Gang caught up.

"Blumpf."

"I know," Oliver said. They should have kept moving,

but he needed to see his friends once more, in case it was the last time. Blumpf helped Oliver up a small incline of rocks, and they continued, running through the trees, following the Gang.

A shadow passed overhead. It floated through the fog, and Blumpf wrapped his arms around Oliver to protect him. Nasty appeared in front of them, majestic, wings spread wide, with the tail of an unlucky rodent dangling from his beak.

"Nasty!" Oliver cried.

"Oooh!" Nasty said as he spit out a heap of bones. "These Dark Forest creatures have truly rotten meat!"

"I'm sorry."

"Don't be! I *love* it!"

He lunged at another rodent and slurped it down, then flew low, keeping pace above Blumpf's head as they ran.

"How did it go back in the city?" Oliver asked.

"Sigil is just as rotten and scary as always, but it went as well as could be expected. The children are alive and headed to the Twisted Tower. Judging by the speed of travel, I'd say they'll arrive several hours before you do. The clock should take a few hours to finish, then they can turn back time, save their mother, and we can get you out of here."

Oliver nodded.

"And the Pribbles?"

"I've tasked our little bird spies with keeping a watch on them. With the *CORTEXIA*™ screen broken, they can't track us or zap to our location again, which is most fortunate. The city should provide a timely distraction, and I believe we can finish everything before they arrive."

"Then you should follow Cora and Jack," Oliver said. "We'll be all right."

"Blumpf," Blumpf said.

Nasty nodded. It was hard for him to leave Oliver, though it was true that his narration duties were needed with Cora and Jack. He searched the woods, hoping to see some sign of the tall, hooded figure. He would feel much better if he knew the Author was near, ready to help if it came to it, but he was nowhere to be seen.

"Goodbye, Oliver," Nasty said, landing on a stump. He held out his wings, and he and Oliver shared a warm hug of feathers and limbs.

"I'll see you at the end," Oliver said, and Nasty flew on, up above the trees, aiming his course toward the Twisted Tower and wishing that what Oliver said was true.

Hands That Are True

I t was evening when Cora and Jack finally arrived at the Twisted Tower, though it was difficult to tell time in the Dark Forest. The trees blocked out the sun, and toxic gases from the swamp collected in the sky, forming black clouds that rolled above them. The line of trees ended abruptly at the edge of the swamp, their trunks burnt in half, almost like the green, bubbling liquid had belched upward and killed everything in its path.

The carriage poked through the last tunnel of black trees and crossed a bridge of spongy ground lined with torches that cut through the swamp. Putrid green water gurgled at the path's edges. They raced toward the Twisted Tower. It was a massive structure up close—taller than the castle in Dulum, taller than the Great Staircase of the Old Mountain Guard. It looked as though a million trees had burst apart and that their splintery remains had been caught in a tornado that spun in place, sharp pieces sticking together at ugly angles. It was a mass of spikes and windows and torches, twisting together to form an ominous corkscrew of doom.

Nasty felt weak at the sight. He dipped and searched for a spike to settle upon as the carriage stopped in front of the door. The moment his feet wrapped around a piece of wood, he stifled a cry. A splinter had lodged in his flesh, and a ribbon of blood trickled down his talon. He hopped to another spike, and another splinter pierced his foot. It was almost as if the wood itself was another adversary fighting against him.

The carriage slowed to a stop, and Sigil emerged, pulling Grayson behind him. Cora and Jack were next; two guards grabbed them and pulled them through the large black doors.

Nasty poked his head through a window. The inside of the tower was an evil place. The bottom floor was a round room lined with shelves of magic books. Fire burned in a hearth, flickering orange light on glass vials filled with potions. A long, circular staircase bordered the room, going up, up, up, passing smaller rooms on each level, reaching all the way to the highest floor, where Cora and Jack's father waited.

"Take them to our timekeeper," Sigil commanded, and the guards obeyed. Nasty watched as a guard grabbed the satchel and another grabbed the barrel wood. They pulled the children up the stairs, starting the long, slow march around the circumference of the Twisted Tower.

Sigil stood in the center of the room and waved his hands in a circle. His body glowed and he began to float, rising, flying above the children to the tower's very top. He stood outside a door and waited, arms crossed, an evil smirk on his face that revealed his sharp, silver teeth.

Nasty flew, settling outside a window, just enough that Cora and Jack could see his shape and know he was with them. Grayson passed by the window first, staggering. He was blindfolded, and his hands were tied. His gray hair seemed to glow in this dark place. Cora passed next. She nodded to

Nasty's shadow, and he flew on, higher, watching them ascend the staircase, around and around until they arrived at the thin landing in front of the room where their father must be waiting.

"Horace!" Sigil yelled in a singsong voice. "Look who I brought!"

He kicked the door open and Cora gasped when she saw a thin figure hunched in the corner of the room. It was unmistakably her father, but this was a frail, sickly version. He lay by a small, flickering fire. It was a smoky place, all wood and beams and rust without a single bit of color. At the sight of his children, Horace forced himself up and hobbled to them.

"Cora?" he asked, wiping his eyes with the back of his hand. "Jack?"

Sigil pointed a finger, sending a thin bolt of magic that knocked Horace down to the wooden floor, howling in agony.

"Stop it!" Jack yelled. He ran to his father and wrapped his arms around him. Horace had Jack's round face and Cora's piercing eyes. His hair was gray, and a large, patchy beard hung from his ashen face. He was dressed in brown rags, which were peppered with holes burned by Sigil's magic.

"What have you . . . " he began, but his voice trailed off. Cora rubbed his cheek.

"Father?" she asked, tears running down her face.

"What have you *done?*" he asked.

"My bidding," Sigil answered, marching across the wooden floor. He summoned the guards to lay the pieces from the spell on a workbench that stood in another corner of the room. Then the guards tied Grayson to a chair.

"Your children are quite impressive," Sigil said. "They brought me everything I require, risking their lives for my glory."

"Why?" Horace whispered, but Cora and Jack were silent. They couldn't bear to look at him, to see the pain in his eyes at this betrayal. He would understand soon, and then he would be grateful. Wouldn't he?

Sigil waved his hand out the window, in the direction of the city of Dulum.

"Soon, there will be no children left. Once the clock is complete and time has been altered, your children requested to serve me. They knew they were on the losing side of the battle and chose wisely, hoping I would extend mercy in exchange for their loyalty. Still, I can't escape the feeling that something else drove them, some *other* motivation."

Sigil nodded, and two guards grabbed Cora and Jack, binding them with rope and throwing them in the corner of the room beside Grayson, holding knives to their necks.

"I'm not so foolish as to believe the tales of children," Sigil said. "Children are wicked creatures not to be trusted. Now build me a clock or your children will die."

Sigil tossed Horace's bag of tools to him.

"Finish by sunrise, my *hands that are true*, or they won't see another day," he said, turning on his heels and exiting the room.

Horace watched, gaping, looking back and forth between

the guards and the children. There was no option left but to work. He pulled his frail body to the workbench and arranged his tools, laying the items from the spell on the floor.

This clock would be much smaller than others he had built, half his height and width, and he could make quick work of it.

First, he broke the jewel into pieces and ground the shards into smooth bearings, setting them in the center of the gears. He spun the gears with his fingers and they gave a pleasing *whirr.*

Then he placed a wooden disc on the table and stretched the skin of the cave eel over it, wrapping it around the edges and nailing it in place. He rubbed the textured blue material with his fingers, smoothing it down, and then held it to the fire. It sparkled in the light, an otherworldly thing. He affixed the hour markers in twelve evenly spaced locations around the edge, saving the "watchmaker's four" for last. He had taught Cora long ago that the fourth hour should be noted with four bars, or *IIII,* instead of the traditional Roman numeral *IV.* This improved balance, he'd said, but nothing in Dulum was balanced anymore.

Horace laid out the wood barrel pieces from the Old Mountain Guard and then pulled a saw from his bag. He began to cut, creating a rectangular casing. It was splintered and rough but refined enough to serve its one awful purpose.

Horace was a master craftsman, each movement of his hands steady and planned. Jack and Cora watched as the pieces they had risked their lives for were slowly transformed into a clock. He was nearly finished when the first bloom of light appeared on the horizon. The sun would soon be up, and Sigil would return, expecting the clock to work. And it *would* work, Horace was certain. Years would pass, his children would age in a flash, and then they, too, would be lost to Sigil's power. How could he stop it? He searched his mind for an answer that would let them all stay alive but could find nothing to believe in.

Sigil's guards watched him work, their knives pointed at his children's throats, ready to slice if he stopped.

When the clock was almost complete, they cracked open the door to give a signal, and Sigil appeared, clutching Grayson by the fabric around his neck. Sigil pushed Grayson into the room and circled the clock, licking his lips in delight.

"When will it be ready?" Sigil asked.

"Soon," Horace said.

Horace felt, in that moment, that all hope was lost, but had he glanced outside, he might have seen shadows poke through the edge of the forest, looking up at the bright window at the top of the tower.

Oliver, Blumpf, and the Gang of Impervious Children had arrived and were circling the swampland, waiting to strike.

The Edge of the Swamp

The journey through the Dark Forest had been difficult. Oliver's arms and legs were scratched and bleeding from the dense branches, and he had the odd sensation of being covered in sweat and freezing cold at the same time. Luckily, it was impossible to get lost. The tower was so large that it provided a constant point of reference for their journey. As long as it was in view, he could be certain they were headed in the right direction.

They had chased the tower through the night, sometimes veering off course to avoid pitfalls or cliffs but always keeping it in front of them. At some point, a series of sharp, percussive bursts echoed across the swampland and through the surrounding forest.

He's working, Oliver thought, imagining Horace hammering away at the case of the clock. And if he was working, that meant Cora and Jack were still alive. Oliver had to hurry. The tower grew bigger in his vision but always seemed far away. Blumpf grabbed his hand and pulled him along, throwing him over a large tangle of weeds.

When the swamp was finally in view, the Gang of Impervious Children fanned out at the sharp-edged tree line. The thick water gurgled in front of them. Rodney bent down and dipped his finger in it, recoiling when it blistered his skin.

Rodney shook his head at the others in the Gang and pointed to the bridge that led to the main door at the base of the Twisted Tower. It was lined with thorny bushes and limbs that stuck from the mud like the arms of sinking creatures.

"They'll see us," Hazel whispered.

Walter nodded and picked up a stick.

"We'll fight."

"We have no other choice," Rosemary said. "They'll have to see us eventually."

"Yes, but it needs to be the right time," Oliver said, looking up at the flickering window at the top of the tower. Something moved around the window's edges—a silhouette of beak and wings. "We'll only get one chance."

"Blumpf," Blumpf nodded.

Oliver's stomach bubbled like the swamp. As soon as they reached the tower, they would start the final chapter of the book and head into unread territory, where anything could happen. Grayson had seemed to think that was a good thing—that they could write their own ending, shaping it to their will—but Oliver wasn't so sure.

"And in the darkness, the Gang of Impervious Children ran to the tower. The tall, gruesome thing stood like the shaft of a clock, and they were nothing but hands upon the swampy dial, being moved by time," he whispered to himself.

Those had been the last words in his copy of the story. In his mind he'd assumed the story ended with good triumphing over evil, but there had always been a small worm of doubt wriggling in his mind. *Things always get worse,* he thought.

Wasn't that the one truth he had come to understand? Not all stories have happy endings.

Above, Nasty's shadow descended from the tower, lit in bursts by the torches lining the path. He settled on a high tree limb and addressed the children.

"The clock is nearly complete," Nasty said. "Now is the time to strike. When you enter the tower—"

He stopped midsentence and cocked his head to the sky, listening to something.

Sharp chirps rang out, overlapping one another, frantic.

"No time for speeches. *Get going,*" Nasty said. He waved a wing at the children, who followed his command, and then flew above the trees in the direction of the chirps. He yelled down to Blumpf, "Protect Oliver! Don't let him in the tower until the battle is over! He only has one life left, and he's not going to die here if we can help it!"

Nasty looked at the sun over the horizon, and in the blinding light, saw three black dots flying toward him, screaming their little heads off.

Bird Spies, Part IIII

"H"orses!" Weasel cried.

"Horses!" Worm cried.

"Horses!" Walnut cried.

Nasty flew on, squinting.

"What is it, friends?" he called out, and they continued chanting the word over and over. He got the sense that they were trying to tell him something about horses.

He swooped down, back into the forest, where the trees' shade provided a welcome relief from the blinding light. The three birds followed, landing on a small branch close to the ground.

"Horses," they said in unison, flapping their wings and looking wildly about. "Horses!"

"Settle down," Nasty said. His little bird spies were shaking, their beaks sputtering open and closed. *Horses.* I heard you. Now tell me what happened. Are the Pribbles still working on the city?"

"Horses," they all said again. They seemed to be stuck on the word.

"Yes, yes, horses," Nasty said. "What about them?"

It was Worm who spoke first. She jumped up and down on the branch, trying desperately to regain her thoughts.

"They know how to *ride* them!" she screamed.

The words had no sooner escaped her beak when the row of trees behind Weasel, Worm, and Walnut were ripped from the ground. The gnarled branches melted into dust all the way down to their roots and slithered away.

Nasty pumped his wings and flew backward. In that moment, it all became clear. He had been so preoccupied with watching the construction of the clock that he had taken his focus off the Pribbles and the rest of Dulum for a few crucial hours. They must have finished their work in the city and taken horses from Sigil's guards, using them to travel through the Dark Forest faster than Nasty had anticipated. The glow of the rising sun had hidden their progress, and all of the kingdom was now gone, save for the Twisted Tower and the surrounding trees.

Perhaps Nasty should have stayed with the Pribbles, but as a narrator, he couldn't be in two places at the same time. Hadn't the children's story been more important?

This, he thought, *is precisely the reason narrators aren't supposed to get involved.*

Nasty could hear the *clip clop* of hooves and saw the small shape of Mr. Pribble bouncing on a black horse, looking like he might fall off at any step. He held the *CORTEXIA*™ clumsily between his hands, waving it in unpredictable movements at the surrounding forest. Mrs. Pribble was beside him. Unlike her husband, she was a natural rider, sitting sidesaddle with a straight back, gracefully gliding over the wide expanse of nothingness. She charged ahead, teeth bared, a warrior ready for battle.

"Follow me, friends!" Nasty yelled. He glanced back at the tower and saw the small shapes of children scaling its splintery sides. Oliver was still in the forest, and Nasty would have to tell him to ignore his earlier advice. The final chapter took place in the tower, which meant that at the moment, it was the only safe place to be.

"Weasel, can you distract them?" he called out, extending his arms to swoop toward the edge of the forest in a wide arc.

"Weasel?"

There was no answer.

"Worm? Walnut?"

Silence.

He looked back. The three birds were flapping their wings as hard as they could, caught up in a draft of disintegrating trees. Their little bodies stretched to strings, so long that they looked like they might break apart. They continued to fly, fighting against the pull of the *CORTEXIA*™, but it was no use. On they flew, eyes filled with terror, trying to escape the awful machine. Nasty remembered what it felt like when the nozzle had been fixed on him, how terrible it was to have your very being stripped away.

"No!" he cried, diving at them. "You can't take *them!*"

He had put these birds in this danger, and he'd risk his own life for them now. He flew closer, watching as the machine worked its way up their bodies, to their necks and skulls, until each was devoured—*pop pop pop*—by the nozzle of the machine.

Weasel, Worm, and Walnut were gone.

The cracked canister sparkled with blue light, and Mr. Pribble continued to ride, circling the tower, collecting rows of trees. He didn't know what he had just done or who he had just taken, and that only made Nasty more angry at the theft.

He changed course, flying toward Blumpf and Oliver, determined to finish this book once and for all.

Blumpf's Protection

I have to go," Oliver said, but Blumpf would hear none of it. He had promised to protect the boy until the battle was over and the clock was in their possession, and that is what he would do.

"Blumpf," Blumpf said, pointing at the tower. The Gang of Impervious Children surveyed the tower and sketched a plan of attack into the ground. Two of them ran across the bridge, trying their best to stay hidden behind the flickering torches. With the light from the rising sun, they could move in the shadows, and it wasn't until they were within striking distance that the guards spotted them.

Adeline and Phineas made quick work of them, leaping to attack and kicking their rods from their hands. The children grabbed the rods out of midair and spun them around, knocking the guards across the head.

Then the entire Gang charged, half of them waiting at the door, and the other half climbing the jagged wood of the tower. Blood dripped from their hands and arms, and the soles of their shoes were shredded by the splintery wood.

"Come on, Blumpf," Oliver said. He wanted to race into the tower and run up the stairs, enter the final chapter, and get to the end before any more damage could be done to Dulum and his friends.

Blumpf bit his lower lip and shook his head. The children were forty feet up the tower, climbing with all the strength they had left in their bodies. The rest of the Gang entered the tower, creeping around the looping staircase, being careful not to alert the guards as they ascended.

Outside, a shadow soared overhead, coming directly at them. Oliver braced himself, peering out from behind Blumpf to see a beak and a flurry of feathers.

"Go!" Nasty screamed, motioning wildly at the Dark Forest. "The Pribbles are coming!"

Oliver felt that odd sensation in his head again, like a bubble had burst and a fog had wrapped around his thoughts. He looked back through the rows of trees and saw limbs and trunks and roots rip from the ground, turn to dust, and disappear.

"Into the tower!" Nasty cried.

Blumpf saw the fear in Oliver's face and understood what had to be done. He picked Oliver up and cradled him in his arms, running around the bank of the swamp, being careful not to touch the toxic liquid. When he arrived at the bridge, Blumpf leaned back and tossed Oliver forward, giving Oliver a head start to the tower's door. A few dozen feet and he'd be there, safe inside for the moment. Oliver pressed on, running hard, searching for dry spots in the soft ground. Sweat ran down his face and blurred his vision.

Was the clock almost complete? How much longer until the Gang reached the room at the top of the tower?

He continued running. When the door was fifty feet away, he called out to Blumpf, but there was no reply. He glanced back and saw two horses burst through the forest, rearing up at the bridge. The few remaining trees surrounding the swamp bent toward them like blades of grass and then broke apart, piece by piece. Mr. Pribble spun the *CORTEXIA*™ toward the swamp and the water lifted from the ground, revealing wet mud and stones underneath. The green water spun in the air, circling the tower like a whirlpool. Gas bubbles popped and oozed, and the rotten stuff continued to spiral, entering the nozzle. Then the mud and sludge joined the cyclone, leaving only gray dust behind.

Blumpf ran through the mayhem, his large feet making sucking sounds in the disappearing mud. There was nothing left surrounding the empty swampland but a few loose trees.

"You!" Mr. Pribble called out, clearly still cross about his altercation with Blumpf on top of the mountain. "I said you shouldn't be here!"

Blumpf glanced back and forth between the Pribbles and Oliver.

"Author!" Nasty cried, flying over the scene and then perching on the tower, high enough to see everything. "Help us, Author, we really need you now!"

This time, however, the Author was nowhere to be seen.

Blumpf tripped in the mud and fell. He pushed himself up and pointed at Oliver, the features on his loosely defined face revealing nothing but love for the boy.

"Blumpf," he whispered.

Blumpf smiled at Oliver and pounded a fist to his chest.

He pointed at the tower, then turned to face the Pribbles, spreading his arms wide and howling at them.

"Step aside, big man," Mr. Pribble said. He yanked his horse's reigns and aimed the *CORTEXIA*™ at Blumpf's chest.

"Blumpf!" Blumpf screamed.

"Is that the only word you can say?" Mr. Pribble asked. He rested his finger on the trigger, squeezing it just enough so that the machine began to hum. Blumpf's hair swayed, as though a gentle ocean breeze was blowing.

"You ruined the chapter on the mountain."

Mr. Pribble squeezed the trigger harder, and now Blumpf's hair began to stretch into long strands. His skin smeared along the edges and went translucent, evaporating into the air.

"You've caused me and my wife tremendous pain."

"*Blumpf,*" Blumpf growled. He charged at them. With each step he faded a bit more. His feet lifted from the ground and his body shrank.

"This is over. We won't be late for the end because of *you,*" Mr. Pribble said. He pulled the trigger, engaging the full power of the *CORTEXIA*™. Blumpf leapt at them, and his body seemed to pause in the air and break apart into a swarm of dust. Swatches of red and brown and tan and black all mixed together to circle the Pribbles and then disappear into the machine.

"No!" Oliver screamed.

"Goodbye, friend," Nasty whispered.

Oliver continued running to the tower, tears stinging his eyes.

A fog was closing in, blocking the sun, glowing pink and orange, constricting around the tower. Oliver couldn't see through it. He could only see the shapes of the Pribbles galloping on, chasing him into "A Timely End."

Oliver threw his body against the door and it swung open. He entered the bottom floor of the tower, where rows of magic books were shelved along the perimeter and vials of liquid littered the iron tables. He grabbed a plank of wood from a pile by the fireplace and jammed it across the handles of the door—not that it would do much good in delaying the Pribbles. Then he leapt to the stairs, taking them two at a time, racing up toward the very top.

Oliver wouldn't allow himself to think about what he had lost. He had to keep moving now that he was inside the final chapter of the book, where his actions alone would determine the ending.

CHAPTER EIGHT

A TIMELY END

Horace wound the mainspring of the clock a quarter turn to prove he was done, and the hands began to move around the dial, seeming to vibrate, like the magic was alive inside it, fighting to get out.

Time moved forward at a predictable pace, *tick tock tick.* The hands made one rotation before stopping.

Horace fell to the floor, massaging his fingers. His work was complete.

Cora glanced at Jack, seeming to talk to him with her eyes, planning when to strike. They would only have one chance to attack, and if they failed, their entire quest would have been for nothing.

"It appears that everything is in order," Sigil hissed.

The clock was surrounded in light, an otherworldly aura that could only mean that Cora and Jack had indeed brought him the pieces needed for the spell and that Horace's hands were true.

Sigil rubbed the clock's scaled dial and then opened its back paneling to peer inside, holding his face close to the gears. Red light from the jewels shone in his eyes. He pulled up the hood of his cloak over his head.

"*Children*," Sigil said, "are such a burden. They're the worst thing that ever happened to Dulum."

Sigil pulled Grayson to his feet and laid the boy's hands on the clock, then pointed a knife at his back.

"Good riddance to them. Wind the mainspring," Sigil commanded.

Grayson glanced at Cora and Jack and turned the key one rotation.

The hands of the clock shuddered and began to move. Grayson continued to wind the mainspring, around and around, until the key could no longer be turned. *Tick tock tick* echoed through the room. Sigil raised his hands above his head and squealed with delight. He looked at his guards and motioned to Cora and Jack.

"I no longer need them," he said, pressing the knife into Grayson's back.

Horace screamed and the guards advanced, but Cora and Jack were ready. They leapt to their feet, ducking out of the guards' grasp and charging Sigil.

"Stop them!" Sigil screamed, waving his knife in the air.

Cora and Jack were halfway to him when the tower began to shake. They fell to their feet as the floorboards of the room buckled and dust poured around them.

Grayson spun and pushed off from the clock. It wobbled precariously and began to fall beside Horace, who made no attempt to save it. Nasty swooped inside the room, steadying the clock and returning it to the table.

"What is this?" Sigil screamed, swatting at the bird. He

looped his other arm around Grayson's neck and pulled him to the window, peering down to see that the water and trees surrounding the swamp had vanished. The whole structure seemed to be sinking into the gray ash.

"What did you do?" Sigil hissed. He leaned farther, trying to get a better look.

"Now!" Nasty called, and the children who had climbed the tower poured through the window, legs and arms flailing wildly at the guards. Half of them surrounded Sigil, ripping the knife from his hand and blocking Grayson from him. Cora and Jack changed course, wrapping their arms around the clock to protect it from the rocking motion of the crumbling tower.

The clock was fully built and fully wound. Their quest was complete. All they had to do was change the time, setting it back to when their mother was still alive.

Sigil fell to his back, his fingers crackling with sparks of magic that had no effect on the children.

"Let go of me, you rotten cretins!" Sigil screamed. He looked to his guards. "Get them!"

Sigil's guards were busy swinging their rods at the rest of the children, but they were vastly outnumbered. More children surged in through the window and Nasty flapped around the room, batting his wings against the guards' faces and whacking them with his talons while the children pummeled them with their fists.

The glow of the clock filled the room with an eerie light, and the whistling of the *CORTEXIA*™ echoed outside.

Suddenly the door to the top room of the tower burst open and the remaining members of the Gang of Impervious Children entered.

"What are you waiting for?" Haydn asked. "Change the time!"

"Where's Oliver?" Cora asked.

"He's still below," Greta said.

"We can't finish until he's here," Jack said, and Nasty flew to the door to see where he was.

The Pribbles Arrive

Oliver had made it up one rotation of the Twisted Tower before the doors were ripped clean off their hinges. The tower shook, creaking and groaning.

The Pribbles followed him inside and then leapt from their horses, their boots slapping against the stone floor. Mr. Pribble spun the *CORTEXIA*™ around and slurped up the horses from mane to tail. The poor beasts never saw it coming.

"We won't be needing them anymore, I imagine," Mr. Pribble said. He licked his lips and then took in all the wicked details of the tower.

"Are we almost finished?" Mrs. Pribble asked, her eyes fixed on Oliver, who was still looping up and around.

"Yes, very soon now. This is the final chapter, dear, and I'll make quick work of it. Look at all these wondrous *books!*"

Mr. Pribble positioned his round body in the center of the room and held out the *CORTEXIA*™. He pulled the trigger and began to spin clockwise, sucking up the walls of the tower and all the items on the bottom floor. The great structure began to lean from the sudden loss of its foundation, and when Mr. Pribble had finished a full rotation, it collapsed a dozen feet, as though sinking into the ground.

Oliver took the steps three at a time, but it wasn't enough to escape Mr. Pribble's quick work. The Gang of Impervious Children had already reached the top floor of the tower, swarming in to help Cora and Jack.

Mr. Pribble sucked up more and more of the tower, plank by plank, level by level, and when he arrived at Oliver, he slowed his pace, relishing the opportunity to make the boy struggle in his climb.

"This is for that mishap on the mountain," Mr. Pribble said, giggling.

He aimed the *CORTEXIA*™ at Oliver's feet, ripping the stairs out right from under him. Oliver hopped from one disintegrating stair to another; he could feel the pain in his toes as the pull of the machine grazed the soles of his shoes. He continued on as best he could, but his pace was slowing, and the muscles in his legs burned.

A quarter of the tower was gone now, vanishing slowly into the gray ground. The mist of the disappearing black wood filled the chamber, coating Oliver's clothes and stinging his eyes.

"Stop running!" Mr. Pribble yelled. "Let's reach the end together."

Oliver ignored him, staying one step ahead of the *CORTEXIA*™. He could see the door to the room high above him. Inside was the end of the book, and if he could get to it before Mr. Pribble took his friends, then they could change the time, finish the story, and exit before everything was taken.

He leapt to the next step, but Mr. Pribble was growing

impatient. He sucked up the wood under Oliver's feet, and Oliver crashed to the ground below.

Instantly Mrs. Pribble was on him, restraining his arms and holding him tight. Her red nails dug into his skin.

"You've made this a *very* unpleasant tale," she whispered in his ear.

"Quite," Mr. Pribble said. He waddled over to Oliver and patted him on the cheek. "All's well that ends well. It's been a tough journey, but we're finally here at 'A Timely End.' You see? It was pointless to fight us."

The Pribbles pressed their backs together and the three of them spun, the *CORTEXIA*™ inhaling the walls of the tower until all that was left was one rotation of stairs and the very top room.

Mr. Pribble extended his hand toward the steps and pushed Oliver by the small of his back.

"After you."

The Truth

With a thunderous crash, the floor of the top room hit the ground and the spiked ceiling cracked in the middle.

The door to the room fell flat on the floorboards. The Pribbles pushed Oliver inside the room, and Mr. Pribble assessed the scene in front of him. He looked at Cora and Jack and the glowing clock with disgust.

"No, no, no!" he whined. "This is all wrong!"

Nasty flew to the clock and perched on top of it.

"And why is that blasted bird still around?"

The Gang of Impervious Children looked at one another, clearly confused at what was happening.

"This *isn't* how the book is supposed to end!"

"What is he talking about?" Grayson asked.

Mr. Pribble lifted the *CORTEXIA*™ and waved it around the room. He sucked up the guards first and then moved on to the nearest members of the Gang. Arthur, Hazel, and Greta disappeared, pulled into the blue light of the canister, followed by Marlowe, Phineas, and Rosemary. In his haste, he took out a chunk of the tower near the roof, and the ceiling and support beams groaned. Through the hole in the wall, they could see glowing fog press around them, backlit with colorful sunlight.

"Who are *they*?" Sigil hissed, his dark eyes darting between the Pribbles. His fingers began to sparkle again, readying an attack against these strange adults.

"Oh, quiet, you," Mr. Pribble said, pointing the *CORTEXIA*™ at Sigil and pulling the trigger before Sigil could zap him with his evil magic.

Sigil screamed, his pale body melting from head to toe. It flew through the opening of his hood, corkscrewing around the room until he was nothing more than a blur of pale colors and slipping into the nozzle with a dull *whoosh*. Sigil's black robe floated to the ground, resting in a pile beside the clock.

"Well, that takes care of *him*," Mr. Pribble said. He turned to Oliver. "You've changed the ending."

Oliver stared at his feet.

"Why would you do that?"

"Tell him," Nasty said.

Oliver was silent.

"Tell me what?" Mr. Pribble asked.

The tower had gone deathly still. All of the remaining children watched in silence, for fear that speaking would make them a target for the strange machine.

"I never *read* the ending," Oliver said.

"You what?" Mr. Pribble asked, his eyes widening behind his round glasses. He walked over to the clock and rapped his knuckles on the eel-skin dial.

"What is he talking about, love?" Mrs. Pribble asked.

"Surely this is the ending. The clock is done. Let's set back the time and save their mother so we can go home."

"You didn't finish the book?" Mr. Pribble whispered. "Why ever not?"

That was a long answer best summed up in a quick sentence.

"I'm a thief," Oliver said, hanging his head. Though he had confessed this fact to everyone else in the room save for Horace, it was still a difficult thing to say. "I stole books from the library—books I didn't think anyone would want—old books and musty books, books that were ripped and yellowed and incomplete. *The Timekeeper's Children* was missing the final chapter, and I checked it out eleven times before I took it. That's why the library said I returned it, and that's why it wasn't there."

The wood of the tower groaned again. Splinters sprang from the beams.

"Well, that's wonderful news!" Mrs. Pribble said. She clapped her hands together. "To think that he's had the book all this time, Edmund! We really should have asked him at the start. Since we purchased the contents of the library, I do believe that means it is *our* property. If you return it today, we won't press charges. Now can we please *leave* this rotten—"

"I can't," Oliver said. "I tried to return it, but it was too late. The library was already closed, and when the garbage trucks came to take the rest, they took it, too. I'm sorry, but it's gone forever."

The top of the tower cracked further, and streams of light poured into the room. All was silent.

"You never read the end of the book," Mr. Pribble said, still trying to process the information he had just received.

Oliver shook his head.

"And this is what you thought happened?" Mr. Pribble asked. "You thought the clock was built and time was set back and everyone was happy for the rest of their days?"

Oliver looked at Mr. Pribble and nodded.

"Oh, Oliver," Mr. Pribble said. He lowered the nozzle of the *CORTEXIA*™ and moved toward him. "Then you don't know the twist."

A Twist in the Twisted Tower

"T"he end of the book is what I remember best," Mr. Pribble said.

He turned to Cora, Jack, and Horace.

"The clock is broken in the battle. Horace has a chance to save it, but he doesn't. As a timekeeper, he believes that time is a circle. It loops and loops, going ever forward, and that is the way it must go—forward. Events in the past should not be changed. Good or bad, what happens happens, and the only thing to do is move ahead, one day at a time. Isn't that right, Horace?"

Cora and Jack's father looked at them, whispering, "It's not right to change time, children, even if it's what we all want. Our lives will continue, and—"

Mr. Pribble lifted the *CORTEXIA*™ and pulled the trigger just hard enough to take in Horace with one gulp.

Cora and Jack screamed, and Nasty felt a shiver through his body. He had never considered that this might be the end. How could it be so?

"Yes, yes," Mr. Pribble said. He stepped toward Cora and Jack. "Your lives *do* go on. With Sigil captured, Grayson resumes rule of Dulum, and Cora and Jack live with Horace for the rest of his days. Cora, of course, becomes the official timekeeper of the city, and Jack leads the guard. What happens after that is left to the imagination, though I'd like to think that Grayson and Cora marry and live happily ever after, ruling Dulum with love and fairness."

Cora and Grayson glanced at each other but did not respond.

The tower cracked again, this time irreparably so, and large chunks of wood began to fall. Mr. Pribble was ready for it. He crouched and swung the *CORTEXIA*™ in a looping figure eight pattern until every last piece of the tower was sucked away and all that was left of Dulum was a wide expanse of gray ground and thick fog. Grayson stood by the clock, alongside Cora and Jack and the pile of Sigil's robes. Nasty jumped from the clock and hid behind it. His heart beat in his chest. As the narrator, he felt compelled to change what had happened, but what could he do?

"That's it, I'm afraid. *The end of the book.* I'm sorry, Oliver, that things did not work out as you thought."

Mr. Pribble pointed the *CORTEXIA*™ at Cora, Jack, and Grayson.

"Who wants to go first?" he asked.

Tears streamed down Oliver's face, and shapes began to swim in the corners of his vision, turning into letters that formed the words THE END. Underneath, the word EXIT was now available. All he needed to do was reach out and grab it and everything would be over. He'd return to the Pribbles' dining room, and the story would be gone forever from his mind.

Mr. Pribble readied his finger on the *CORTEXIA*™'s trigger and was just about to squeeze when his wife said, "Look, Edmund! What is *that?*"

Everyone turned.

Through the fog, a tall, hooded figure emerged.

The Tall, Hooded Figure

It was just a blur at first, but as the tall, hooded figure walked closer, the fingers of fog parted and its full shape appeared.

"Oh, Author!" Nasty yelled, hardly able to contain his excitement. "You're here! I knew you'd come! We sure could use your help!"

"*Author?*" Mr. Pribble asked.

"That's right!" Nasty said. He flew out from behind the clock, suddenly emboldened by the presence of the Author. Surely nothing bad could happen now that Malcolm Bloom had arrived!

Nasty struck a pose, arching his back and extending a wing.

"Mr. and Mrs. Pribble, I would like to humbly introduce you to the author of *The Timekeeper's Children*, Malcolm Bloom. I imagine he is none too pleased with what you've done to his story!"

The figure moved closer, gliding beside the clock and placing Grayson's hands on the dial.

"What are you doing, sir?" Nasty asked. "Take care of the Pribbles!"

Cora and Jack watched as the figure turned from Grayson

and walked past them, raising an arm to cover Nasty's mouth.

"Mr. Bloom?" Mr. Pribble asked, lowering the *CORTEXIA*™ and stepping closer. "Is that really you?"

"Yes," Nasty said, laughing. He spit a bit of the figure's sleeve from his mouth. "All authors put a piece of themselves in their books, and now you'll have to deal with him directly. Good luck to you!"

The tall, hooded figure's head shook back and forth.

"No," it said. Its voice was oddly familiar and seemed to come from the center of its belly.

"No?" Nasty asked.

The figure extended its arm, and the robe separated and floated to the ground.

Cora and Jack gasped.

Oliver gasped, followed by Nasty and Grayson and the Pribbles.

All in all, there was an awful lot of gasping, because Malcolm Bloom was not underneath the robe. It was another *Oliver*, and perched on top of his shoulders was another *Nasty*.

"Someone needs to explain to me what is happening," Mrs. Pribble said. Her eyes darted back and forth between the two copies of Oliver and Nasty.

"Quite," Mr. Pribble said.

The other Oliver stepped forward and placed his hand over the nozzle of the *CORTEXIA*™.

"We're not so different," Other Oliver said to Mr. Pribble. "We both stole a book we loved."

The clock still glowed in the center of the gray expanse, and the hands of the clock ticked forward.

"You can't go back in time, Mr. Pribble. Not really. You loved this book as a child, but you didn't understand it. Children aren't a threat."

For once, Mr. Pribble was speechless.

Other Oliver turned to Oliver and Nasty.

"You thought it was the author following you and helping you through the story, but it wasn't. It was *you*, well . . . *me* all along. Once a book is written, the author is gone. They're only able to give half of the story, anyway. " Other Oliver tapped the side of his head and looked at the Pribbles. "The other half happens here. This is my book, too. I created it along the way, making it different and better than the author could ever dream. This story belongs to me, Mr. Pribble. It isn't yours to steal, but it is mine to share."

Other Oliver pointed at the clock.

"You know what to do, Oliver."

Turn Back Time

The truth was that at that precise moment Oliver *didn't* know what to do, but as he glanced around, a plan came to him, so instantly that he felt it through his body, a strange tingle that went all the way to his toes.

The two Olivers moved at once, as if they shared a brain, which, I suppose, they did.

Other Oliver jumped toward Mr. Pribble, wrestling the *CORTEXIA*™ from his grip.

"What are you doing?" Mr. Pribble sputtered. He fell onto his backside and kicked his legs like an upended turtle.

Oliver picked up Sigil's robe from the ground and turned it inside out, revealing the familiar dark material. He motioned for Nasty to perch on his shoulders, then wrapped it around them, forming the tall, hooded figure that had followed them since the start of the book.

Other Oliver held the *CORTEXIA*™ above his head, and the canister pulsed and sparkled. There were the sounds of howls and bird chirps, running water and tumbling rocks. Deep inside, they could hear a distant cry of *"Blumpf."*

Cora and Jack looked at Oliver in amazement, slowly realizing what was happening.

"I'm sorry about your mother," Oliver said.

"I'm sorry about yours," Cora said. "But I suppose we all need to move forward."

She turned to Grayson and nodded, readying his hands on the clock.

"Just this once, we can break the rules of time."

Other Oliver slammed the *CORTEXIA*™ down and the canister shattered. There was a deafening *whoosh* as massive waves of color surrounded them, flowing around them and into the air, full of life and noises.

The tower began to build around them, under their feet, lifting them high into the air. The swamp water filled the muddy basin, and the dark forest reappeared, tree by tree. Far in the distance, the tallest peak of the mountain became visible as it reformed in a reverse avalanche, the rocks tumbling on top of one another, returning to how they once had been. Beam by beam, the towns of the Old Mountain Guard were rebuilt. Past that, swatches of green and brown reconstructed the Green Lands and the exit of the Cave of Horrors, and far beyond that lay the Land of the Giants.

Oliver watched it all, the words THE END and EXIT still floating at the top of his vision. He felt a buzz in his head, as if his brain was vibrating against his skull.

"Let's do this again," Oliver said to Nasty. "But this time, I control what happens."

"Turn back time!" Jack shouted, and Oliver guided Grayson's hands with his mind. Grayson turned the hands of the clock just the right number of rotations, and brilliant light exploded from the dial. Everything began to spin, faster and faster. The ground moved under their feet, and the world smeared around them. Sounds dulled, and Nasty clung tight to Oliver's shoulders, the black robe flapping in the twisting current of particles. Cora and Jack seemed far away, small dots amongst the twirling light.

It ended as quickly as it started, and Oliver found himself dropped into darkness, lost in a thick forest of trees and brambles.

The ground shook and *BOOM BOOM BOOM*s echoed through the trees.

"Are you still there, Nasty?" Oliver whispered.

"I am," Nasty answered, his voice muffled under the black robe. "I can't believe that worked."

"Of course it worked. It's my imagination."

Oliver saw a boy running directly at them.

"I do believe we're at the beginning," Nasty said.

The boy came closer now, and Oliver could see it was *him*, back at the beginning of the story, looking positively terrified as he ran through the trees.

In the clearing, he saw Mrs. Pribble waving a lantern through the fog, her husband close behind.

"I'm so very sorry to do this to you, Oliver," Mr. Pribble said. "Since the records show that you returned the book to the library, I'm left with no other choice. It seems to have vanished and could be anywhere in the world by now. Of course, that means that the last remaining copy lives *in your mind*."

The Past Oliver continued to run.

"Here we are, Oliver, in the land of Dulum. Chapter one of *The Timekeeper's Children*: 'A Theft in the Land of the Giants.'

The *CORTEXIA*™ is a special software tool we created—it will allow us to take the story from your mind, page by page, until the entire tome is ours. You won't miss it, will you?"

Past Oliver jumped over roots, and when he saw the tall, hooded figure move through the trees, he skidded to a stop, opening his mouth and preparing to scream. Nasty stuck a talon out of the black fabric and motioned for Past Oliver to be silent.

"I remember this," Oliver whispered, watching Past Oliver prepare to run just as Mrs. Pribble clenched her hands around his throat and pulled him toward her husband.

"Yoo-hoo! Edmund! He's over here!"

Past Oliver screamed and kicked, but Mrs. Pribble's grip was too tight. There was no sense helping him. Cora and Jack would arrive soon, and they would pummel the Pribbles with stones and then take Past Oliver captive.

Oliver reached up to pat Nasty's talons, then placed his index finger above his left ear, tracing it to the middle of his forehead. He wrapped his fingers around the word EXIT.

It was time for him to write his own story, but first there was something he needed.

A Bloody End

Oliver lurched forward in the Pribbles' dining room, crashing into his bowl of roast beef. Blood from the meat trickled down his face and pooled in the little crevice above his chin.

He forced himself to his feet, feeling dizzy and weak from the adventure he had just escaped.

The Pribbles sat beside him, still absorbed in their goggles. They would exit soon, too, and he had to make it to his father before they could stop him.

He threw the goggles inside his backpack and began to run, as fast as he could, down the book-lined hallways of the Pribbles' mansion and past the elaborate reading rooms. His rubbery legs and arms felt disconnected from his body, and he steadied himself by running a hand against a bookshelf. His fingers were bloody from the roast beef, too, and left a smear across the cleanly colored spines of the Pribbles' library.

"Where are you going?" a worker asked as Oliver turned a corner and crashed into him, sending him reeling back into a beanbag chair. "Look what you did to the *books!*"

Down the hall, familiar voices yelled at him.

"Stop that boy!"

"Oliver, wait! We must talk this instant! Don't leave!"

Oliver continued to run. He crossed a Pribble logo embroidered in the purple carpet—a giant golden *P* that sparkled under the skylights, then slid into the great entry room of the mansion.

The clock above the door told him the time. *An hour and a half.* It felt as if he had been gone for weeks. How could it only have been an hour and a half?

"Someone stop him!" Mrs. Pribble yelled.

The Pribbles' butler was fifty feet in the air on a sliding ladder, dusting the high bookshelves. He slid down to give chase but was too late. Oliver flung open the front door and sprinted to his father's car. He clawed open the car door, threw in his backpack, and dove into the passenger seat.

"Oliver?" his father asked. "Done so soon?"

"GO!" Oliver yelled, just as the Pribbles hobbled into the sunlight.

Oliver's father eyed the dried blood on his son's face and hands. "What *happened* to you?"

"*GO!*" Oliver said again, and this time his father obeyed, punching in their home address just as the Pribbles came within reach of the window.

The small car shot off, and the Pribbles' shouts followed them as they careened down the drive.

"Don't let him get away!"

"Come back!"

But Oliver was already gone.

The Author of the Story

Oliver's father reached over and wiped a bit of blood from his chin.

"Did you cut yourself?"

"No," Oliver said. "The roast beef was undercooked."

His father nodded, though that answer was hardly sufficient as to why they had fled so suddenly from the Pribbles' mansion.

The story buzzed in Oliver's head.

He remembered it all, every place, every plot point, every feeling and emotion. The broken canister of the *CORTEXIA*™ had released it all in his mind, but it was different now. It was *his.*

The roads zipped by, and Oliver watched as large expanses of yards and mansions slowly transformed into smaller and smaller homes with ill-maintained lawns and boarded-up windows. Children and adults sat on porches and steps, their heads tilted to the sky, the lenses of their goggles glowing blue.

"What happened back there?" Oliver's father asked for the eighth time, and for the eighth time was answered with nothing but silence.

Oliver closed his eyes, leaning back in the seat and tightly gripping the seat belt. The scenes from the book played vibrantly in his mind—Cora and Jack in the woods, Nasty in the cave, and Blumpf helping them up the mountain. He missed them already, but he could still feel them with him, bouncing around in his head.

When they finally arrived home, the car had hardly stopped before Oliver unlatched his seat belt and opened the door, taking the stairs three at a time and jumping on his bed. The soft mattress was a luxurious treat after long nights of sleeping on rocks and mountainsides, and he relished the feeling. He slid to the edge of the bed and peered over, lifting up the blanket to reveal the spot where his stash of stolen books used to be.

Sitting there, all alone, was the leather-bound journal from Ms. Fringlemeier. It was perfect in every way—not at all like the books he had stolen.

It's time for you to write your own story, she had told him that final day at the library. *I know there are amazing things happening in your mind.*

Oliver pulled the goggles from his backpack and secured them to his face. He switched them on and felt the room spin and twirl until he was back in Dulum, right where he had left off. The black robe was wrapped tightly around him, and Nasty was perched on his shoulders.

"I'm back," he said.

"I knew you would be."

"I'll need your help narrating," Oliver said, and it was

good that Nasty's face was hidden, because at that moment the emotion he felt was overpowering, and tears welled in his beady black eyes.

"It would be my honor," he managed to say.

Together, they crept along the woods, watching as Cora and Jack made their appearance and took Oliver captive, then they followed the three children to the Land of the Giants, where Oliver's head was removed from his body for his first awful death.

"That's much worse to watch now that I like you," Nasty said.

Oliver smiled. He performed the exit motion and lurched back to his bed, grabbing his journal and a pen.

"Where do I start?" he said aloud, staring at the blank page—a fright for every author.

Nasty answered, still audible inside his head.

"You must start with something overly dramatic, Master Oliver. Something that will hook the readers from the very first page and propel them forward."

Oliver began to write, his hand moving as though controlled by Nasty's wing, and continued throughout the afternoon.

From time to time his father cracked open the door to check on him, occasionally dropping off a plate of food and a glass of water. He watched as Oliver scribbled, his hand sliding over the pages of the leather journal like a boy possessed. Words turned to sentences and sentences into paragraphs. Pages filled and characters took shape. As Oliver wrote, the world seemed to come alive in his mind, as bright and loud as it had been with the goggles strapped to his face. Nasty narrated through him, his melodic voice buzzing in Oliver's brain.

The next day was Sunday, and Oliver threw on his goggles and continued in the Cave of Horrors, watching as Past Oliver led Cora and Jack to where he had pointed, off the main path of the story and into the other chamber filled with bats and spiders and rodents. Oliver and Nasty stayed close, concealed by the robe, constructing the new room from Oliver's own imagination. He filled in details that the Author had never added, making the story bigger and better than it had been before.

Monday morning, he wrote for the entire thirty-seven-minute bus ride to school, seated next to the same boy who had let him try his goggles just a few days earlier.

"*Now* what are you doing?" the boy asked, watching as Oliver's ink-stained hand tore across the page.

"Writing a story," Oliver said, and the boy watched in wonder as he created, ripping words and pictures straight from his imagination.

"What's it about?" the boy asked.

Oliver considered the question. It was difficult to summarize.

"Tell you what," he said. "I'll let you read it when I'm done."

The boy smiled and nodded, then slid his goggles back over his face.

"Cool. I'm Sam, by the way."

"I'm Oliver."

Oliver wrote over recess and on the bus ride home. He wrote after dinner and through the night, balancing every free moment that week between wearing the goggles and writing.

On the banks of the River of Escapement, he stood and constructed a raft to help them on their journey, and when Cora betrayed them in the lagoon, he appeared from the trees and imagined her grip loosening on the knife.

Then he and Nasty were off, flying to the banks of the Loosely Rendered Town, just in time to hear Past Nasty's calls for help from the Author.

Oliver obliged. He imagined the town, creating its every detail inside his mind, then he hid underneath the grain storage structure until Cora kicked Blumpf through the hole and down to the ground. When the massive mountain man landed in the soft mud, Oliver grabbed him and stared into his eyes, creating a character that had never been in the book but would now be crucial for its success.

"Blumpf," the man said, and in a rush, all emotions surged through him. Love and fear and anger and courage. He jumped up and down, clapped his hands, cried, and laughed. "Blumpf," Blumpf said again, understanding in that moment that he must do anything to protect the children, even if it meant sacrificing himself.

"Blumpf," Oliver repeated, and the man climbed the ladder and raced toward the children.

Oliver and Nasty watched as the Great Staircase burned and fell, then took the long flight to the top of the mountain to save the children from the Pribbles. Oliver changed the story again, sending the *CORTEXIA*™ spinning as it fell down the mountain, inhaling rocks, creating the avalanche that would plummet Blumpf and the children to the ground.

"Perhaps you should have been more careful," Nasty said under the robe, but it was too late to change that. The only thing they could do was move forward. They flew to Dulum and hid in the streets of the city, appearing on cue to save themselves from the Gang of Impervious Children.

Days ticked by, and Oliver continued writing, following his past self to the Dark Forest, where he watched Mr. Pribble slurp up the swamp and the Twisted Tower. When it appeared that all hope was lost and the remaining bits of the story would be stolen from his mind, he appeared through the fog, removing the black robe to talk to Mr. Pribble.

"This story belongs to me, Mr. Pribble," he said. "It isn't yours to steal, but it is mine to share."

He looked at his past self and pointed at the clock.

"You know what to do, Oliver."

They moved in unison. One Oliver grabbed the *CORTEXIA*™ from Mr. Pribble's hands and smashed it on the ground as the other wrapped Sigil's robe around himself. Grayson turned back time to where the story began again, a circle that loops and loops, going ever forward, like the hands of a clock.

Tick tock tick.

When Oliver was done writing, he held the book in his hands, flipping through the pages to read what he had created, excited to share it with others.

A MILDLY SAPPY (YET HOPEFULLY SATISFYING) EPILOGUE

A Gift for Mr. Pribble

The Pribbles' sprawling mansion seemed to glow in the morning dew, like a fragile castle made of ice, baking in the radiant sunlight. It was Saturday morning, and the Nelsons' car navigated up the winding driveway. Oliver held a small package on his lap, wrapped in brown paper, and his pinkie finger nervously twisted around the bow like a baby worm.

When the car was parked under the portico, Oliver walked to the door and knocked until he heard the echoey pitter-patter of footsteps.

The door opened and the Pribbles' butler appeared, his face twisting from annoyance to confusion to surprise at an impressive speed.

"*Oliver?*" the butler asked. "It's . . . it's . . . *you*. You're all they've been talking about this last week. We weren't . . . *oh* . . . I mean to say . . . wait here!"

He turned and ran down the hall, calling out, "Mr. Pribble! Mrs. Pribble! *He's* here! *Oliver Nelson!*"

From the car, Oliver's father smiled. He had read the book the previous night, and despite his anger at the thought of the Pribbles trying to steal the story from his son's mind, had eventually come around to the plan.

"I'm so proud of you, Oliver," his father had said. "I don't know anyone else in the world who would do this."

And he *had* to do this. Here he was, back at the mansion, his fingers trembling on the package.

Mr. Pribble appeared at the door, unshaven and wearing a bathrobe. He ripped off his glasses and rubbed his eyes, as if the small boy in the entryway was a mirage.

"Oliver?" he asked. "I didn't expect to ever see you again. You left in such a hurry the other day, and . . . I never got to apologize."

"You don't need to, Mr. Pribble. I understand why you did it. We're both thieves, remember?"

"Indeed we are. Still, it was wrong of me to try to steal *this* story from you. Had I known what it meant to you, well . . . I probably still would have tried. But you loved that book more than I did, and you understood it in a way I never could. I was wrong. You've shown me that with your brilliant imagination. Children aren't a threat. They're the best thing to happen to books. I'm sorry."

Oliver smiled.

"You may never find the book you're looking for, but I hope this helps."

He held out the package to Mr. Pribble, who took it carefully and peeled off the paper to reveal a leather-bound journal filled with Oliver's small handwriting.

"Oh, Oliver," Mr. Pribble said, tears trickling down his face. He ran his fingers along the cover. Mrs. Pribble appeared from the picture book wing and glided through the great marble entryway. She leaned over her husband's shoulder as he flipped through the pages, arriving at chapters containing hideous giants, dark caves full of bats and rodents, gangs of impervious children, and a magical clock that could control time.

"It's *The Timekeeper's Children*, even better than the original. This is the best gift I've ever received," Mr. Pribble said, and an idea came to his mind so suddenly that he jumped back, nearly knocking over his wife. "I believe I have something for you in return."

The End

A line of school buses crested the hill, each packed tight with children. They were quiet, mostly, all curious as to why they had been summoned to the Pribbles' mansion. The moment they entered the bus, their goggles had stopped working, and they'd been forced to stare out the windows, watching the parks and buildings of the city pass by.

Oliver, Oliver's father, Ms. Fringlemeier, and the Pribbles had worked through the previous night, preparing the house for the children's arrival.

"These shelves are much too high," Ms. Fringlemeier had said, her librarian skills still as sharp as ever. "And why aren't the books organized by genre? Come help me, Mr. Nelson. Let's move this display over here, and grab that stack while you're at it."

Oliver's father obliged, helping Ms. Fringlemeier hang signs above the various wings and prepare tables full of recommended reading.

"If this goes as intended, we could use both of you in the future on a more permanent basis," Mrs. Pribble said.

Considering that neither of them were currently employed and they enjoyed working together very much,

358

Ms. Fringlemeier and Mr. Nelson agreed.

When all the work was done, Mr. Pribble looked at the new arrangement of books and wiped sweat from his brow.

"To think," he said, his eye twitching slightly, "in a few moments, thousands of greasy fingers will be all over the pages of my books."

"Isn't it wonderful?" Ms. Fringlemeier asked.

When the buses arrived at the sprawling estate, some parked under the portico and others filled the front lane leading to the entrance.

Soon the property was teeming with children. The doors to the mansion were flung open and Mr. Pribble waved them inside. Children filled the atrium and the hallways, browsing the shelves and staring in wonder at the rows and rows of perfect books, filled with stories that could change their lives forever. Oliver followed Mr. Pribble down the halls and they pointed at select titles, sharing enough of the plot inside to entice a young reader to its pages.

"Our home," Mr. Pribble said, "will forever be open to any child who wants to read. That is my gift to you."

"Hey, Oliver!" a familiar boy yelled, appearing from a reading room. "This place is amazing, isn't it? It's full of those paper book things you like so much! Look at that one! And that one!"

"Hi, Sam," Oliver said.

"Is this one of your friends?" Mr. Pribble asked, and before Oliver could consider the answer, Sam nodded and pointed at the leather-bound journal in Mr. Pribble's hands.

"Did you finish writing your story?" Sam asked.

"Almost," Oliver answered. He turned to Mr. Pribble and asked, "Could I borrow that for a few more minutes? I need to write the ending."

"Oh?" Mr. Pribble asked with a smile. He pulled a fountain pen from his breast pocket and handed it to Oliver. "I'm glad to hear it. I didn't like the thought of those children stuck in a loop forever, with me as a villain constantly in pursuit."

So while the other children perused the shelves for books and curled up in reading rooms, Oliver wrote a mildly sappy, yet hopefully satisfying epilogue, which Nasty proudly narrated once again, flying in circles around his imagination.

Oliver returned to Dulum one last time, where Cora and Jack were waiting for him in the tower. Sigil was defeated, the clock was destroyed, and the canister of the *CORTEXIA*™ was smashed to bits, spilling the stolen contents of the story back over the land.

"This is the end," Oliver said. "You'll need to go on without me."

"We'll manage just fine, thank you," Cora said, flicking the hair from her face, but there was a slight smile on her lips.

"What will you do when you get back to Garden Grove?" Jack asked.

"I don't know, but I think I have a friend now."

"You have lots of friends," Cora said.

"Blumpf," Blumpf said, nodding. He wrapped his arms around Oliver for a powerful hug before the boy disappeared.

The group walked down the spiraling staircase of the tower and traveled back to the city. Time moved forward, never again turning back. Days turned to weeks, weeks

to months, and months to years. Grayson took over rule of Dulum, moving Cora, Jack, and their father to a large stone home next to the castle, where Cora was trained to be the official timekeeper of the city. It's said her clocks were the most beautiful devices ever created by human hands.

"Would you like to train to be in my guard?" Grayson asked Jack, but Jack held a piece of the giants' jewel between his fingers and let the light sparkle in his eyes.

"I have another idea," he said, and today there is hardly a person in Dulum who doesn't wear a ring crafted by his nimble fingers.

Blumpf took lodging in the castle and was perfectly content to care for the animals in the stables and sweep the stone entryway, where he was known to look at the sunset and remember the face of the boy who had given him life.

Nasty made a home underneath the clock set into the top tower of the castle. Through the years, he observed everything that happened below and told stories to anyone who would listen, though he never found a more attentive audience than Cora and Grayson's children.

And that, Oliver decided, was exactly how the story should end.

When he was done, he wrote the only title that seemed appropriate along the spine: *The Thieving Collectors of Fine Children's Books*. Mr. Pribble filed it in the north wing, under *N* for Nelson.

That is where it sits to this day, waiting for you to find it and make it your own.

Acknowledgments

While stories may be a creation between the reader and the author, there is a whole team of people who work to bring a book to life. I would like to thank my agent, Alex Slater, for being the first to believe in this story and for helping me make it the best it could be.

The entire Little Bee/Yellow Jacket team has been a joy to work with—my editor, Charlie Ilgunas, who provided invaluable story insight, as well as Ariel Palmer-Collins, Dave Barrett, and Kayla Overbey. And thank you to Paul Crichton and Tristan Lueck for helping get this book into readers' hands.

I'd like to thank Natalie Padberg Bartoo for the design of the book, and David SanAngelo for bringing the cover illustration to life.

Special thanks to my friends and early readers, who provided excellent suggestions, ideas, and encouragement: Kelley Rose Waller, Shawn Smucker, Cliff Lewis, John Cashman, and Robert Swartwood. You're the best.

Lastly, love and thanks to my family, especially my wife, Andrea, and my children, Wyatt, Everett, and Marlowe. I couldn't do it without your support and understanding, especially when a sticky plot point can make me act, dare I say, a little Nasty.